Praise f

D1622376

Never Isn't Long Enough...

"The rebuilding of the South after the Civil War brought industrialization, urbanization, and technological advances to rural American farms. Railroads spread commerce and opportunities to every corner of the land. In a saga set amidst these transformations, F. Diane Pickett captures how they affected a rural Georgia family. Life on the farm, the coming of the automobile, moonshiners, the Roaring Twenties, the movie house ... they're all here! A fascinating story."

—Dean Debolt
University Archivist, West Florida History Center,
University of West Florida, Pensacola

"Diane Pickett joins a distinguished parade of colorful Southern writers from William Faulkner to Fannie Flagg, who have managed to capture the inexplicable logic that is endemic to so many Southern clans. Written with great humor and insight."

—Robert M. Fulmer, PhD
Author of *Newcomers in Paradise*

Never Isn't Long Enough

F. Diane Pickett

uphill publishing

Miramar Beach, Florida

Published by: Uphill Publishing
          2ll Eagle Drive
          Miramar Beach, FL 32550

Cover art & design: Brad Wallace Design
Author photo: David Roth Photography

First Edition

Printed in the United States of America

For bulk orders, please contact BookLogix at 470.239.8547 or sales@booklogix.com.

Publisher's Cataloging-in-Publication Data

Pickett, F. Diane.

    Never isn't long enough / by F. Diane Pickett. – Miramar Beach, FL : Uphill Publishing, c2014. p. ; cm.

    ISBN: 978-0-615-87659-7
    Summary: A humorous Southern family saga spanning the years from the Civil War through World War II featuring the doomed romance between a young farm girl and a wealthy older man called to God and commerce.–Publisher.

    1. Southern states–Fiction. 2. United States–History–Civil War, 1861-1865–Fiction. 3. United States–History–20th century–Fiction. 4. World War, 1914-1918–United States–Fiction. 5. World War, 1939-1945–United States–Fiction. 6. Historical fiction. 7. Love stories. I. Title.

PS3616.I2854 N48 2014   2013956583
813/.6—dc23   1405

1 3 5 7 9 10 8 6 4 2

To Pick ~

In loving and powerful memory

Contents

Acknowledgments

I AM TREMENDOUSLY GRATEFUL TO MY DEAR AND LOYAL FRIEND Dewey Ray, who has been my mentor and guide throughout this long process. He has done all the heavy lifting on computer issues and the endless morass of publication details. Writing the book was far easier than the publication process, and without his help and support I would never have taken on the task. In addition, his thoughtful and insightful comments helped me give some of the characters additional depth. He added greatly to my courage in writing this book and is absolutely the world's best cheerleader!

My friend and most avid reader, Annette Robson, has been "with me" from the beginning of this work, constantly praising and urging me on. Her enthusiasm for the story and its characters has been immensely gratifying. It was rewarding to know she eagerly awaited the next chapter as it was constructed. We spent long hours together reading and refining. My only previous experience with fans was when I was queen at Mardi Gras in New Orleans, but that involved way too many beads and beer!

My concept editor, Lora Lisbon of Blessingway Authors' Services, has been amazing in her attention to detail and I am so thankful for her hours of patient labor and her expertise. Her fingerprints are on all the pages as she labored over the smallest word. I would also like to thank my wonderful illustrator, Brad Wallace, for the dynamic cover.

Many friends, especially Brenda Ray, Debra Channell, Bill Linne, Julie Lopp, and Malca Lebell, were very generous with their time and interest in previewing this book and adding encouragement and helpful comments along the way.

THANK YOU ALL. WE DID THIS TOGETHER.

Author's Note

EVERYONE FANTASIZES ABOUT WRITING A BOOK THAT KEEPS readers turning the pages. To do so, you need interesting people to write about. I set about re-creating the lives of two Southerners and their individual journeys in an attempt to reveal who they started out to be and who they actually became. She had an intense desire to get out of poverty—at any cost—and never look back; he was called to God but answered the call to a different life. Although their paths crossed only briefly and chaotically, they were to forever change each other's lives.

Set against a playful rendering of almost a hundred years of Southern history, their saga raises fascinating questions: Did either of them get what they wanted? Could they have altered the course of events that changed their lives so dramatically?

Theirs is not a love story but rather a tale of betrayal leading one of them on a bitter journey that injects its poison into the character's every encounter. In the process of recording it, I have learned that not every

story has a happy ending and some, like life itself, end
with a question—in this case, Just how long is never?

1.

Never

HILL EXPLAINED ETERNITY TO HIS CHILDREN. IMAGINE, HE said, an eagle that comes once a year to Stone Mountain to sharpen his beak and when the mountain is worn down *that* is eternity. They could understand it easily because they were born in the shadow of Stone Mountain at the start of the war. It was actually World War II, but in reality it was a war between their mother and life.

They learned about "never" from their mother. She was seriously absorbed with it. So, eternity and never became the same thing for them.

The first time they remember hearing the word *never* was when one of their beautiful aunts would say something like "That woman was no lady, and if you want to be a lady you must *never* do what she just did." That had a huge impact, because in the rural South of the 1940s every female of any age was judged on beauty, manners, and a smile so gracious it would blind just about everyone within striking distance. All girls aspired to be a lady. To do otherwise meant you were stuck in that perpetual hell of husband hunting with no chance of getting one.

Such a girl would remain the pity of every Sunday school teacher in the South. Brains were not particularly necessary, but winning the bake contest at the First Baptist Church Picnic was absolutely essential. And every girl knew if she went to college she could drop out as soon as she captured Mr. Wonderful or some version thereof. He might not remain Mr. Wonderful for long, but he would have to do because divorce wouldn't do. Finding one husband was hard enough; getting a second one was next to impossible. No lady would ever divorce—unless, of course, it would result in a large chunk of money, a guaranteed place at the head table of the Woman's Club, and the right to talk about the wages of sin at every church function. Church was a mighty big deal and sin the number one topic, so you had to establish bragging rights right off the bat.

The goal for college was not to get an education but to get a husband, and Mrs. was the most popular degree offered. Even Ivy Leaguers had that curriculum down pat.

Their mother—known to everyone else as Faye—had taken a shortcut. From the moment she had slipped out of the birth canal and fixed her beady eyes on her surroundings, she didn't like what she saw. She figured she was destined for better things. She was not about to waste her life on farmhands and cotton fields. She was going to Atlanta. For every true Southern woman, Atlanta was the closest to heaven you could ever expect to get, and you had to bake a heck of a lot of cakes to get there.

Faye didn't have to bake as many cakes because she was gifted with flaming red hair, a great set of knockers, and a fierce determination to get off that farm. She also had a figure that was as firm as a casket. That comes with the territory of pulling corn, hoeing cotton, and picking peas. Playing baseball and football with her four brothers also helped. She later put that hand-to-hand combat practice to good use in the wrestling match of dating. She didn't like to lose that one too often—but hey, Atlanta was the goal here! A girl's gotta do what a girl's gotta do. Faye was in a hurry, so she had to work fast.

In a family with nine siblings, somebody was always in trouble, about to be in trouble, or asking for trouble. Faye was just plain trouble. Her mother, Mae, used to say that Faye was born high-tempered. That was Victorian code for bitch. Her red hair dueled with her screaming outbursts that could explode into a volcano of outrage whenever her demands were not met.

She had watched three of her four sisters do the college thing and get husbands. Her fourth sister, June, still a child, was a work in progress and couldn't be much help to a girl in a big hurry. Besides, June's already budding dark beauty was in sharp contrast to the redheaded and fair-skinned girls in the family. She was obviously going to be a local tobacco queen, and Faye planned to have an Atlanta address by the time that particular competition started.

Faye knew everything about farm life, but what she wanted to know about was excitement. There wasn't much of that on the farm unless the heifer ran off with the neighbor's bull or the pigs got loose in the vegetable garden. She also craved attention. It was difficult to be noticed in such a large family, but Faye quickly figured out that red hair, temper tantrums, and attention went together.

She learned to be bossy and enjoyed her power over the younger children in the household: Larry, Wallace, Sara Mae, and Vernon in addition to June. She had two older sisters—Gwen and Garland—and an older brother, Ollie Jr. She didn't get far bossing them around, but the five younger ones were easy prey. She pounced on them like a flea on a dog. They went round and round through the house and out into the yard. They would run, and she would yell.

She came by the yelling naturally. It was in her DNA. She had also perfected it while learning to call the cows and pigs from the pasture into the barn, and the skill did not desert her in later life.

It didn't take much to get her going, and once in gear there was no brake on her vocal cords. She resented her station in life and had plotted since early childhood to escape to a different world. She had envied her city-bred well-to-do cousins, who lived in a small town, *not* on a farm. To Faye's eye, they had lovely clothes and housemaids and were comfortable in what she considered gracious homes. Besides, there was not an entire basketball team of them, so they each got lots of attention.

Her own home was a small wood-frame house with a screened front porch and a back porch containing the well from which water was drawn. This typically Southern farm-home, with no running water or electricity, was too small for such a large family and offered no privacy. Sometimes you even had company in the privy at the back of the house. The little bedrooms were arranged in a row across from the equally small living room, dining room, and kitchen. When the entire family gathered in the kitchen for meals, it was akin to a crowd of food fanatics registering for a convention.

Bedtime was a bit like musical chairs since there were eleven people and only five beds. They slept two or three to a bed, and Faye made sure she got to the biggest one first to claim her space. The sisters and brothers bedded down in separate rooms, and no one had a room of their own, not even their parents. Faye didn't like going to bed early, but there was little to do in the evenings except more chores, which did not interest her since she was already tired from the day's work.

Her day began at dawn, helping get breakfast cooked for all eleven of them on the wood-burning stove. Then she had to make enough biscuits for breakfast, school lunch pails, and after-school hunger pangs. After breakfast, she helped dress the younger ones. In addition, tiny June and Vernon needed changing, feeding, and bathing. Gwen and Garland, meanwhile, made the beds and washed the mountains of breakfast dishes in a tin pan. The water for washing was brought in by pail from the well on the back porch.

The older boys, Ollie and Larry, had no time to spare either. Their morning chores consisted of one of them chopping and bringing in firewood for the stove and getting it hot enough for cooking while the other took the younger boy, Wallace, out to the barn to feed the chickens and hogs.

Usually Faye left for school feeling more like a housemaid than a student. In the summertime, the days were longer and harder since instead of going to school she had to work in the fields alongside her brothers and sisters. There her fair skin burned in the sun, causing freckles to mar one of her best assets. She wanted out and thought of little else.

She had heard the story endless times of her mother's misfortune in giving up the teaching profession to become a farmer's wife. Faye had absolutely no intention of going that route. More than once she'd said, "I would rather ride to hell on a one-wheel bike than make that mistake." Every time she heard that story she winced and became more determined than ever to be a glamorous woman in the city.

Faye's mother, Mae, was an educated woman who had been born to teach, but her life took a side step when she married a farmer. Nonetheless, she still taught—even if it was only her own large brood of children. Faye paid enough attention to her lessons to at least learn how to write because she planned to send lots of postcards home from Atlanta.

"But how am I going to get there?" she would ask herself. The farm was five miles out in the country from Brookfield, a candy store whistle stop for farmers on their way to slightly larger Tifton, to sell their cotton, tobacco, corn, or peanuts.

Cotton was king, and "whacky tobaccy" had not yet been invented. Yet the post-Depression rural South was awash in golden tobacco that was auctioned off at the end of every summer. It was an exhilarating time for farm families. Auctions were almost like fairs, and each year's beauty queen was named the Tobacco Queen of Tift County. Sara Mae, the seventh child in the family, was a three-time winner. Mae Mae, as she was often called, was a petite and intelligent replica of her beautiful mother, right down to her red hair. Only Sara Mae didn't wear her hair in a braid; instead, she let it flow in long, saucy curls down her back. After her third win, someone shouted, "She's just too damned beautiful—why don't we try hogs next time? Maybe Myrtice can stand a chance. She bakes a damn good pound cake, too!"

Tobacco time was not only for tobacco queens but for cash registers as farmers brought their golden goods to bulging warehouses. Long rows of bright leaves were bundled and tied into big white sheets looking like plump ghosts waiting to be brought to life by the tongue-twisting auctioneer with his singsong litany of prices.

A successful auction meant that the farmer had cash for supplies, seed, food, and equipment. Faye's father, Ollie, didn't have a tractor yet; he was still plowing with a mule. He wouldn't get his first tractor until his son, Wallace, came back from the war with a fistful of dollars—soldier's pay saved out of four long years of grueling combat. Ollie always said he would have done without a tractor if it meant keeping his sons safe. Four sons went to war, and four came home. But Ollie Jr. came home in a casket.

Cash-heavy farmers attracted all sorts of salesmen from far and wide. Eager to part the farmers from their money, car salesmen were among the frontrunners in the competition.

Enter Hill Pickett, also known as Pick. He was a first-class ticket to Atlanta about to be punched.

2.

Pick

PICK WAS THE OPPOSITE OF FAYE. HE WAS A TALL, DIGNIFIED, elegant, laughing man with blue eyes and hair that had prematurely turned snow white. His hair had probably turned white from fright due to his many adventures. He had lived every moment fully and was prepared to continue his carefree lifestyle forever. He almost succeeded—and then he met Faye.

By the time they met, Pick was a mature man living in Atlanta. He had never married and was content with his bachelor life. There had been endless women, and he sampled all those he could but had not found a permanent place for his restless heart. Life, to him, was the open road, and he had spent endless hours driving coast to coast in search of automobiles for his rapidly growing business. America was in love with the automobile, but none more so than Pick. Cars were the love of his life.

To understand Pick, you had to know something of his background. Thrust into life in 1900, at the height of the Victorian Era, Pick was the product of a stern autocratic father—a buggy-driving, circuit-riding Baptist preacher—

and an equally stern mother who was often left alone on a small mountain farm in North Georgia struggling to feed her growing and nearly starving family of six sons and one daughter. Born in Talking Rock (named after the Cherokee term for "rock that talks"), Georgia, Pick was fated to talk his way through life. He was meant to be a preacher, but his cathedral instead became The Church of the Car Dealership.

He learned to drive, based on his experience with farm equipment, when he was nine years old, in 1909—the same year Henry Ford brought the Model T to the masses and the same year Pick's father died. Although Pick had seen a car once before, the first time he ever drove one was after being sent on horseback to fetch the doctor to attend the Reverend Thaddeus Pickett's bedside. He found Dr. MacDonald only a few miles away, recognizing him by his furiously red hair and the outlandish plaid coat he always favored. Dr. MacDonald had come over from Scotland only a few years before and quickly discovered that the wearing of the kilt would not be tolerated deep in Southern territory. Nor did his big hairy legs appeal to the ladies. So the plaid coat became his trademark.

When Pick found the doctor, he was lurching and teetering along a rutted road in some kind of black, noisy machine that soon became stuck in a mud hole. The more Dr. MacDonald tried to go forward, the more the wheels of the contraption got stuck in the mud.

Well, Pick knew a thing or two about mud holes, as did every farm boy in America. He figured if he could get a cow out of a mud hole, he could get the doctor out of one too. Fueled by desperation, he gave the doctor his horse and told him to ride on ahead to the reverend and he would bring the car. He had no idea what to do with this particular piece of equipment, but he had been around enough farm machinery to recognize a gearbox and a crankshaft. Long and strong for his age, he engaged the gearbox and decided to treat this gadget like his pet cow, Jezebel.

Jezebel was so named because she had an amorous nature and, like other females of the time, wanted what she wanted when she wanted it. Trouble was, what she often wanted was the bull on the farm next door. She knew she was the most beautiful cow in Pickens County and could have her pick of any of the bulls. Her eyelashes were so long that when she blinked it was like a tidal wave of fur. Her full, huge mouth was a triumph of careful cud-chewing, and she could manipulate those lips over the most moist and sensuous grasses. So whenever she saw Mr. Wonderful, she was apt to leap the fence, all the while batting those long eyelashes at full window-wiper speed. Upon landing, she wouldn't stop to comb her tail but simply ran like hell until reaching the pothole at the bottom of the hill that separated the two farms. Sometimes she got stuck in all the muck, especially during rainy seasons. Then she'd get scared and start hollering and thrashing about, getting stuck all the more. Pick had to go rescue her and learned early on that the best thing was not to pull her forward but to back her out. So that's what he did to Dr. MacDonald's Model T.

Once in the driver's seat, Pick noticed that the Tin Lizzie, as the Model T was known, was an amazingly simple machine. It had three pedals on the floor: one on the left marked C for clutch, which also functioned as first and second gear, one in the center marked R for reverse, and one on the right marked B for brake. There were also two levers on the steering column—the right one for gas and the other for spark/advance.

It seemed to Pick that the simple thing to do was to put this contraption in reverse and, as with Jezebel, back it out of the mud hole. That method worked fine, but he was at the bottom of a hill moving full-speed upward and backward, unable to see where he was going without hanging out the side of this clattering calamity that seemed hell-bent on destruction. Soon, he was hollering just like Jezebel as he mounted the crest of the hill and thought about beginning a demented descent down the other side.

Again, simplicity was the answer for the Model T. Pick, in an act of inspiration, stepped on all three pedals at the same time, stopping the Tin Lizzie practically in midair. When it settled down to earth, Pick surveyed his position. He could only see through the extremely high steering wheel, not over it; but if he went backward, he could hang out the side while holding the steering wheel with one hand. He could then gauge distance and obstacles behind him. He figured that steering Lizzie was about like steering a horse—take the reins firmly and hold on, but in reverse order.

He had backed slowly and carefully down the hill before encountering a new obstacle: home was forward, but he was moving backward and was familiar with only one gear: reverse. So he tried to turn the thing around but kept circling until he got the back of the car pointed toward home. Knowing that gear well by now, he took off in reverse under full power toward home.

As he approached the barn, he stood up on all three pedals and came to a shuddering halt a few feet from the door, exhausted but exhilarated by the adventure. Then he dashed into his house, only to learn that the Reverend Thad had gone on to Glory, the victim of a horse accident he'd experienced upon returning from his latest famous revival. In Pick's mind, his father was now finding out if the God of the Baptists he had been proclaiming for the last forty-five years was a reality or if God just had a great press agent.

3.

Starvation or Salvation?

TO BETTER UNDERSTAND PICK, YOU HAD TO KNOW NOT ONLY his background but also his papa's background before him because that's who molded him. By the time of Pick's birth, his father had become a well-known preacher in the dusky foothills of the Blue Ridge Mountains. To the young Pick, and indeed too many churchgoers for miles around, Thaddeus Pickett was the equivalent of a modern-day rock star.

Yet, Thaddeus had not intended to become a preacher. His parents had emigrated from North Wales to North Carolina and eventually moved on to the mountains of North Georgia, where they became prosperous farmers. Thaddeus, at age sixteen, was in line to inherit the family farm when the Civil War broke out and his Celtic blood called him to battle.

A crack shot and avid hunter, Thad decided to get in the game before the Southern boys whipped the "damn Yankees." He assumed that victory was certain, and he didn't want the fun to be over before he'd had a chance to play. So he snuck off early one morning before the rooster could crow and headed for Virginia.

Trouble was, he didn't quite know where Virginia was, so he spent several days looking in all the wrong places, including the tops of some very tall trees. It was there that Thad uttered his first prayer, saying, "Oh my Gawd, should I shoot the bear that's up in this tree with me or those damn Yankees camping below?" Apparently God was also on duty that night because he gave an executive order that brought the tree, the bear, and Thad down all at one time. The bear distracted the Yankee captain by taking a large chunk out of his behind at the very moment the powder in Thad's rifle went off in the campfire, sending the Yankees flying for cover. Not knowing what was happening but fearing an enemy attack, the soldiers panicked and fled in all directions. However, Thad's ammunition going off in the fire illuminated the entire campground for easy pickings. Or so the story goes.

Hailed as an accidental hero by his comrades-in-arms, Private Pickett went off to war with the 65th Regimental Georgia Infantry, Army of Tennessee, to fight the Army of Northern Aggression. It was an experience he would never forget. In fact, memories of the horrors and sacrifices of the war would often permeate his future sermons, along with tales of his exploits and how he had decided to become a preacher. Thousands of young men on both sides had never been away from home before. They, like Thad, had gone to war as unsupervised teenagers—brave, ignorant, and eager to show off. By the time the war was over four years later, it had become the largest military conflict in the Western world and had cost 600,000 American lives, more than both World Wars combined. It had also brought vast social and economic changes, not just through emancipation but through an altered financial system and a changed relationship between the states and the federal government.

At the outbreak of the war, Thad was concerned with none of these things. Like other soldiers, Northern or Southern, he expected quick victory and a return to business as usual. Yet, as the war grew more desperate and hopeless, many troops became "born again," their battlefield conversions giving new meaning to the song "Onward Christian Soldiers."

Having grown up on a remote mountain farm with deeply religious parents, Thad as a full-time soldier quickly became as accustomed to bullets as he was to prayer. He often muttered, "Dear God, don't let 'em hit me when my pants are down," for diarrhea was common and severe. It didn't take him long to figure out that hunting humans was a far cry from hunting squirrels and rabbits for food and that faith under fire couldn't always protect him.

Other than during the heat of battle, army life was basically boring and left much idle time in which to make a great deal of mischief. So at every opportunity, Thad got in touch with his inner rascal and created havoc. He was a quick thinker, and when the captain said, "Private, what are you boys doing down there on your knees? Shooting craps?" Thad's response was, "No sir, cap'n. I was just holding a prayer circle!"

His best feat was turning water to wine. Thad had stumbled across an abandoned still, and soon the entire regiment had gotten so drunk that he was able to round up all their uniforms and weapons and singlehandedly march them naked down to the creek for a mass baptizing. When they came to the next day, the universal complaint was that the Yankees had swept them up on a tide of religion and left them to repent instead of shooting them.

Thad liked the sound of that and decided then and there that he would take up where the Yankees left off and preach to one and all—sometimes the Yankees and sometimes the Rebs. He simply snuck back and forth between the lines, which, as a man of the cloth, was easy to do. And since neither army commonly deployed embedded clergy, Thad didn't have to declare himself a minister.

He knew he was called to preach, and he could hold an audience captive for hours—especially since there was no place to run off to without risking a bullet. And there wasn't a hell of a lot to do in the parking lot of horses and wagons they lived in between battles either. Consequently, soldiers were always eager for entertainment, and Thad gave it to them.

Preachers were known to be frustrated actors, and Thad was no exception. His two main subjects were heaven and hell. And his descriptions of the hereafter and the hell-after were akin to glittering stage sets of monumental proportion. Think Ziegfeld Follies on steroids.

Although serving as a full-time soldier, Thad preferred the stage of the pulpit; but there were a couple of things he had to do first, and they both included bullets. The first bullet event was the battle of Pickett's Mill in May 1864. This site was to become an important strategic base of operations for Sherman as he moved toward Atlanta. He lost 1,600 men in that campaign while the Rebs had just 500 casualties. The ferocity of the battle delayed Sherman's eventual capture of Atlanta by at least a week and allowed Thad time to reload his musket as well as refill his lungs for another assault on the devil. Tent revivals had become his specialty, and he had begun to wage war against Satan with as much ferocity as the rebel yell. He soon became known as Thumping Thad because he pounded that Bible so relentlessly.

Thad's second bullet event emerged a month later, on June 27, 1864 with the outbreak of the Battle of Kennesaw, which was to become Sherman's most significant frontal assault against the Confederate Army of Tennessee under General Joe Johnston. The fighting ended in a tactical defeat for the Union with 3,000 casualties for Sherman and 1,000 for the Rebs. The Rebs were later outflanked, and on September 2, 1864 Sherman entered Atlanta.

However, he arrived without Scarlett O'Hara, who had "Gone with the Wind" and returned to Tara, and without Thad, who had been wounded in battle.

Wounded, weak, and weary, Thad was one of hundreds of soldiers mustered out of the army and left to fend on their own. With no money, no hope of work, and war still waging, Thad considered his prospects. He concluded that while the theater of the pulpit might not earn him much money it would provide him with food and, generally, shelter. In no time at all, Thumping Thad had them packing the joint.

4.

The Road to Redemption

FOOD WAS SCARCE AFTER THE CIVIL WAR, AS WAS SALT. NOT only was salt needed for flavoring but it was required for the curing and preserving of meats. So Georgia's Governor, Joe Brown, ordered that salt be supplied to wives and widows of soldiers serving the Confederate Cause. Thad took it upon himself to do the deed, reasoning that if he had salt he also had a sermon to deliver. And so it all began.

Wisdom has it that the road to hell is paved with good intentions. Thad said to himself, "That may be, but as long as there are some sweet potatoes and cornbread in the potholes, I don't care. I can find redemption on a full stomach as easily as on an empty one. I'm hungry, and I'm gonna preach a sermon that will empty every picnic basket in that revival tent!" He knew about the contents of a picnic basket because in the very early days of the war, women would pack food baskets and take their families to distant hills to watch the battles unfold, certain of glory and victory. However, the carnage and feelings of defeat that followed left them as empty as their food baskets.

Scholars have made it abundantly clear that religion stood at the center of the Civil War for both sides, each believing God was on their side. Southern leaders chose *"Deo Vindice"* ("God will avenge") as their national motto. As for the slaves, feeling convinced that God was on their side gave them courage to take the Underground Railroad and, filled with pain, hope, joy, resignation, and rebellion, run away into the arms of the Northern Army. With that kind of support from both sides, Thad, amidst scattering salt to the widows and wives who came to his revivals, felt all set to preach.

Most Americans believe that the Civil War was about one thing—slavery. Yet, the Civil War was primarily about the high tariffs on the agricultural South and its dispute over states' rights. For example, the state of Georgia was about 25 percent black, with the exception of the north Georgia mountain counties where there were almost no "Negroes." The hilly terrain was unsuitable for the type of large plantations down state that made slave labor essential, so the mountain Georgians were basically unsympathetic to the slave question. Yet, when war was declared one-sixth of the entire Pickens County population enlisted—for states' rights.

After the war, traditional concepts of race in the South had to be moderated to cope with extreme changes caused by both the war and the emancipation of blacks. The entire social balance had been altered. Not only had the North ravaged the lands of the South but the war had torn apart families that had come into armed conflict with each other over differing political, economic, and religious ideologies. Since the abolition of slavery had decimated their old traditions and economies, Southerners were forced to adjust to an entirely different way of life. In response, Southern churches had begun denouncing the North as sinful and decadent, saying it had turned from God.

Details about the circumstances into which Thad had been thrust during and after the war have since come to light.

Philip Shaw Paludan writes, in *Religion and the American Civil War*, that religion was a large cultural system in the post–Civil War South, where many evangelicals preached the moral consensus for slavery. In addition, many of them defended the South's use of slavery as biblically sanctioned and ordained by God. They also frequently preached against materialism, defining sin and evil as greed.

In his book *A Consuming Fire*, Eugene D. Genovese argues that Southerners viewed their slave practices as a valid system of bonded labor that created conditions favorable to Christian behavior and advancement. On the other hand, he says, they regarded demands made by the Northern capitalist market as having forced people to choose between Christian ethics and materialism.

This was powerful stuff for a young preacher, and Thad would use the material in some of his most thundering sermons! Only twenty years old when the Civil War ended in 1865, he knew he was a veteran of many battles but had no idea his next one would be a duel to the death with the devil and would last a lifetime.

5.

Pump and Circumstance

PEOPLE WONDER HOW THE ORGAN GOT ITS GIG AS THE CHURCH musical instrument of choice. It turns out that the pipe organ is actually older than Christianity. Ctesibius of Alexandria, a musician and engineer, built the first one in 246 BC.

Pipe organs were not permitted in early Christian churches for they were thought to be too secular and not suitable for religious music. However, around AD 800, when Charlemagne was crowned King of the Franks, he set about uniting the warring tribes in Western and Central Europe, ultimately launching a revival of art, culture, and religion through the medium of the Catholic Church. He subsequently declared that the pipe organ would be the favored instrument for church music.

Well, don't you just know that every pope was determined to get one and keep up with fashion? If you don't believe popes are fashionistas, consider those long dresses and silly hats they wear. On top of that, they only have to work one day a week and get to ride around campus in a glass cage waving at people they have never met. Then they scoot back to their secret city surrounded by secret agents called cardinals, whose only duty is to collect money and keep it hidden in vaults in the Secret City.

Pipe organs came to America in great numbers in the 1600s and 1700s, and then, like the churches themselves, suffered terribly during the Civil War. Not only were instruments and churches destroyed but the economic ruin left behind made replacement of either one almost impossible.

Preachers of the time needed a great variety of things. Foremost among them was a wife, a church, and music. Since Thad was without these commodities, he set about trying to get them.

Ellen, a mountain girl Thad had come to know, had an organ and could play it. Thad thought about this for a long time because he was also terribly smitten with another mountain girl who was beautiful, but she could neither sing nor play. Unable to make up his mind, he finally consulted his father, Joseph, who advised, "Marry the girl who can sing 'cause the congregation can't carry a tune by itself."

Thad was an arresting figure of a man. He was black headed with a biggish nose and a thin line of a mouth that seldom turned up. Tall and slender yet with a wide frame, he had a high forehead and deep-set blue eyes with eyebrows that could pass for spruce trees. He wasn't exactly handsome, but you couldn't ignore him either. Certainly, Ellen couldn't.

So on Christmas Day 1866, Thad and Ellen were married in Talking Rock, Georgia. On their wedding night, as Thad gazed forlornly at his plain-looking wife in her nightdress, he recalled his father's advice and cried out, "Sing, Ellen, sing." Or so the story goes.

Three phenomena dominated life in the rural South of the late 1800s: family, farming, and religion. For survival, the entire family worked the land. There wasn't much else to do. There were few cities, libraries, or concerts, and certainly no radio, TV, or other theatrical forms of entertainment. There were no national newspapers, magazines, or even rural mail delivery. Books were scarce and expensive. So aside from working the land the farm families built their world around religion, not only for their spiritual salvation but for their entertainment as well. The church shaped their everyday lives and the preacher was the focus. Thad, as a fire-spouting, demon-chasing preacher, added a dash of theater to the pulpit and proved to be a talented entertainer as well.

Ellen's role was also ready made. Healthy, yet not all that tall, she'd reach those pedals with her short legs flying like a second grader's with her first bike. Watching her play with the vigor required to keep the bellows going was quite a sight. By the end of the first hymn at any service or event, she felt like she was personally battling for Christ in hand-to-hand combat.

When she married Thad, she was only sixteen yet fully capable of handling the rigors of a circuit-riding, buggy preacher. But she had never been out of the county, so some days she felt like Moses in the wilderness, losing her way in the heavy brush, or like Noah in the ark, when it rained for forty days and forty nights.

Thad, meanwhile, preached that "the demons are upon us," often sounding much like an inspired demon himself.

One day, Ellen muttered to Thad under her breath, "There don't seem to be many people who believe in demons anymore. How are you going to handle that?" to which Thad simply replied, "Well, we will just have to convince people that there *are* demons."

Mountain music was made up mostly of fiddlers and banjo players, so the organ became a hot item whenever it appeared. Unlike most Baptist preachers of the day, Thad was not opposed to a little dancing for a good cause now and then, and the organ added an unusual flavor to the popular and necessary barn dances of the day, as well as the house-raising celebrations.

The Estey Organ Company, established in Battleboro, Vermont, in 1852, designed organs for missionary work. These were reed organs that generated sound with foot-pumped bellows. Smaller, cheaper, and more portable than pipe organs, reed organs could be folded down into themselves to become a rectangular box with leather strap handles on the ends for carrying and then easily strapped onto the back of a wagon or buggy.

Barn raisings and house raisings were preceded by log rollings at which the men would clear land, cut trees, and burn debris. Then the logs would be left out to season and later used to build barns and houses. Neighbors from adjoining farms would gather to "raise" these barns and houses using the seasoned logs—events often leading to quite a party.

For folks basically cut off from the outside world, work was also a form of social interaction, and great feasts would be held following these events. Thad was usually there to bless the food, and Ellen to play a few hymns before the festivities got off to a rollicking start.

Visitors to their small world were few and far between. So with the 1883 arrival of the railroad in Jasper, the tiny capital of Pickens County, Ellen welcomed the music and expanded social life. Thad, for his part, delighted in the new opportunities to preach, especially to the hundreds who came by train for the gospel-singing contests held in May and September on the steps of the courthouse. It was an 1800s version of Woodstock minus the drugs and sex, of course.

The gospel songs of the Deep South were a uniquely American and deeply emotional style of religious music that could be traced back to early American folk music and African American spirituals. At the end of the festivities Ellen would play a haunting closing hymn that would linger over the dusky blue mountains as the families made their way home, eager to arrive before dark and avoid encounters with hungry bears on the trail.

In addition to Thad's circuit preaching, the couple was kept busy blessing the food at amusements such as box suppers, which were held to raise money for various causes. For these suppers, young ladies prepared special baskets of delicious meals that were calculated to appeal to their sweethearts. Each box was auctioned off to the highest bidder, with the sweetheart often having been apprised of his lady's box—whether by a special ribbon or other means. Fights sometimes broke out at these events, but with Thad on hand they refrained since few wanted to spar with him. It wouldn't be a fair fight anyway because they would either go to hell for fighting with the preacher or the devil would make them go ten rounds with him!

Corn shucking was another occasion for merriment. In addition to completing the chore of pulling the outer husks off ears of corn, there was also the benefit of a drop of "corn likker" for those who wanted it. The rivalry was robust, not just for the one who shucked the most corn but also the one who found the most red ears. If the corn got liquefied, the fiddlers might play till the moonlight became the sunrise. With her organ having been safely packed away early in the evening, Ellen didn't like to stay overlong at a corn husking.

Native Americans often appeared at these functions, where their skills and hard work were warmly welcomed. After all, Pickens County had been "The Land of the Cherokees" until their forced removal in 1838, when their terrible death march of 1,000 miles led them on the Trail of Tears to Oklahoma and the unknown "Land of the Setting Sun." Still, some had evaded the US soldiers and lived off the land, though they were hard to find in their mountain habitats.

The Cherokees were highly regarded, and their degree of civilization was indeed incredible. Among much else, they were the only Indian tribe to use a written language, which had been developed by their chief Sequoyah between 1809 and 1824. In devising this writing system, Sequoyah had given his people an enduring gift allowing the greatness of the Cherokee Nation to live forever.

Sequoyah was a mixed-breed Cherokee born in Tennessee who later fled to Georgia to escape the incursion of whites. While there, he learned silversmithing and began to sell his work. A buyer suggested he sign his work just as the white silversmiths signed theirs. Unable to write, he enlisted the help of a wealthy farmer, who showed him how to spell his name. Following this, Sequoyah became convinced of his people's need for literacy. So using a phonetic system in which each sound made in speech is represented by a symbol, he created "Talking Leaves," the eighty-five letters that now make up the Cherokee alphabet. Within months, thousands of Cherokees had become literate. By 1825, much of the Bible and numerous hymns had been translated into Cherokee. And by 1828, the Cherokees had published their first bilingual newspaper, the *Cherokee Phoenix*, along with religious pamphlets, educational materials, and legal documents.

Because of his knowledge of the alphabet, Sequoyah later became an Arkansan delegate and appealed to the federal government to defend Indian lands and people from encroaching whites—to no avail. President Andrew Jackson ordered the removal of Indian people to "Indian Territory." The Cherokees on tribal lands were the last Indians subject to removal in any state east of the Mississippi, except for the Seminoles in Florida. As for the Cherokees who lived on private lands rather than communally owned tribal lands, they were exempted from removal and became integrated into the white community. Ellen was often thrust into their company and even taught one of the women to play a simple tune on the organ, much to their mutual delight.

Thad now had a wife and an organ player, but he still didn't have a church or money—which made little difference to them as there was hardly anything to buy. What small trading was done had to be on credit and based on the constantly depreciating confederate dollar, with which corn could cost $1,000.

Thad and Ellen were no different from the other mountain folk. They lived remote from cities and railroads and made an honest living through hard labor. Thad's father had been a farmer before the War and afterward returned to that labor with a few hoarded seeds and some fruit trees that had been spared Sherman's destruction.

After their first child, Lillie, was born in 1869, Ellen longed for a life more stable than tearing around the mountains in a buggy, hanging on for dear life, while her husband practiced preaching to every rock and tree along the way. She soon decided that the missionary organ had been invented just to torment her.

Thad was like a spinning top, rolling full-speed down a mountainside, laying waste to everything in sight. There was no stopping him. He was never quiet and never satisfied unless he had some poor soul quivering in the audience fearfully awaiting his fate—heaven or hell, what would it be? Thad always kept them in suspense right up until the last minute and only gave them relief when the organ began to blast out "Come to Jesus, all ye weary laden," usually played by Ellen praying for a rest on the pedals.

So Ellen took Lillie to their small farm and was happy to rock her baby instead of leading "Rock of Ages." She kept hoping to inspire Thad to ease up a little, but her prayers were never answered!

Thad was a self-proclaimed preacher steeped in the Word and convinced he was put on this earth to save every last soul, whether they wanted it or not. Once, riding up to one of his circuit sermons, he took off the saddle, put it under the building, and announced, "It's gonna rain." Since there had just been a long drought, the crowd was pretty skeptical, but one hour later it indeed rained. Thad was in mid-sentence, and the rain came down so hard that the creek overflowed, meaning there was going to be some serious baptizing. People came from all around the next Sunday to see both the baptizing and the amazing young man whose sermon had simultaneously called down the wrath of God and the rain. Now that's entertainment, folks.

6.

The Man Came
Down from the Mountains

Excerpt from the *Atlanta Journal* (July 12, 1900):

And the man came down from the mountains of Hepsidam and preaches to the sinners of Buckhead. Now he comes to Atlanta as Nineveh, calling on sinners to repent and flee from the wrath to come. "In Atlanta," said he, "church spires go up to heaven while sinners go down to hell," and he calls for a revival of the old-time religion with a preaching of the plain old-fashioned gospel, which he declares has become unpopular.

He further says that "statesmen and faithful ministers of the gospel never get rich. Only imposters in religion and demagogues in politics ever succeed in that. Consequently, I am a poor man. The old-fashioned gospel is not popular. I know it because I preach that kind."

In this, Mr. Pickett epitomizes his own career. He has been a Baptist preacher in the mountains of North Georgia for many years, and in the intervals of his ministry has found time to run for Congress twice. . . . From this it may be inferred that the Reverend Thad Pickett is not a preacher of the stereotypical type. He is a picturesque figure, a fine specimen of physical manhood. His style of delivery is easy and tone conversational until he rises to a climax, when the voice develops explosive qualities like the detonation of a bomb thrown high in the air. He walks the floor gesticulating with suggestive force. He speaks rapidly and fluently. His mind is saturated with the language of the Bible. He seems to think out loud in scriptural terms. His diction is a blending of the homely speech of everyday life with the sublime style of Job, the pregnant passages of Paul, or the brilliant metaphors of the prophets. He brings into the city the free spirit of the mountains.

In another sermon, Mr. Pickett pays respects to the unoffending clergy. He is down on preachers who want the good opinion of all. A large crowd gathered under the tent . . . near Inman Park last night to hear the Reverend Thaddeus Pickett deliver one of his characteristic sermons. "Now I mean to say exactly what I please about the preachers," said he. "They are home folk. If you people out there don't like it, just call it a family row and settle it among ourselves."

BY THE TIME THAT ARTICLE WAS PUBLISHED, THAD WAS known far and wide as a fearsome follower of the gospel who went from a buggy-riding circuit preacher to an ordained minister with the ability to draw an audience of hundreds, if not thousands. Sadly, Ellen was no longer by his side, a victim of one of the many fevers of the time or simply worn out from pumping that damn organ! When she died on September 28, 1880, Thad was off on one of his many wild rides and received word of her death from an Indian runner. Ellen's father, a physician, had been unable to save her.

So Thad was back to where he started—no wife and no organ player—but he did have an eleven-year-old daughter, Lillie, who needed mothering. As he combed the country-side looking for sinners, he also kept his eyes open for a new wife. He frequently encountered a devout family named Worley. They were sympathetic to his plight in general but specifically attuned to the fact they also had an eighteen-year-old marriageable daughter named Laura.

Never indecisive, Thad decided to propose and went to put on his courting clothes. They were the same as his working and Sunday go-to-meeting clothes. In fact, they were the only clothes he owned: a black frock coat, black wool pants, a homespun shirt, and boots that he polished as often as possible with a mixture of water and chimney soot.

Thad and Laura were married December 2, 1880, slightly over two months after Ellen was buried. Laura could not play the organ, but she could produce sons, and their first one, Orestes, was born exactly nine months later, on September 2, 1881. He was sickly at birth and did not improve with age. Like many children born in the nineteenth century, he would not survive much past maturity.

Orestes was a peculiar name for a Southerner to choose as it had its origins in Greek mythology. According to Homer in his *Odyssey*, Orestes was the son of Agamemnon, king of Mycenae, and his wife, Clytemnestra. Homer writes that Orestes was away when his father returned from Troy to meet his death at the hands of his wife's lover. Upon reaching manhood, Orestes avenged his father by killing his mother and her lover.

It was also an unlikely name choice since Orestes, like Laura's later sons, was deeply devoted to his mother. Explaining the choice of name, Thad said: "On the day he was born, I was at my desk comparing the mythological Greek gods to the one true God of the Bible. I read this story and liked the way the name rolled off my tongue. The name was so powerful you could almost taste the sound in your mouth. Naturally, I had to give him a strong name because he was not born a strong boy and would need all the help he could get."

Soon Laura was managing a growing household of six sons and a daughter. Over an almost twenty-year period, from 1881 to 1900, Laura continued to produce her large brood. In addition to Orestes, there was Roscoe, Golden, Thad Jr., Ed, and finally, Hillyer, the youngest, who would later become known simply as Pick. Her only daughter, their middle child, was named Dainty Lenora. Her stepdaughter, Lillie, remained a beloved part of the household until her own early marriage a few years later. Lillie and Laura were only seven years apart, so they simply grew up together.

In addition to managing the household, Laura also managed a thriving ministry for Thad. She was quiet but determined. He became the preacher for Talking Rock Baptist Church, where he and Ellen had been married. He also ministered Friendship Baptist Church, which had started in 1840 with eleven members. It was housed in a log structure measuring thirty-two feet by twenty-six feet with only a small doorway to let in light. There were no windows because glass was not available, and besides there was no ready money to make the purchase. Actually, the lack of light also made it a lot easier to sleep through a sermon!

Church services were not held in the mountains every Sunday because there were no full-time preachers and thus circuit riders were utilized when available. You needed a good horse and expert riding skills to do that for a living. You also needed to be grateful for "love offerings." Preachers, who were seldom salaried, were dependent on whatever funds a congregation could spare in the spirit of love. Since money was hard to come by, an offering might simply be comprised of peas and potatoes.

Thad was a much beloved preacher, but that was not always the case for his competition. After sermons delivered by other preachers, the congregation was sometimes known to triumphantly sing, "I am resolved no longer to linger."

With few church buildings standing, tent revivals and camp meetings were very popular. As church was the primary source of entertainment, religious events were held under a variety of circumstances. It helped if you were a "true believer," but most folks went to church as much for the social activity as any religious fervor. It was one activity enthusiastically approved by the entire population, particularly in the rural South.

Camp meetings bringing farmers and festivities together often started on a Friday. They could run from ten days to two weeks, when there was always a "dinner on the grounds" for participants and picnic baskets filled to the brim with special dishes for lunch. There were usually three services a day—at 8:00 am, 11:00 am, and 3:00 pm— and, in the absence of electricity, a candlelight service at night.

When people really caught the fever, services could last all day and into the night. Penitents would go to the anxious seat (mourner's bench). As for the rest of the congregants, in addition to the praying and preaching there was also lots of singing and fiddling. This was perfect entertainment for an isolated population, and they loved it.

Friendship Baptist Church tells the story about how on one occasion the Reverend Thad was preaching and everything seemed "cold." The night before, some of the brethren told him to just preach a short sermon in the morning then close the meeting, but Thad was having none of that: he began preaching at 8:00 am and did not stop till 11:20 am. At the end of the meeting, fifty people were baptized. Some were believers, and others had been frightened into a frenzy created by the thundering sermon.

You didn't have to be a swimmer to be baptized, and Thad was determined that if he saved a soul for redemption he sure wasn't going to lose it to a drowning, so he held them tightly and took them to the shallow end. Baptisms were usually done in a nearby mountain creek and had become yet another special occasion for food, festivities, and gossip. A favorite form of entertainment was observing how the sinner "took" the baptizing. Did he go easy or did the congregant thrash about like a fish on a hook?

7.

The Great Adventuress

FAYE'S MOTHER, MAE, WAS A DEEPLY RELIGIOUS WOMAN whose faith sustained her throughout her 103 years. She possessed a great sense of adventure, as was evidenced by her early life, and she was an educated woman, which was unusual at that time. Women were rarely schooled beyond the basic skills, as their role would be confined to the home. Educating a housewife was thought to be frivolous.

Caroline Mae Love was a shining figure with a mind so bright you could almost hear it crackle. She wore her red hair in two braids that she twisted around on the top of her head like a crown. When she took it down to wash it, her hair was so long that it hung down to her knees and would shimmer like rubies in the morning sun as she brushed it, holding one long piece at a time over her shoulder.

Her demeanor was in almost comical contrast to that of her husband, Ollie, who was 6 feet 2 with a dark Cherokee heritage and a quiet, controlled manner. Mae was always busy talking, sewing, reading, teaching, or cooking. Ollie said little and smiled often. His soft, sweet smile was striking on such an imposing figure. The children all thought it was magic to sit on his lap by an open fire. Being held so gently and tenderly, they were lulled into a feeling of such safety that even when he slipped his finger into a mouth to pull a loose tooth, they were too entranced to cry.

While fresh out of college, Mae had left her home and her fiancé in Tennessee, to pursue what she loved most—teaching. Wanting to teach three sessions a year instead of only a winter one, she had answered a newspaper ad for a teaching job in a place she had never heard of: Brookfield, Georgia. The three-day train trip to Brookfield required connecting in Atlanta, which was bustling and post-Civil War busy at that time. But Mae was in a hurry to get to her dream, so she reluctantly left Atlanta behind and pressed on. She was full of smoke from the coal-spouting train engine, as well as excitement and anticipation, when she finally reached Brookfield.

All she needed now was a place to live and a church to attend. Right away, she took a room in a boardinghouse that came with an organ, a piano, and a handsome man. The handsome man sang while she played the piano, which led to courting then progressed to buggy rides, church socials, and cakes. Mae was a superb baker who nonetheless knew that she was too intelligent and ambitious to be completely satisfied as a farmer's wife, which would have been her fate had she not left home. It was a close-run call, but the handsome man, Ollie, won the toss. She threw over her fiancé in Tennessee, married the handsome man, and started to have lots of things in the oven—nine altogether.

Even so, Mae never quit teaching. She taught all nine of her children at home till second grade, using a piece of oil cloth mounted on the kitchen wall to create words, numbers, and games as the children patiently sat at her feet shelling peas, shucking corn, or churning butter. Even story time became a lesson as she spun tales of fairies and goblins who could not only count but also read and write stories about their cats and dogs. Soon every child was counting the pigs on the farm or reading their own stories to placid cows busy chewing their cuds.

8.

Cars in My Eyes

James Hillyer Pickett was nine years old when the Reverend Thad died in 1909. The youngest of six sons, he had a beautiful older sister, Lenora, and an older half-sister, Lillie. The baby of the family, whom everyone adored, Hillyer, as he was known at the time, was a precocious little boy, not only highly intelligent but full of energy and questions. He also had an insatiable taste for adventure.

After the shock of his father's death, Hillyer realized that life on the farm would now consist of an endless stream of dawn-to-dark days filled with nothing but work. The mantra of the Pickett household had always been "If you don't work, you don't eat," implying that everyone on the farm had a job to do and, if it wasn't done, everybody suffered.

Hillyer's job was to rise before dawn, cut and gather firewood and start the fires in both of the family's fireplaces and the wood-burning stove. That stove was the most important item in the house because it not only allowed food to be cooked but also permitted water to be heated in a cylinder attached to the back, providing warm water for soups and stews, scrubbing dishes, washing up, and for the occasional bath as well.

If you are thinking cozy hot tub with a built-in wooden frame, bubbles, and candlelight, forget about it. Bathing took place in the kitchen using a small metal pan turned up on both ends so the water wouldn't slosh out. The pan was nearly the width of a kayak and just about as comfortable. *Luxury* was not a word to be associated with bathing; *necessity* was more like it.

Oils and perfumes were unavailable, and the cleanser was a scratchy lump of lye soap made from potash blended with water and lard. Fat was rendered from whatever meat source was available and saved for a variety of uses, including soap and candles. Sometimes that come-hither smell emanating from a shiny clean woman could be bacon fat. If you were hungry for pork, it could be a great evening!

Women usually washed their hair once a month and used Borax or egg yolks for shampoo. Bathing didn't occur each day because water was too precious and too difficult to get into the house. The only running water was provided by young children with large pails running back and forth from the hand pump in the backyard. Hillyer always hoped he would be the first one in the bath while the water was still warm and clean because he, like the others, knew the water wouldn't get changed till everybody had bathed!

After breakfast, Hillyer was off in the woods hunting squirrels and rabbits. Despite his young age, he was a calm and accurate shot. That came from endless practice with his father and older brothers. Hunting for game was not a sport but a necessity. Livestock were too valuable to eat and were either kept for milk and butter or bred for sale. The squirrels and rabbits were supper.

Hillyer attended school regularly and was a star pupil. He particularly liked geography and was always asking questions about other places. He kept saying to himself, "I know there is another world out there somewhere, and I want to find it." He had been to Jasper with Thad a few times and he was determined to get off that farm and look at something that could not be seen from between the legs of a cow or the top of a mule.

Money was scarce. Thad had tithed with fervor, so there was little left for Laura. She often wailed, "How am I going to keep body and soul together and feed this family?" So one by one, her lads, as she always thought of them, began to leave the farm. Slowly news of the changing postwar world began to creep up the mountains as surely as the mountain laurel flowered across the hillside.

In 1909, the average life expectancy was forty-seven years and the average worker earned $200 to $400 dollars a year. William Howard Taft had just been inaugurated the twenty-seventh president of the United States and construction on the Titanic had just begun in Belfast, Ireland. The Army Air Corps was formed as the army took delivery on the first military aircraft from the Wright Brothers, while Admiral Perry, the first man to reach the North Pole, climbed it in 1909, at the same time a French aviator made the first flight across the English Channel. Construction on the Panama Canal as well as the naval base at Pearl Harbor began while the Indianapolis Speedway opened to motorcycles and Ty Cobb stole home in the World Series.

Yet, things were happening closer to home that got Hillyer's attention and started him off on a rollicking, frolicking adventure. From the time he saw a car to the time he backed Dr. MacDonald's contraption home, he knew he was hopelessly, desperately in love with the automobile. He thought, "I don't know what it is going to take, but I am determined to have one of those for myself. I have to get busy and find a way."

That meant he had to get a job, and jobs were scarce in those hills. So at the age of fourteen, he hired himself out to a neighboring farmer, who gave him room, board, and twenty-five cents a week—not much money, but after two years enough to buy a suit of clothes and a railroad ticket to Atlanta. There, with an eye to enterprise and opportunity that came to define him, he hired himself out as a driver for the rich men who could afford to buy cars but didn't have a clue how to drive them.

9.

A Long Empty Road

FAYE WAS ANOTHER ONE WHO DID NOT DRIVE. FOR ONE thing, she didn't know how; for another, there wasn't anything to drive but her daddy's old pickup truck. It had seen lots of use hauling fertilizer and hogs, and on Sundays it was the only means for getting to church. The entire family piled in so closely it looked like a sea of eyes and noses topped with red hair splattered with soot by an occasional brunette. Everybody knew when the Loves arrived at church. Their old pickup looked like a circus truck unloading a troupe of midgets as an endless supply of legs, arms, and bottoms hopped out.

Faye dreaded going to church because she was ashamed of how she looked in her homemade dress and poorly fitting shoes. It didn't matter that her brothers and sisters were dressed in a similar state. She thought to herself, "I deserve better. I want all those things the town girls have—their pretty clothes, their houses, their family cars and especially their parties." Envy was becoming her middle name.

She might not have pretty clothes, but she knew she had a pretty face and was spotless in whatever meager outfit she wore. She kept thinking as she sat in church with her family, "I might be poor, but I am always clean and neat. Nobody will ever be able to say that anything about me is dirty."

Her oldest sibling, Gwen, had once made an offhand, hurried remark to Faye, exclaiming, "Get away from me, you stinking little ole thing." Not only was Faye humiliated at the time, but it marked her for life. She would still think about it years later while sitting next to Gwen in the pew. Church attendance was a requirement in her household, and she didn't dare miss a sermon. She might not listen, but she would dutifully be in her place in the pew.

Both her parents were deeply religious and passed their strong beliefs down to their children. Faye believed she believed, but what she really believed in was not the road to heaven but the road to Atlanta. So far, the road looked pretty empty, but she was still young and hopeful.

10.

Mae's Beautiful Garden

WHILE PICK COMPETED WITH THE ELEMENTS, FAYE COM-peted on the home front in Tift County. One of the poor farm girls who attended high school in town, she had to ride the school bus to get there. She hated the noisy bus that traveled from farm to farm collecting rural students. It was cold in the winter, hot in the summer, and always dusty. She especially hated the dirt that she could almost feel creeping through the windows. She lived on a dirt road on a dirt farm and now had to ride on dirt to school every day as well. She kept herself busy on the ride by picking the slightest specks of dust from her clothing. She was fanatical about cleanliness. That was the only thing in her life she could completely control.

Her own family occupied a large part of the bus, and she wanted time away from them. She thought, "I want to be by myself for a change, left alone without somebody else always looking over my shoulder." That was a rarity she didn't often experience. Everything had to be shared—not just space, clothes, shoes, and food but even time itself.

Although there was always competition on the bus to get the best seat, all Faye cared about was staying as far from the windows and door as possible so as to keep herself clean. Therefore, she only competed for the aisle seat in the back, and woe betide the person who got there before her.

She was used to competition as she was born into a family of beautiful people. Her mother, petite and redheaded, had been touted the most beautiful woman in Tift County. Her tall, dark-haired father was equally handsome. They produced nine children who were evenly divided between redheads and brunettes, with one blonde thrown in for good measure.

Gwen, the oldest, was a redhead who mothered her younger brothers and sisters with sweetness and kindness. She would retain her mother figure role throughout her life and was always the one to calm the angry seas of family dramas. With such a large brood of redheads, tempers could flash like wildfire.

Garland was the second born who would later change her name to Betty. She hated her name, but not her hair. She was the blonde and had a stern and serious side to her. Garland seldom laughed as she didn't see much to laugh about in a large and busy household where she had so many responsibilities.

Ollie Jr., the first son and third child, was a brunette with a smile and eyes that could charm a kitten without using a saucer of milk. His calm and gentle manner was much like his father's. He was also blessed with dark good looks and the keen intelligence all the children had inherited from Mae.

Faye was the fourth and a full-out redhead with a temper to go with it. She, like all her brothers and sisters, had inherited their mother's short stature. Yet at only five feet, Faye felt tall by comparison to her mother, whom she often called "Shorty." While petite in every way, Faye was a beautiful female specimen with blue, intelligent eyes and a perfectly formed figure. She never wore her hair in pigtails, even as a child. She liked to feel it swinging down her back as she prissed and posed, always expecting to be admired.

The only thing that marred her perfection was the crippled ring finger on her right hand, the result of a deep cut from a saw blade. One day as a young child, she had been playing on the front porch while her father did some carpentry on the steps. Her curiosity ultimately got the better of her, and she slipped and fell. Fortunately, her father managed to catch her before she crashed down the steps, but her finger suffered a serious cut. It never healed properly, and she was left with a deformed finger for the rest of her life. However, she learned to write with her left hand and exhibited beautiful penmanship. But she also learned to use that story any time sympathy was required as it always got her the attention she craved. She would cry out, "I can't do that because of my crippled finger." She eventually developed a repertoire of pitiful stories to be dragged out at a moment's notice.

Her young brother Larry was also a redhead, but a sweeter one. He didn't have much of a temper, but he didn't need to. His talents lay elsewhere. He had enough stubbornness to make a mule shake his head in despair. No one was ever able to change his mind about anything. He was argumentative and bull-headed, driving everybody crazy when he refused to shift his position on any matter. Debates with him were always losing propositions. Yet he was always kind and loving.

The sixth child, Wallace, was spared the red hair but got some of the temper nonetheless. His dark hair was rich and thick and waved across his forehead like a flag in the breeze. Wallace seemed a bit aloof, which added a layer of mystery to his good looks. It was often said that he was so like his older brother, Ollie, that they could have been twins. Wallace took his responsibilities very seriously and eventually would be the one to manage the family farm.

Sara Mae was the seventh child and a redhead as well. She inherited her mother's beauty as well as her brains. An intellectual who craved learning, she would eventually become the most educated of all her siblings. She went on to earn a master's degree and teach on several levels, including an occasional stint at the university. She had a tremendous spirit as well, and her curiosity would take her on great adventures all over the world.

Vernon, or "Bunny" as June called him, was the eighth child and full of mischief from the day he was born. He loved to tell jokes and pull pranks on others. He and June were very close as they were only two years apart. They also shared a wonderful sense of humor. Bunny had a great time having a great time. In fact, he was way too much fun for his own good and always up to something that *was* no good. He was another brunette with dancing dark eyes and a devilish smile and attitude to go with it. A born heart breaker, he played the role to the hilt. Women would always adore him, but none more so than his mother. He was her "baby" and would remain her favorite all his life.

The last flower in Mae and Ollie's beautiful garden was June. Mae was thankful when she arrived, but said to Ollie, "I hope God does not send us any more because I don't think I can do this again. I am too old at forty-five to tend to any more young 'uns." Though June and Sara were five years apart, they would remain close all their lives. However, there were times when June felt left out among all these busy and fiercely focused people. Although just as intelligent, ambitious, and beautiful as any of them, she was so far down the line that she sometimes felt forgotten.

She was very creative, musically gifted, and artistic as well. She loved arranging bouquets and felt at home among the beautiful flowers of her mother's extensive garden.

She had hair black as the night and snapping eyes to match. Her olive skin set her apart from the fair complexions of the others, so much so that she laughingly called herself "Little Black June." She laughed constantly at herself as well as all the others in the family. Her humor would become her trademark.

Life in this household was a constantly noisy experience. In addition to children clattering and chattering everywhere, there were the constant household noises: chimes of pots and pans, dishes being washed, wood being cut, floors swept, windows washed, dogs barking, pigs squealing, and animals braying. Faye couldn't wait to get away.

11.

Swinging a Pick

Hillyer's first job in Atlanta was driving one of the city's most successful doctors on his house calls up and down the famed Peachtree Street. Hillyer found it fascinating and exciting. The beautiful women he constantly met in the company of the good doctor particularly excited him. Occasionally he was invited to pick a young peach off the tree. One of them, however, had not quite ripened, and consequently Hillyer had to make a hasty departure to another employer.

While Hillyer loved driving the cars, he was no closer to owning one. So he took the train back to Jasper, said goodbye to his mother, Laura, and went to work for The Marietta and North Georgia Railroad, digging holes for the telegraph poles that ran alongside the rail lines.

The railroad had come to North Georgia in 1883 and brought jobs and wealth to some of the towns along its route as the vast resources of the Pickens County marble industry began to emerge. The Cherokees had quarried marble by hand for carvings and other decorative uses. They also made the stone into projectile points. With the arrival of new European immigrants, the Cherokees were forced from their homeland and the former Cherokee lands were redistributed through lotteries to the new arrivals.

Among them was Irish stonecutter Henry T. Fitzsimmons, who recognized the huge potential of the high-quality marble and quickly established a productive marble works. Through the Civil War and for a couple of decades afterward, the industry limped along, limited by the difficulty inherent in moving the heavy marble products. With the arrival of the railroad in 1883 and this new capacity for marble to be shipped across the nation, the industry began to thrive. During the marble boom of the 1930s, Georgia marble was utilized for the figure of Lincoln at the Washington Memorial, the Longworth House Office building in Washington, DC, the US Supreme Court Building, the Puerto Rican capitol, the New York Stock Exchange, and later for the renovation of the east wing of the US Capitol Building, as well as many other projects.

Hillyer didn't hang around for all that. He went to work on the railroad with one thing in mind and that was to make money so that someday he could own a damn car. Like his father, he was long and strong, and his young back could handle the strain of hauling around his awkward and heavy tools. The pick, shovel, ax and other necessary one-hundred-fifty pounds of equipment outweighed Hillyer, but he still managed to carry it with him as he made his way down the line. Hillyer didn't need to worry about making time during a busy week to "work out." His was grueling labor digging holes with a pick and a shovel, but it made him as strong as Tarzan! He kept thinking to himself, "This is hard work, but it is going to get me a car someday, so I can do it."

After Samuel Morse, a professor of arts and design at New York University, patented the telegraph in 1837, it became an essential means of communication. The device soon changed how news was communicated over distances—

now it arrived in hours instead of weeks—and in 1851 the Western Union Telegraph Company was founded in Rochester, New York.

Early telegraph networks were mostly constructed alongside railway lines. The standard practice was to hang them from insulators on telegraph poles, which meant establishing a pole route in advance along a continuous strip of land between the points to be linked. This required a lot of land, and the telegraph companies didn't own any. So to obtain rights to erect their poles they made agreements with landowners, which required continuous negotiations with them as well as a host of officials.

Eventually it was the railroad companies themselves who became the first serious customers for this advanced technology. Since the telegraph could transmit messages faster than a train could move, it became key in communicating arrivals and departures of trains up and down the line.

This was Hillyer's work, so he had a lot of job security as each mile of telegraph required about thirty to forty poles. He was becoming stronger and stronger each day. At the end of the day there wasn't much to look forward to because bed was going to be a boxcar, which certainly didn't include room service, a minibar, or cable TV.

The railroad crew was made up of varying degrees of smart, stupid, lazy, and mischievous young men. The smart ones learned early on not to mess with Hillyer because he was not only strong but fast. As with any group, there is always a stupid one who can't quite figure it out—that would be Henry. He was not new to the railroad, but he was new to Hillyer, and Henry decided to teach the newcomer a lesson. Henry was no match for Hillyer, so it was over very quickly. But Henry was not entirely stupid: he jumped off the train at the next station early the following morning, and by the time Hillyer arrived there later that day, carrying his tools, Henry was set to make some money. He had organized a fight with the local bouncer and was taking bets that Hillyer would whip him. That proved to be the case. Hillyer said to himself, "I don't have a choice except to fight, because if I refuse I will have the entire railroad crew to deal with. They have all laid bets and will gang up on me." So he slugged it out bare-fisted till his opponent finally dropped.

It got to be a pretty regular routine: Henry would be the advance man, set up the fights, take the bets and then split the profits with Hillyer. They didn't win every time, but often enough so that Hillyer was soon making more money fighting than he was digging holes. Folks in every town along the route began to hear about Pick, the Iron Man. Henry kept the bets coming by singing, "Pick Pickett and you've got the winning ticket." Soon Hillyer became known simply as Pick.

It didn't take many fights for Pick to figure out that he lacked the temperament for the ring, so he handed in his tools, took his winnings, and headed back to Jasper and his Pickens County roots. He had enough savings to buy a horse and start a new career where Thad had left off—as a circuit-riding preacher. Because of his upbringing, Pick knew that Bible so well he could rattle off any chapter and verse at any time.

Before long, Henry was back in the picture taking bets on who could trip up Pick on the Bible. It never happened. After a few months of preaching and several miles of riding that horse, Pick decided he might have been "called" to preach but wasn't going to answer the phone. He wasn't cut out to be a preacher, and the pain in his ass, acquired from too many hours in the saddle, agreed with him.

12.

Pieorgis and Polkas

PICK STILL DIDN'T HAVE A CAR AND HE STILL WANTED ONE. He couldn't be a circuit rider, but he could he could ride the trains. So telling himself, "There are only two things that have ever made me any money, my fists and my faith," he took his last few dollars and, with Henry, boarded the train from Jasper to Chicago. To give himself some rest between bouts, he decided to preach in one town one day and fight somewhere else the next day. Henry, of course, wasn't going to miss out on making a buck, so he had Pick dubbed "The Fighting Preacher" and took bets on who was going to win, the Lord or the devil. If Pick won, the devil made him do it, and if he lost, it was the Lord's will.

Pick arrived in Chicago with a few more dollars than he expected. That small amount of money, however, would not last long, and jobs and housing were scarce. Chicago had become the transportation hub of the United States with its road and rail and the waterways of the huge Lake Michigan. That city was where all the main rail lines from the East Coast ended in and all the western ones began. Over thirty rail lines entered the city, which made it a natural distribution point for goods. Further fueled by industrial expansion, Chicago was a magnet for immigrants from Eastern and Southern Europe.

Chicago in 1918 was a city of great ethnic diversity, its thousands of immigrants contributing to political diversity as well. Pick had no experience with any of this. Being from the rural South, he was the first to admit that his food and politics were limited to pork chops and preaching.

Yet, he was fascinated with everything he saw and eager to explore this strange and exciting new world. He found a room that he shared with four other men, in a rundown boardinghouse owned by a Polish woman. Soon he learned to drink Polish beer, dance the polka, and speak some Polish words, thanks to the landlady's daughter. He taught her some new words as well, but she never understood how to say no in English.

His introduction to Polish culture was intense. He soon graduated from the pork chops of the South to the unfamiliar tastes of *bigos*, a hunter's stew made of sauerkraut and *kielbasa* sausage and cabbage and served with *piwo*, or beer. He came to love the meat- or fruit-filled dumplings of Pierogia and the stuffed crepes of Nalesniki swimming in sour cream. His first taste of *wino* and *wódka* made the dancing that followed far more enjoyable. He particularly favored the *trojak*, a double-partner dance with one male and two female dancers in which the boy dances with one girl while the second one dances alone and then the boy switches partners. Now Pick was certain he had encountered bliss, and was swept up in the energy of the music, the swirling women, and, of course, the vodka. His first dancing performance became legendary.

He had never before had beer, much less vodka, and the hangover he had the next day would have crushed Superman. When he woke up, he was afraid to move. His head hurt with such intensity that he thought he had been in a fight and lost. That was pretty much the case, except he had lost to the very thing Thad had always preached against — the evils of drink. Well, Pick reckoned if he was going to hell he might as well get on with it, then took Henry's advice for "the cure" and did it again.

After he got the drinking part figured out, he had to tackle the religious angle. He had never met a Roman Catholic before, but determined to find out if their God was different from his he went to the cathedral. He was confused by all the business of people moving their hands over their chests and considered it some sort of hand signal for a game they were fixing to play. Nor could he understand what was being said, only to find out later that no one else could either. Polish was hard enough for him to grasp, but Latin was impossible. And at first, Pick thought they were "speaking in tongues," as some fundamentalists groups were known to do.

Everyone else just smiled and knelt down on some piece of wood that didn't look big enough to hold a Bible, much less a person. There he heard moaning going on up front at the altar, but Pick finally realized it was some kind of chant. He had heard the Cherokees do that sort of stuff when he was a kid and expected them to break out the communal pipe at any minute. Instead, this fellow in a dress talked some more and pretty soon marched down the aisle with his buddies, ringing some sort of bell. Pick thought it must be the dinner bell, so he trotted out behind them, hoping for dinner on the grounds! Or so the story goes.

Pick decided he better stick to the Baptists. They knew how to put on a good feed, and they didn't chant when they sang. Their gospel music was rich and vibrant, straight from the heart, and sung with enough volume to keep the devil at bay till the next Sunday.

Soon Pick had a new job in the tire warehouse at Sears Roebuck. His shifts lasted ten hours a day, six days a week.

The average workweek was fifty-four hours, but Pick worked extra hours to make more money. The average annual wage at that time was $875, a value equivalent to about $12,679 today. The average house cost $6,716. Other than Sundays, the only time Pick had off was for baseball practice. The US government would not implement a forty-hour workweek or the Fair Labor Standards Act until 1938.

Sears was still a catalog company with no retail stores, meaning everything was shipped directly to the customer. The massive fourteen-story Sears Merchandise Building had been constructed in 1906 with the help of seven thousand men who laid down 23 million bricks and 15 million feet of timber to construct the world's largest store and business complex. Soon a clubhouse, tennis courts, dining hall, and athletic field were added to this complex where company baseball rivaled many of the minor leagues.

Pick knew he could easily make the team and set about doing so. A skilled and graceful athlete, he was also fast and gifted with quick eye-hand coordination and a great arm. Soon his time in baseball practice was looking and sounding like a tennis match. The sounds of plop, plop were, like tennis serves, being returned as hits were made, and balls were caught and sent flying back with a constant rhythm of hit, catch, throw. Those combined assets made him a brilliant outfielder in a game he was to adore for the rest of his life. He loved baseball as much as he loved the Bible.

The work at Sears was messy, smelly, and cold, and consisted of very hard physical labor. He was used to that, but he was not used to union workers. He didn't even know what unions were, though he soon found out.

Chicago had a wide range of unskilled workers employed by the railroads, manufacturers, slaughter and meat packing companies, metal-working firms, garment manufacturers, and iron and steel producers. Most of these unskilled workers were immigrants with little, if any, education. Most also possessed an intense desire to better themselves. Union leaders persuaded them to organize for better pay, hours, and conditions.

Pick had to think about this in his new environment and calculate his risks and rewards. His work on the farm had meant long hours, little pay, and terrible conditions. His thought was, "So what is different here? If I join the union, there is no guarantee things will improve, and if I don't I will still have to fight my way to work every day among those who *have* joined."

He finally decided he had had enough fighting, and besides, that pretty little Polish girl was learning too many English phrases, including "marry me." So he and Henry jumped a boxcar and headed west to San Francisco.

13.

Dogs and Derelicts

PICK AND HENRY WERE USED TO SNEAKING ONTO TRAINS AND living in boxcars, but this trip was especially hard. The 2,500-mile train ride from Chicago to San Francisco usually took three days with stops in Iowa, Nebraska, Colorado, Utah, and Nevada. But this trip took much longer. The United States had entered World War I on April 6, 1917, and on December 28 of that year President Woodrow Wilson nationalized the railroads for troop movements and to long-haul necessary supplies for the war effort.

Railcars jammed with soldiers and supplies made for crowded and cramped conditions. There was hardly room to swing a cat without getting fur in your mouth. Yet, reprising his role as Preacher Pickett, he had managed to talk his way on board. By this time, he looked considerably older than his years. The harsh Chicago winter had inspired him to grow a beard, and it now wrapped around his face and neck like a fur coat on a frog. The only thing you could see was his nose and those piercing blue eyes.

His sermons on board the train became less about salvation than about survival and he continually comforted young men not much older than himself, as they anguished about the slaughter they were about to face upon entering the war. Europe had been on fire since 1914, with guns and ammunition igniting every major European border since the sobs of wives, mothers, sisters, and daughters had not been enough to change the minds of the politicians. The fighting in open trenches indicated it had become a war of attrition and whoever had the most men would ultimately win.

The third battle of Ypres lasted from July to November of 1917, during which the British casualties had run as high as 310,000 and the Germans 260,000. Because of the enormous losses, many soldiers began to refer to the battle as "Wipers." Adolf Hitler at the time was a German corporal who reportedly served as a regimental runner behind the frontlines. He was later awarded the Iron Cross for saving a wounded comrade. Hitler is probably the most studied and analyzed individual the world has ever known, but historians still disagree on his exact role in the war and what effect it may have had on his later life.

Europe had been running out of young men by the time the United States entered the conflict. The war was finally brought home to the United States after the British intercepted a coded message from Germany to Mexico. In it, the Germans promised portions of US lands would be returned to Mexico in exchange for Mexico joining the war against the United States.

With the army constantly requiring more troops, President Wilson shifted its enlistment status from volunteer to conscription. In June of 1917, the first draft since the Civil War began with the Conscription Act requiring all males between the ages of twenty-one and thirty-one to register. Later in the war, the age would be downgraded to eighteen.

Still only eighteen years old, Pick survived the train trip, but his heart was heavy as he watched men march off to an almost certain death. The romance of war had long faded for him, and while he was too young to be called up, he was just the right age to be called to San Francisco, and he meant to enjoy every minute of it. He had heard wild tales about the place from everybody on the train and was eager to see what it was all about.

San Francisco in 1918 was a humming, bustling, cosmopolitan and vibrant city. Its unique position, perched as it was on the hillsides of the Pacific Ocean with one of the world's largest known natural harbors, meant goods could be imported and exported worldwide. It had gone from the pioneer boomtown of the Gold Rush of 1849 to an elegantly rebuilt city after almost total destruction in the earthquake of 1906, which had left nearly a third of its population homeless.

Pick was immediately fascinated but told himself, "The first thing I need is a good shave. San Francisco looks very fancy, and I look like a bear!" That meant he had to find a room and a bed. He followed his nose down narrow, winding, busy streets jammed with sights and sounds he had never experienced. He knew he had to find something cheap, so he kept track of the dogs and derelicts along the way and when they started to lie down he figured he had found an affordable neighborhood.

After a quick shave, he was back on the streets, taking in the vibrant city life with big, wide eyes. He kept looking for Chinatown, which he had heard so much about. He had never seen an Asian and hoped they were as agreeable as the Poles he had met in Chicago, especially the girls.

After hours of hiking up and down steep streets, however, Pick felt a little frustrated. He was amazed at the trolley cars clanging their way through crowds, but he didn't have the money to waste on a ride, so he just kept walking. He had absolutely no desire to climb on one of those crazy machines and try to cling on like the rest of the folks seemed to be doing. In Chicago, he had seen electrically powered ones, but not going at 100 miles an hour down a sleep slope like these appeared to be. He figured the safety of sidewalks was better than a clanging calamity!

Suddenly, he turned a corner and there it was—the noisy, smelly, jingling, colorful, intoxicating, and exotic world of the Far East. He had to stop and catch his breath. Every single color, sight, sound, and person was more amazing than the next. Nothing in his young life had prepared him for the scene laid out before him like an unending buffet. All he could do was stare in awe as each and every one of his senses was bombarded again and again.

His farm life had been dull and dreary, and sensory indulgences had been limited in every way. There, clothing was almost exclusively black or brown, and made from wool, coarse cotton, or flannel. Here in Chinatown he saw the brilliance of purple, red, orange, yellow, gold, and silver streaming at him from all directions in the form of clothing, food, furniture, or painted faces. He touched silk for the first time and was astonished at how it slipped through his fingers like gravy over mashed potatoes. He vowed then and there, "Someday I will own silk ties, dress my ladies in silk, and sleep on silk sheets."

That would not be happening in the near future, however, because San Francisco was expensive and he was running out of money. Pick, inspired by the city's huge import-export industry, quickly found a job in another warehouse, where he struggled on for a few weeks. Then he heard that Alaska was the best place for a young man to be, and he decided to give it a try.

But there was one more thing he had to do before leaving San Francisco: he wanted to see a painted lady. He had heard about them from Henry, whose description was confusing but tantalizing as he raved on in ecstasy about them. Henry, of course, couldn't be counted on to tell the truth about much of anything, so you had to keep one eye closed and both ears open when he got to going on about something. Besides, he was no more an expert on women than Pick had been when they first met.

Pick kept looking at the delicate Chinese girls with their beautiful skin, elongated eyes, and shy smiles. Pretty soon he was smiling himself, as he learned some new skills under the colorful silks. His previous experience with women had pretty much been limited to industrial-strength farm girls and the generously proportioned Polish girls. Allured by the delicate Chinese flowers, he began learning enough Chinese to work his way through a large and beautiful garden. All the while he prayed that he hadn't "left fertilizer on any of those flowers."

Still, he wanted a painted lady! When he found out a painted lady was a Victorian house decorated in colorful, rich hues, he immediately summoned Henry, packed his bag, and caught a steamer for Anchorage. It was back to dogs and derelicts.

14.

Anchorage Away

I N LATE SPRING OF 1918, ANCHORAGE, ON THE SAME PARALLEL as Oslo and Stockholm, was just beginning to wake up from its winter's sleep. The town had been formed only four years before as a major construction camp for the northbound Alaska Railroad. It remained a tent city built of mud and dreams, where memories of the Klondike gold rush of 1899 still echoed. All of Alaska, in fact, was a sprawling, cold mystery. It had been bought from Russia fifty years before and finally organized as a territory in 1912. Its culture orbited around Alaskan Natives, with bows to Russia's ongoing fur trade and all that fiery vodka

Little had changed in Anchorage by the time Pick arrived. His sea journey on what turned out to be a relentlessly creaking steamer had been long, wet, and cold. The only entertainment on board had come from the constant howling of dogs in the cargo hold. By now, Pick was used to fun and didn't do boredom very well. To liven things up, Henry devised gambling scenarios and started taking bets on who could stand up the longest in the pitch and dive of the waves. After a bit, he took bets on everything from who could tell the biggest lie to who had the oldest coat. There was only one woman on board, whose name was Mary, so dancing was just about out of the question till they got Pick drunk. Because he was slender, an attribute that also applied to his feet—which were a mere size 9 and thin for a man—the passengers dressed him up in Mary's clothes and high heels then took bets. The first bet was about whether Pick could stand up in Mary's shoes. When he showed he could, the next bet pertained to how long and the third to whether he could dance in them. "Well," he muttered under his breath, "I didn't do all that polka stuff for nothing." Then he proceeded to fly around that floor as fast as the fiddle could twitch until a giant wave spilled them all in a heap with Pick on top of Mary, who apparently also loved to dance. They danced this way every night, it seemed, or at least they *claimed* it was dancing.

Pick's arrival in Anchorage was both dazzling and depressing. Not only was there glistening ice in the distance, but the town itself was surrounded by treacherous mudflats. Ships couldn't dock, as a wharf had yet to be built. Thus, passengers came ashore in shallow draft-boats, balancing on their heads whatever meager supplies they possessed. Once ashore, things were not much better as the foul city still had open sewers, and harried pedestrians clung precariously to wooden plank walks, which became Pick's means for getting to a logging camp.

Anchorage existed only for the railroad and was the major transportation hub for Alaska. The city was in constant chaos with a steady stream of men, horses, wagons, and supplies, arriving and departing.

While Alaska had been essentially lawless during the great gold rushes of 1849 and 1899, it had apparently been home to many passing preachers as it instituted Prohibition on December 31, 1917, two years before the law was passed in the United States. The intent, no doubt, was to limit alcohol intake by Eskimos and Native Americans.

No liquor could be sold in Anchorage itself or within a five-mile strip on either side of the railroad, which made bootlegging profitable. In the winter, liquor came over in sleds pulled by dog teams. In the summer, with shipping channels open, it came inside bales of hay or canned tomatoes.

Pick didn't much like the looks of Anchorage, where all the Chinese were men brought over to work on the railroad expansion to Fairbanks. In fact, there were almost *no* women. Everything seemed to be ordered from either Sears Roebuck or Montgomery Ward, so Pick immediately suggested to the camp leader, "Why don't we order up some *women* from those catalog companies? And if you can order up a mail-order bride, why not a cook too?"

There would be plenty of work for a cook as none of the men had a clue how to make a biscuit, and he was dreaming about a big, fluffy warm mound of flour dripping in butter and loaded with blackberry jelly. What he got instead on his first night there was a piece of day-old salted cod and a plate of beans, his first forkful of which he spat out, saying, "These damn things taste like the open fire they were cooked on." But since there was nothing else to eat, he learned to get them down.

The few women in the camps were either married or wanting to be married and had come to Alaska to find a rich husband, an idea left over from the long-gone goldfields. Pick decided a wife was not a household item he needed, so he canceled his order and got back to working on the railroad. He had considered other career moves, but copper mining, fishing, working in salmon canneries, coalfields, or oil fields were not jobs he felt would look good on his résumé, so he stuck with what he knew.

15.

Ice Pick

AFTER THE FIRST TWENTY MILES OF LAYING TRACK OUT OF Anchorage, Pick took a leave of absence from the railroad as the work had been backbreaking and he still had his mind on silk sheets. He decided to go to Fairbanks.

Shortly after his election, President Wilson had appointed the Alaska Engineering Commission to study where a new government railroad should be built, and Fairbanks had won the toss. Fairbanks lies 120 miles south of the Arctic Circle and 400 miles north of Anchorage. The Gold Rush had raised it from a mere trading post to a town of almost five thousand people by the time Pick had caught wind of it.

After deciding to go to Fairbanks, he learned that the overland route from Anchorage was by packhorse and dogsled, guided by an amiable Eskimo equipped with enough food and furs to make the long trek. Unbeknownst to the Eskimo, Pick had medicated himself against the fierce cold and ice with some fiery Russian vodka. He thus survived the trip in a happy, though hazy state.

Sliding into town on a slick patch of ice and suddenly spotting a hotel, three churches, two banks, and a sawmill, he shouted, "Hallelujah!" He checked into the Palace Hotel for a few days, using the hefty wages he had earned from laying cold track in a time when World War I had sucked most men from work on the rail lines. Pick fervently hoped his joyful view of Fairbanks would be extended by the young ladies of the town, and set about trying to find out.

Fairbanks was not as elegant as San Francisco, but it had sewers and water and, *yes,* women! Pick decided to try his luck at church and, by happenstance, chose a Russian Orthodox one. Having been to the Catholic Church in Chicago, he now had some idea what was going on, but was still bemused by the rituals and ornate interiors. While there were many similarities, he wasn't going to be fooled a second time. So when the dinner bell rang, he didn't expect food and therefore was unprepared for an invitation he received from the priest to join the congregation for a social. The event proved to be a little wine and cookies in a back room. Churches were permitted altar wine, and Pick discovered this stuff was strong enough to change a Baptist to a Presbyterian.

The Russian Orthodox women, while very polite, were a bit aloof, whereupon Pick realized this was going to be a long campaign complicated by small-town gossip and social politics—not something he was skilled at or interested in learning. He decided his interests could best be furthered with a substantial amount of cash, so he took a job as a logger for a sawmill and lived at the camp in a leaky cabin with a woodstove for warmth and cooking. At the time, trees were felled by crosscut handsaws, then the logs were pulled by horse and chains to the sawmill, where they were cut into products for fish traps, crates for canneries, dock pilings, and mine shafts. Lumber was left green as there were no kilns to dry it. The frame houses, built too quickly from green lumber, were often twisted and warped, and hence were dry but cold in the winter—nothing like using the seasoned logs of home, thought Pick.

The mill was owned by a third-generation Russian named Ivan Netrov, who was blessed with beautiful twin daughters, Agnessa and Ksenia. Both were excellent cooks and house-keepers eager to find husbands. They often visited the mill, bringing Ivan food or other supplies.

One day while Pick was hauling a load of logs to the mill, the horse reared and broke the chains, causing a log to snap backward and pin him to the ground. The blow to his head knocked him out. When he came to, he found himself in the delicious arms of Ksenia, whose name, he knew, meant hospitality. He thought to himself, "Thank God it wasn't Agnessa, whose name means chaste and holy!"

Pick was taken by dogsled to the Netrov household, where the only doctor in town called to his side. Yet another Russian, the doctor was known to prescribe for himself and kept a "medicinal" supply of vodka on hand at all times. Medicines were scarce; kerosene, tobacco juice, and whiskey just about summed up the available pharmaceuticals. Kerosene was used to treat small open wounds and other surface disorders; although fiery, it served as an acceptable cautery when nothing else was on hand. Tobacco juice was useful in treating bug bites and insect stings. The whiskey (and vodka) substituted for anesthesia and encouraged sleepiness; they also encouraged fights, dancing, and other distractions that led to more open wounds, more kerosene, and more whiskey.

A fellow could use a good still in Alaska, and there were plenty around, hidden in dense forests of virgin timber. With little else to offer, the doctor handed out his prescribed medications to one and all. When he saw Pick was coming round, he said, "I left you a little medicine nearby." Pick drank it all in one gulp.

Ivan felt guilty about the accident, and Ksenia felt grateful. After all, she held the man of her dreams right there in her arms — and in her own bed. Ivan, ever the watchful father, ordered her from the room and stood guard for several hours. Eventually the vodka tempted him, and soon he was snoring on the floor while Ksenia crept back in to see how her handsome man was faring. Unfortunately, just as she was beginning to heal some of his wounds, Agnessa rolled in the door, snatched Ksenia by the hair, and marched her out again.

After a few painful days and a terribly sore head, Pick was able to make his way back to the logging camp and review his situation. Fall was already in the air, filling his lungs and eyes with a feathery frost and knowledge that winter was well on its wicked way. If he remained in Fairbanks, housing would be a real problem as the logging camps would soon close. If he stayed, he was in danger of succumbing to Ksenia, and he wasn't ready to be tied down despite Ivan's offer of a share in the sawmill.

While Pick was pondering his fate, word came that President Wilson had lowered the draft age to eighteen. Although Alaska was not yet a state, Pick felt he should go back and register for the draft anyway, then he got word that his mother was terribly ill, instantly sealing his decision to go home to Jasper. He left Alaska as quickly as possible, sailing through the already gathering ice that floated in the sparkling rivers and streams.

In 1918, Alaska was still a mysterious frozen wasteland with few inhabitants, most of whom were natives. A few hardy souls braved the miserable journey over icy tundra to occupy the territory. Once there, many remained to eke out a living in fur trading or salmon fishing. Those who left were said to have "come out" of Alaska to return to civilization. Pick came out. He would miss this land of glittering grandeur with its vibrant and colorful cast of characters and beautiful creatures, but he would not miss Ksenia. He wanted to buy a car, not a woman.

16.

Laura's Lads

A S PICK ROLLED ALONG SEEMINGLY ENDLESS MILES OF RAIL heading back east, his thoughts naturally turned to his mother. Laura had been a widow almost ten years and was now fifty years old. She had been an only child and after the death of both her parents and the loss of the Reverend Thad, she had no one to turn to except her children. Following her husband's death, she had remained in Jasper for a few years, struggling to provide for her remaining children. She raised apples and peaches for sale and grew vegetables for the table, but that pitiful income did not go far, and one by one her sons left home.

The eldest, Orestes, had followed his father in death three years later, and the other five boys needed to find work to support themselves and their mother. Roscoe was now the oldest and had completed law school at the University of Georgia. He had opened his practice the same year Reverend Thad died.

Golden left school in the ninth grade and was now working in Dublin, a small town in south Georgia. He was doing research on hog cholera, which, at that time, was epidemic. Everyone thought Golden was a dreamer because he seemed to see into the future and visualize things that were not apparent to others. One of his visions was that Stone Mountain would become a destination resort. He had another vision of a completely modern planned city, and he was instrumental in bringing that to fruition. Peachtree City, thirty miles south of Atlanta, was a dot on the map in 1958, but by 1972 it had its own zip code and become a model for future planned communities all over the United States.

Laura had lived with Golden for a while, but returned to Atlanta to be near her other sons. Thad Jr. now worked as an ambulance driver at a big hospital there, and Laura kept house for him for several years until her sons joined forces and bought her a small home of her own back in Jasper.

Ed was the least educated of the boys because he had left school in fourth grade. To help meet expenses for the family, he took odd jobs until he was old enough to get hired as a clothing salesman for a company in Chattanooga, Tennessee. He worked in several retail stores and learned the delicate business of women's clothing. By 1934, he had become a prominent Chattanooga merchant and civic leader. That year, he opened his own store, called Picketts, downtown on Market Street. Over the years he guided it to amazing success. Picketts sold ladies goods of exceptional style and fine quality, and soon became a hallmark of women's apparel, known throughout the South. Ed was tall, courtly, and impeccably dressed, with an ever-present rosebud in his lapel, his lack of education was never a stumbling block.

At that time, formal education was not considered a necessity as America was still primarily an agrarian society and children were kept at home to work the land. In 1900, only half of all first graders went further than sixth grade, and barely a third completed the typical eight-year school course, with fewer than one in five going on to high school. That year fewer than 7 percent of seventeen-year-olds were high school graduates, but by 1940 almost half finished school.

While compulsory education had been implemented in a few states, such as Massachusetts, it did not become federal law until 1918, when all states required at least an elementary education. Early laws did not require attendance until age eight or, in the case of Ohio and South Dakota, age ten. The compulsory education movement gained traction in the 1920s, when, in time, all six-year-olds would be required to attend school.

Education was not on Pick's mind as he continued his trek across the continent. He found entertainment on the train scarce except for card playing, so he hunkered down to refine his card-playing skills.

17.

Gas, Glory, and Girls

WHEN PICK GOT OFF THE TRAIN IN JASPER THERE WAS good news and bad. The good news was that his mother had survived the terrible flu epidemic of 1918 and that the armistice had been signed on November 11. The bad news was that he had lost most of his money gambling his way across the continent, becoming more and more reckless as he got closer to home. It was a lesson he wouldn't easily forget. He wouldn't quit gambling, but he vowed, "I will sure as hell quit losing."

By this time, soldiers were returning from the Great War and available jobs were quickly snapped up. So far, Pick's résumé included farming, driving a car, fighting, preaching, digging holes, laying track, warehousing, logging, and gambling. He had also become a smoker. He had learned to roll 'em and smoke 'em and now was never without them. The cigarettes didn't do him much good on the job front, but he knew they added a certain flair to his character. His long, slender fingers seemed to magically slide out of his pockets with a perfectly rolled tube of tobacco and light it with a single strike of a match. He loved to talk with his hands, and the cigarette was his graceful signature, signaling the beginning and end of his entrancing stories.

He knew cigarettes and stories weren't going to make him money. There were Bible stories, but he reminded himself, "I'm definitely over that!" His brother Roscoe had started a law practice in Jasper, and Pick thought maybe he could be Roscoe's driver and take him around to his cases in the various courthouses in North Georgia. After all, Pick was still one of the rare men who could actually drive a car.

But he was in for a blow upon discovering that Roscoe didn't possess a car! In fact, Colonel Pickett, as he was called, had never owned a car in his life. He either walked, rode a horse, or took the train to get to the center of town, where his office and the courthouse were located, without ever worrying about a parking ticket. The fact that he was called Colonel Pickett didn't mean that he had been in the cavalry; it was simply a courtesy title conveyed on lawyers in the South at that time.

Suddenly fate stepped in and Pick was offered a dream job, whereupon he bellowed out the greatest "hallelujah" of his entire preaching career. A man named Branson would buy Pick a car in exchange for delivery of certain goods in a timely manner to Atlanta. This would be a fast car because Pick would quite possibly have several other drivers wanting to ride along behind him, in pursuit. The goods were varieties of mountain moonshine. Prohibition was coming, and everybody was getting ready!

Distilled spirits were nothing new to the mountain folk. The early pioneers were mostly of Scots-Irish stock and they knew about distilling whiskey. They brought with them their copper kettles and recipes. They also liked to drink it, a skill Pick had perfected during his sojourn to the "icy frontier." He had also learned from his travels that immigrants did not consider drinking a crime because they came from cultures that drank as a normal part of life. The job certainly fit in with his plans.

Farming had become prosperous during World War I as food and other war shortages in Europe had caused markets to boom. And of course, after Armistice the market went bust. Corn had been a stable and dependable export for American farmers, but now their markets were evaporating. There had been a temporary Wartime Prohibition Act intended to save the grain for the war effort, but now Prohibition officially began with the Volstead Act of October 28, 1919. Farmers immediately found a new market for their corn.

It was not a crime to purchase or consume liquor, only to make it. One frustrated barkeeper started charging patrons admission to see a striped pig, but once they were inside, the drinks were free. Pig farmers celebrated. The government frowned upon home stills, but hardware stores did a brisk business selling inexpensive home distilleries. Distilling instructions were easy to find in pamphlets issued by the US Department of Agriculture.

Stills were easy to hide in the mountains, stuck into hollows or chicken houses, and covered with native plants and trees. Moonshine or white lightening was sometimes referred to as "white dog." It was simply what liquor looked like before it went into oak barrels and was aged for darker color and flavor. Moonshiners used glass jars for bottling, and large sales of sugar or glass jars often tipped off the feds, so these items were smuggled in the same way white lightning was smuggled out—in fast cars. Cars and trucks roared through the mountains with their cargo carefully concealed in specially made vehicles and covered with cabbage, apples, or hay.

Now Pick had a new position to add to his résumé—runner/hauler! He quickly realized, "This is definitely not a job I can explain to Mother." Laura had specific information on how Jesus had turned water to wine, but unless Pick actually started walking on water she wasn't going to be happy about his new career. So he simply said, "I have a job as a traveling salesman and they are going to furnish me with a car." When Laura asked, "What are you going to be selling?" his reply was, "Glass jars."

Pick's dream had finally come true! "I have wheels!" he exclaimed in utter delight.

They came in the form of a 1918 Dodge pickup named "The Screenside." In actuality, it was a half-ton commercial car built as a full-roofed delivery van with wire screens in place of the usual panels in the back. Its cargo-carrying body and heavier springs made it ideal for the task, and its 35 hp engine outran its 26 hp Chevy competitor. It also had mounted spotlights and a price tag of $885.

Pick had had previous experience with moonshine while in Alaska. One of the Alaskan native tribes had become adept at making its own whiskey after being denied alcohol consumption by the territorial government. Their own body fat, Pick knew, was not the only thing insulating them from the brutal winters.

Farmers in the foothills of the Southern Appalachians had brewed "shine" for centuries, which Pick was pretty sure had produced some powerful conversions during both his and Thad's preaching careers. It also made those tent revivals vibrate with a "whole lot of shakin' goin' on." Speaking in tongues might not be religious fervor so much as delirium tremens.

Armed with his pickup and a pistol, Pick set off on the first of many runs to Atlanta. His theme song was "Corn Goes Bad but Whiskey Never Does." He felt, "I am protecting the livelihood of hundreds of farmers. I might not be saving their souls, but I am helping to save their bacon." After all, a bushel of corn would bring seventy-five cents at market and a gallon of corn liquor ten dollars.

Never was there much in the collection plate at any sermon he had ever preached.

Pick's first stop was a tavern in Buckhead, which was a step away from Atlanta at West Paces Ferry and Roswell Road. Buckhead seemed to have gotten its name when a large buck deer was killed and its head hung in a prominent location for travelers to observe. Buckhead was becoming the new "in" place for wealthy Atlantans who, at the conclusion of World War I, had begun building large estates and mansions in the rolling hills nearby.

The Golden Age of Atlanta was beginning, and throughout the twenties Atlanta society had a full social calendar of debutante balls, formal receptions, an energetic football season, a week of Grand Opera from New York's Metropolitan Opera House, as well as lavish home balls—all of which were fueled with high-octane white lightning. Pick was more than curious about all this activity and determined to get not just a foot but his entire body in the door of those swanky affairs. His plan of action began with the maids who met him at the servant's entrance to take delivery of his liquid stock. After a few moonlight runs, he had enough money to buy a good suit of clothes and set about charming some of those maids. It wasn't too difficult because he was smart, attractive, and fun to be around. In addition, his time in the pulpit had provided him with a great deal of confidence, while his extensive travels had lent him an air of mystery and romance. Few others at that time had been out of their own county, much less their own country. All of this made him absolutely irresistible—and he came with a car! Cars were becoming more commonplace, although only one in three people owned them.

Courting the maids was easy, but Pick decided, "I want one of the young ladies from the big houses. Not just any of them, however. I don't care for fat ones, really skinny ones, and certainly not desperate ones." His opportunity came one evening when the door was opened by a beautiful, graceful blonde named Alice, with hair piled up to heaven and wearing a silk dress. He remembered how silk felt, and he wanted to experience how Alice felt in silk. Alice was fed up with the men she had met in her restricted life of chaperoned parties, dances, and teas. She wanted excitement, and she found it in Pick! He was everything she had been hoping for—handsome, dangerous, and mysterious.

She taught him the ways of Atlanta society, and he taught her all she had ever wanted to know about everything else. She was an apt pupil, and soon that pickup was rocking, as was Pick. The only trouble with Alice was that she got bored easily and was very demanding. She had turned Pick from a country boy into a sophisticated man, and he had turned her into a full-fledged woman with appetites he wasn't quite ready to satisfy. Certainly not long term. Each had gotten what they wanted.

For Pick, life in Atlanta in the twenties was finally being lived in the fast lane. When he wasn't being chased by men down dangerous mountainous roads, he was chasing dangerous women around busy street corners. But he never got caught by either of them, and that was the plan.

He had a few close calls with several women, and closer ones with the revenuers. But the worst one was when he almost got caught by his own brother. Thad Jr. had also learned to drive and had a job at Grady Hospital driving the first motorized ambulance in Atlanta. That was a big step up for Thad, who had previously been shoveling manure from the parking area for ambulances that had been horse drawn. His job back then had been all about push, shove, and shovel.

While his new job relieved him of the smell of horse manure, it didn't relieve him from the smell of the drunks who found his ambulance a convenient place to catch a few winks. He was constantly moving broken bodies in and out. A few were corpses; others, casualties of too many evenings of lavish entertainment. Some nights Thad was too tired to go home, so he just threw the current bum out and slept in the ambulance himself until someone woke him for another shift.

One night, Pick was downtown delivering a load of moonshine when he ran out of gas. There were very few gas stations in the city, so he always kept a gas can in the back of the truck. Unfortunately, he had forgotten to refill it and couldn't make the return trip to Jasper. Grady was only a block away, and Pick thought he would just get Thad to give him a ride home and deal with the gas thing the next day.

Pick had been taught never to miss an opportunity, and the one he saw was just too tempting to pass up. A glorious ambulance parked in the back of Grady had no driver inside. The seats were basically wooden benches, so it was easy to spot occupants. The coast was clear, and Pick hopped in. There were no ignition keys, just a tiller to steer the thing, and Pick started steering toward the mountains. Unbeknownst to him, Thad was on board and soundly asleep in the back, laid out on the stretcher. He had worked valiantly with little rest for almost seventy hours, hauling bodies all over Atlanta following a series of fires and train-crossing accidents. As the ambulance with Pick at the wheel crested the last mountain, Thad began to stir and by the time they reached Jasper he was fully awake and fully furious. Pick had never heard a sermon like the one Thad Jr. proceeded to deliver. Their father would have been proud! But being a quick thinker, Pick immediately explained, "Mother has been asking for you, and this seemed like a good time for you to make a quick trip back home to see her. I was glad to help out."

The trip turned out to be a life-changing event for both men. They were both tired of driving cars in dangerous situations. They got to talking and decided to pool their resources and go into business—the automobile business.

18.

Rich Men's Toys

THE HISTORY OF THE AUTOMOBILE AND THE HISTORY OF America are inseparable and defined the first half of Pick's life. In the late 1800s, there were hundreds of automakers—sons of farmers, backyard mechanics who tinkered with engines, and bicycle mechanics and machinists who understood drives and gearing. Each began adapting their knowledge to gasoline engines, and thus the horseless carriage was born.

Until Henry Ford introduced the production line in 1913, automobiles were manufactured one car at a time in somebody's garage with parts purchased from many different suppliers. The machine was then shipped by rail to the individual buyer who took delivery at the railway station, paid cash on receipt, and had the final assembly of the car completed at a local garage.

Because there were hundreds of manufacturers of all different sorts of cars, repairs were difficult as no parts on any two cars were alike. Tires were treacherously thin—like oversized bicycle tires—and subject to puncture at the slightest insult to their veneer. That made a shovel and rope necessary equipment for the all-too-frequent flat tires, as well as a strong arm to turn the crankshaft. Driving was not for the faint of heart or the weak-limbed, and certainly not for women! The drivers were primarily farm boys with technical knowledge, dexterity, mechanical skills, and a sense of adventure.

Prior to the automobile, American society was separated by class. You were either rich and mobile or poor and isolated. You lived and worked on a farm or you had an entirely different life in the city. From its inception, the automobile was the great divider. Cars were initially available only to the wealthy, who had the cash to buy and maintain them, as well as the funds to hire a chauffeur to drive them and a mechanic to take care of the constant repairs.

Drivers didn't have to be licensed, but some road regulations began appearing at the turn of the century. One such regulation stated that a person had to be sent ahead an eighth of a mile to warn those driving horse-drawn vehicles that a motorcar was on the way; the rationale was that it would prevent horses from spooking at the sight of these strange horseless carriages. In the early days of the 1900s, there were just 23,000 automobiles on what could only be described as uncharted mud roads. Yet, there were 17 million horses. There were also endless mechanical problems associated with the automobile and very few service facilities.

Motorists at that time had to band together to aid each other, and they often traveled in pairs or groups in order to pull each other out of mud holes or ditches. Rarely did they get help from farmers. In fact, farmers created a second income for themselves by digging chuck holes in the road and then charging the hapless auto owners a steep fee to pull them out. Also, cities and villages insisted on absurd speed limits of 4 to 10 mph—sometimes keeping them secret—and imposing a fine of ten dollars per mile for exceeding the speed limit.

Horseless-carriage clubs began to spring up as enthusiasm for the automobile continued to grow. On March 4, 1902 in Chicago, the American Automobile Association (AAA) was founded in response to a lack of roadways suitable for automobiles. At the outset of World War I, AAA had made an appeal that car owners do their own driving in order to free up skilled drivers for the war effort. Pick didn't see that as a problem because, for one thing, there were very few cars in North Georgia and, for another, he knew he could drive whatever was out there and repair whatever befell them.

At the turn of the century, most shopping in rural areas was done through the Sears Catalog. Founded in 1886, Sears had been selling farm tools as well as prefabricated houses, so naturally, Sears began producing its own cars to be ordered from the catalog. The owners just had to uncrate them, do minor assembly, add fuel, and drive home. But by 1912, the Sears Motor Buggy cost more to produce than it was generating in sales, and so it was discontinued.

Initially, bicycle shops simply added automobiles to their showrooms. John Wilys founded the first automobile dealership in 1905. As others followed, their biggest competitors were Sears, Macy's, and Wanamaker's. However, because the department stores lacked showrooms, body shops, and mechanics, they soon phased out their automobile inventory. That left the way wide open for dealerships that were directly connected to the manufacturer, and soon both flourished.

As the automobile became more complex and less dangerous to own and operate, American society became more complex and, in some ways, more dangerous. Courting could now be done in the car instead of on the front porch with parental oversight. Sunday drives began to affect church attendance, and driving vacations generated the motel industry. Even education was changed as students no longer had to walk to rural one-room schoolhouses but could instead be driven by bus to large schools that would otherwise have been out of reach. The new influx of rural students required schools to alter curriculums as well as provide athletic programs, school bands, and vocational studies. They also added social programs through extracurricular activities such as 4-H, debate, language, and civic clubs.

Cars required paved roads, vastly improving driving conditions, and eventually, increasing the number of women drivers. Shopping in towns became commonplace, meaning that rural residents no longer had to depend on catalog shopping. Dining out became ordinary instead of extraordinary as people were no longer confined to their own tables, eating food they had grown and prepared themselves.

During the 1920s there was an explosion of new cars on the market. Automobile production rose from 2 million in 1920 to 5.5 million in 1929, making motor vehicle manufacturing the largest industry in the United States. During this time, the earlier open cars (convertibles), called tourers, were replaced by enclosed vehicles boasting heaters to keep passengers warm. By 1929, radios, which were not yet available from automobile manufacturers directly, could be purchased separately and installed in the vehicles. Radio was an important new part of life, and in 1922 the first commercial broadcast station in the South—WSB, owned by the *Atlanta Journal*—began to air the news, music, and events of the day.

The Roaring Twenties also was a time of tremendous celebration in general for a postwar nation. Women had won the vote in 1920, and the automobile transported women and a rapturous youth into an explosion of rebellion and frivolity. "Skirts are up, and morality is down," blared the preachers from the pulpits. Pick's prayers were now along the lines of "Dear God, go ahead and call the good girls home, I can take care of the bad ones myself."

Cars were no longer an extravagance for the rich but rather a necessity for the masses. Their demand was fueled not just by the robust economy but by the introduction of automobile financing through General Motors Acceptance Corporation (GMAC) in 1919, effectively establishing auto dealer financing. This made life much easier for car dealers, who no longer had to primarily rely on cash sales from rich customers. The country was awash in postwar luxury, and everybody wanted a car, whether they could drive it or not.

19.

Used-up Cars and Brand New Woman

THE PICKETT BROTHERS WERE PHYSICALLY SIMILAR—TALL, intelligent, and hardworking—but otherwise very different. Thad was sweet yet serious while Pick was energetic, fun loving, high-spirited, and fiercely competitive. Thad had married the girl of his dreams, whereas Pick dreamed of all women. He once stated, "Marriage is more of a nightmare than a dream, and I'm not ready to give in to any particular woman. My little black book is as thick as my Bible and contains just as many names." Their automobile business, which they named Pickett Motors, began with three used Model T Fords and two employees— Pick and Thad. They leased a lot on Spring Street in Atlanta, built a small garage to handle repairs, and started scouting for inventory. Early on, they figured out that a lot more money could be made selling new cars than fixing broken ones.

Pick and Thad soon specialized not just in selling cars but in teaching first-time buyers how to drive them. This brought in rich women who wanted to flaunt their new freedoms and wealth. Pick was happy to oblige them in every way, and every day if necessary. Satisfied ladies began sending their girlfriends car shopping and Pick's bank account was soon as fat as his little black book—which was responsible for much of his success.

But before he could do anything more with his black book, he had to figure out the Blue Book—a price list for used cars. The year 1927 was not a good one for car manufacturers: their numbers dropped from 108 to a mere 44. Pick told himself, "The market for first-time buyers is getting saturated, and in the coming months I'm going to have to shift to used cars." Jumping in with gusto, he began searching for secondhand automobiles in excellent condition from new car dealers who had taken them in trade and directly from the public. This required all his powers of persuasion because owners were reluctant to part with their prizes. By 1932, auto production reached its lowest point and used cars had risen to prominence. The Great Depression was in full swing, and what had seemed like magical money in the twenties was now a distant memory.

Pick, however, had established a long list of private clients who could still pay over-the-top prices for specialty and luxury cars. That was the easy part. The hard part was finding the actual cars. His travels took him far and wide, including frequent trips to New York City, where he soon began building entire fleets of cars and shipping them around the country to delighted customers. Although the country was heading for dire economic straits, Pick was doing just fine.

20.

Dancin' Dorothy

B Y NOW, PICK WAS WELL-KNOWN TO BE A LADIES' MAN AND a great catch. Back in the late twenties, he was especially fond of Dorothy MacKinnon, whom he had met in Jacksonville when she was very young. He had watched her grow into maturity and blossom into a phenomenal beauty. Pick had known her mother through a business deal and was considered an old family friend.

Dorothy had long, rich black hair that fell to her waist and amazing black eyes that gave her a soulful expression. Her perfect beauty and statuesque five-feet-nine frame caught the attention of Broadway, and at the age of eighteen she became a fabled Ziegfeld Follies chorus girl. With her Southern charm and polite consideration of others, Dorothy was well liked by the entire company of dazzling dancers. Backstage gossip was a popular pastime, and the dancers chattered like schoolchildren.

New York was a great place to be during the Jazz Age, when the dancing and parties were endless. Pick and Dorothy were among the beautiful people gracing the best tables and the hottest dance floors all around that glittering town. Since she was a professional dancer and he was a quick learner, they drew attention everywhere they went, for their glamour as well as their charm. He had perfect manners, and she had perfect beauty.

Dorothy's best friend, Helen, was a lusty and busty girl from Chicago who had been the victim of numerous short-lived romances. Always alert to mischievous men, she guarded Dorothy as well as she could. She was particularly encouraged about Dorothy's prospects when she heard her say, "I just adore it when Pick is in town. He understands how money should be spent—*on me*. He is so handsome in that darling aristocratic way, and his snow-white hair is the absolute perfect frame for his blue eyes. I do declare, why, they are as bright as the center of a rainbow! Besides, I am so tired of trying to dance with those short, fat, cigar-smoking men who are always trying to squeeze into my dressing room. Why, I can hardly squeeze in there myself and certainly not with all my clothes on!"

Adding that she barely came up to Pick's nose, she told Helen, "It's fun to be able to check his pockets for surprises he's brought me instead of having my chest land on some balding head that smells like Havana."

Whenever Dorothy and Pick would walk into a room, however, the dynamics would completely change— something everybody recognized. When asked about it, Dorothy would say, "I was a bit frightened at first because I thought my slip was showing or something worse." Panty hose had not yet been invented, and it was hell for a woman to get a run in her stocking or be seen when the seams of her stockings weren't straight.

Some time later she told Helen, "For the first several dates I spent a lot of time in the powder room examining my posterior. I soon learned better, though, and started checking out the competition instead." Helen began to suspect that, while Pick was every bit the Southern gentleman, he had eyes in the back of his head when it came to women.

Because he carried himself like an aristocrat, there was no way either young woman would know that he had grown up pushing a plow and saying sweet nothings to a mule instead of a brunette or redhead. Years later, when Helen shared her observations, Dorothy noted, "Oh, Pick was lots older than I was. This was probably part of his magic to me."

Dorothy confessed to another friend, "I was well used to men being in charge because the theater, dahling, is filled with all those sorts. Unlike other men, Pick was totally confident in every situation, though never cocky. That was a relief after all the ghastly bottom-pinchers and bombastic boasters I had to go out with just to get dinner. The theater is exciting, but God, it is exhausting to have to continue to play roles after a performance is over. While death and taxes may be certain, rent and dinner are more immediate needs!"

Pick loved to tell jokes, but you had to pay attention because his wit was very dry, and if you didn't get his humor the first time he wasn't patient enough to repeat himself. Dorothy said, "I didn't want him to think I was dumb, so I hung on his every word. You could tell he was used to that."

He laughed often, with honest joy. When he smiled, his whole face smiled, not just his mouth. His eyes would twinkle like a starry night, and he would throw back his head with the pleasure of it all.

As his friends would easily admit, Pick was a great storyteller. His Welsh heritage made him an engaging raconteur as he enthralled men and women alike with tales of his many adventures. His soft, lyrical voice was especially compelling when the words fell like honey dripping from its comb. He never paused, stumbled, or searched for a phrase—he was, after all, the Reverend Thaddeus's son!

Now aged thirty-six, Pick had already swallowed a very large bite of life, but he was always ready for the next taste. He just didn't want to have to eat the whole bakery if he could have one slice of cake at a time. Women, including Dorothy, tended to disagree with this perspective. If they baked a cake, by God some man was going to eat it!

For his part, despite considerable efforts from the cake culture, Pick had managed to elude capture. He had proposed from time to time, to be able to stay in the game, but he always made sure there was a fault line—he was too old, too young, a traveling salesman, not a college graduate, drove fast cars, chased fast women, gambled, and worst of all, his mother was still alive! No sensible woman would want Laura for a mother-in-law if she could help it. Mother Pickett believed starch was meant for more than cotton and she had made sure all six of her sons had plenty of it in their shirts, and in their backbones as well. Her life as a poor preacher's wife had made her not only pious but parsimonious as well, and fiercely determined to impart these qualities to all her children.

Therefore Pick's friendship with Dorothy MacKinnon, the dancer, came to a reluctant close during one of his car-buying trips to New York. Unable or unwilling to commit, Pick eventually lost her to a well-connected New Yorker. Her dancing days were over, but he was still doing the rumba all over the South.

A swift change in partners came in the form of Miss Mary King of Americus, Georgia.

21.

Faye's Fantasies

MEANWHILE, FAYE'S LIFE IN RURAL TIFT COUNTY HAD NONE of the glamour, dash, or sophistication that had become Pick's signature. She didn't know anything about the automobile business. In fact, she had very little knowledge of anything apart from her hard life on the farm, material she read in her schoolbooks, and fantasies she had created from movie magazines that were passed around by the girls from town. Still, she knew there had to be a path out of poverty, and she had her walking shoes on and was ready to go. Like Pick, she was ready for adventure; unlike Pick, she was a woman, which usually meant you had to wait for a man to provide it. "I am stuck on this farm, and there is absolutely nothing I can do about it—at least not yet," she often said.

By now her two older sisters, Gwen and Garland, were off at college in Tennessee. They both had won scholarships that paid for their tuition, but they had to work in the college kitchen every day to pay for room and board. Faye's beloved brother Ollie had gone "up north" to find work. So she was now the eldest of the clan still at home, and her workload hadn't gotten any lighter. The Great Depression had invaded every household in the country, and money was almost nonexistent. As Faye lay in bed in the room she shared with her parents, she could hear the creaking of their rocking chairs in the living room and their whispers as they sat near the soft fire that warmed the cold rooms.

One night she wanted to cry when she overheard her father say: "Mae, I just don't know what we are going to do. I can grow enough to feed the family, and I can butcher my own hogs and cows—so we will always have plenty to eat. But I can't grow shoes or clothes and all the other things we need. Faye is always dreaming about a fancy life, but she will be lucky if she can find a good man who can provide for her. It won't be long before she can be married. She needs to think about that and get her mind off Atlanta. She is a real pretty girl, but that won't matter to a farmer who needs a wife to help work the land and make a home for him. I know you don't like boys coming around here, but both of you have to face facts; her beauty is not going to take her to the places she wants to go. You need to have a talk with her."

Mae heard about the dreams Faye chattered on about and knew the girl was fooling herself, but truthfully, she didn't want her daughter to marry a farmer either. She had hopes that Faye would use her intelligence and pursue an education, as her sisters were doing. Mae knew that would be her ticket to a better life and her only way off the farm. Faye, for her part, made excellent grades without trying too hard. However, she was definitely not interested in wasting time going to school.

She was eager to get out into the exciting world she saw in the movie magazines. Although she devoured them the minute she got her hands on them, she didn't dare take them home since they were not the kinds of magazines Mae would permit in the house. She called them "trash fit for only a strumpet."

Mae had very firm rules about most everything, a reality that Ollie tempered with his soft manner and sweet smile. No one could get past Mae, particularly when it came to her girls and any boy who approached the front door. Mae guarded her daughters the same way Ollie tended his horses— carefully and constantly. Dating was rarely allowed, and only under very strict supervision. Occasionally when a boy drifted by the door on his way home from a nearby field, he would only get as far as the front porch before Mae would appear, broom and apron in hand, ready for combat.

Faye was only allowed to go to her senior prom under certain conditions. First, the boy had to be someone known to the family. Faye didn't have to like him, but he had to pass muster with Mae. Second, she had to be chaperoned by one of her brothers on a double date. Last, she had to be home by 10:30 pm.

While Faye was elated at the prospect of going to a dance, she thought, "I am ashamed of the dress I have to wear—that old hand-me-down from Cousin Ida in town— and I know *somebody* will recognize it."

She might not have been prettier than any of her sisters, but she certainly thought she was and felt entitled to better things. "It's just not right that as pretty as I am, I still have to wear someone else's old cast-off clothes. I would look beautiful in a new dress of my very own. I want it to be pink with rows and rows of ruffles, just like the one I saw in a magazine." Although Faye had never known hunger pains because her father had always been able to provide plenty for the table, she did have daily pains of shame, envy, and jealousy.

She went to her prom and solemnly vowed, "I will never marry a farmer, and someday, somehow I am going to have a wardrobe of pretty store-bought dresses. I just know there is a way." She had to wait for the right opportunity. She didn't know when that might occur, but she was convinced it would happen—just like in the movies.

22.

Another near Mrs.

ANOTHER MOVIE WAS ABOUT TO BEGIN NOT FAR FROM TIFTON, but Faye would not be the star of this film. Americus, although a farming community only fifty-five miles from Tifton, was a very different place. For generations, Americus had been a haven of culture and civility, refinements it still retained in 1929. Its broad shady avenues were lined with regal oak trees. Their wide, whispering shadows were like long leafy sentinels guarding the private and privileged lives of those ensconced within the abundant Victorian and antebellum mansions filling the city.

These homes were the by-products of wealthy cotton farmers who, following the arrival of the railroad in 1854, had created a distribution center in Americus for their cotton and other goods. Dusty farms were considered no place for a well-bred Southern woman. They were all corralled in luxurious homes in town and catered to by servants.

What had begun as a small courthouse town now bloomed with as much abundance as the cotton bolls for which it had become famous. The railroad brought not only commerce but culture and education. The town boasted an electric streetcar system, a teacher's college, a performing arts center, and Dudley's Opera House, where internationally famed Sarah Bernhardt performed in a five-act play in March of 1916.

The Rylander Theater opened in 1921 with a $5,000 pipe organ, a Typhoon cooling and ventilating fan system, and nearly a thousand opera chairs. There was an orchestra section for five hundred eighty patrons, a balcony for one hundred fifty patrons, and a gallery for one hundred thirty. Due to racial segregation, the gallery was reserved exclusively for black patrons and had its own entrance and ticket windows. The grand opening on January 21, 1921 featured the national touring company and the hit play *Lightning*. The first talking movie shown in Americus debuted at this theater in 1929. Admission prices were twenty-five cents for adults, ten cents for children under thirteen, seventeen cents for "colored" adults, and ten cents for "colored" children. During its heyday the Rylander hosted minstrel shows, vaudeville acts, musical revues, and plays as well as high school graduations.

Americus High School graduations were social events. Each young female graduate walked on stage wearing a long white dress and carrying a dozen long-stemmed red roses. It was her moment to advertise her youth and beauty, the fact that she was now of a marriageable age! Afterward, the graduates were celebrated at home with private balls and parties throughout the city.

Pick was especially interested in this year's round of parties because he was particularly interested in the lovely Miss Mary King, who was among the field of graduates. It was June of 1929, and life for him was still on a roaring tear. It wouldn't rip apart until October of that year, when the stock market and the lavishness it supported would explode and scatter fortunes like cotton bolls in a high wind.

The 1920s and 1930s saw the advent of the traveling salesman, his profession made possible by the newly paved roads and better cars. Salesmen and other travelers generated a need for small hotels and places to eat along the way. Pick had long ago developed a taste for the elegant and so was always looking for hotels that fit the bill.

The massive five-story red brick Queen Anne edifice known as the Windsor Hotel occupied an entire city block in Americus. It opened in 1892 to a grand event in the fifth floor ballroom, with several thousand in attendance. It was a one-hundred-room Victorian masterpiece complete with turret, tower, and a huge veranda spanning the second floor, furnished with rocking chairs. The large, three-story, open-air lobby atrium was an innovation in design for its time and featured centuries old Georgia hand-carved heart pine, and marble flooring from Corona, Italy. By the time Pick got there, it also had electric lights, a telephone, a bar, and an elevator. To his despair, it did not have hot and cold running chambermaids.

Americus was a regular stop on Pick's way to Florida, where he traveled several times a year to buy cars that had either been abandoned or sold for pennies by wealthy visitors. Henry Flagler, founder of Standard Oil, came to Florida at age fifty-three and immediately envisioned "An American Riviera," which he soon centered in St. Augustine, opening the Ponce de León Hotel and Resort in 1888. He built railroads and lavish resorts all along Florida's Atlantic coast that quickly attracted wealthy tourists and the cream of international society. With reliable long distance automobile transport now a reality, wealthy northern tourists would drive down to Florida for the "season" and often take the quicker train route back north afterwards. This left a fertile field for sharp car dealers.

Pick was pretty well-known in Americus by now and had many business associates who entertained him, both at home and in public. He had been invited by the President of the Americus Chamber of Commerce in February of 1928 to attend a dinner at the Windsor Hotel where Franklin D. Roosevelt, a candidate for governor of New York, was a guest. Also attending was Miss Mary King, in the company of her father.

Southern society had very stringent rules, and young ladies were not permitted to appear unescorted in mixed company. Mary was an unusually intelligent, mature, and aware young woman with a wide variety of talents and interests. She had developed a keen early interest in politics and begged her father to take her with him to hear FDR. Now that women now had the right to vote, she was going to exercise that right at the first opportunity. She wanted to be ready.

Pick was certainly ready! He took one look at that towering blonde beauty and was instantly smitten. Mary was almost as tall as he, with an athletic and shapely form and blue eyes that simply bore into his soul. He was so paralyzed upon seeing her that he could hardly respond to the introduction by her father. For the first time in his life, words failed him. "My God, have I lost my tongue along with my heart?" he asked himself. At first, he thought he had suffered a stroke and was relieved when his words and his breath finally returned.

He knew he had to compose himself and made an effort at conversation. He and Mr. King were old acquaintances and Pick, as it turned out, was among the small party invited back to the King home to entertain FDR for the remainder of the evening. Charles King had no idea of the desperate beating of Pick's heart and the space his daughter occupied in the mind of someone he considered to be an older man. Mary, after all, was still only a child, barely seventeen, and Pick was pushing thirty, with a wheelbarrow load of desire.

Americus was accustomed to famous visitors, yet the Southern Code was still practiced to the highest degree. Every granny in town still bore the scars of the "War of Recent Unpleasantness," and they were determined that no Yankee was going to slip through their closely guarded lines. Nor would any stranger make their mark in that small society of Uptight and Upright Matrons without a serious review of their credentials. Their collective memory bank still included the horrors of the Andersonville Prison that had been built only seventeen miles from Americus during the Civil War. It had housed forty-five thousand Union soldiers, and the grannies maintained a stern lookout for any possible escapees remaining in the South.

Pick made it through the first round because many of the grannies still remembered his father, the Reverend Thad, whose fame had even spread to that distant little enclave. Just to be sure he was up to snuff, though, the grannies invited Pick to preach at the First Baptist Church Homecoming Service. That was an absolute windfall for Pick. He polished his shoes, his hair, and his Bible, and thundered out a sermon that would have made Thad proud! His delivery was so flawless and his desire for Mary so profound that with the closing hymn of "There Is a Name I Love to Hear," he almost shouted, "Mary!" but managed to holler, "Hallelujah!" instead.

Homecoming was an important event in a rural Southern Baptist's church life. It was celebrated once a year with an invitation from each Baptist church to anyone who had ever been a member to return for a day of remembrance. The ladies of the church made a mighty fortress of their own and reigned over the day, each one bringing her best dish to share. The endless long sturdy tables were topped with mountains of homemade food, such as Heavenly Hash, the ever-popular salad composed of marshmallows, whipped cream, cherries, pineapple, and pecans. Finer food could not be found, nor could a more appreciative audience. Homecoming turned eating into an Olympic event, and by the time it was over, its remnants looked like the first meal of the returning Confederate cavalry after the Civil War.

Baptists worked up an appetite during those long sermons, and the constant hymn singing simply prolonged the agony. Pick was hungry himself, so he blessed the food with the shortest prayer he thought he could get away with and let the food frenzy began.

Good-byes were lengthy affairs as it was the Southern habit to stand and wave until the last person had gone, all the while murmuring, "Now, y'all come back soon and tell [so and so] I said, 'Hey.'" The bigger the family, the longer the litany of Heys.

The men of the church had their own special homecoming chore also deeply rooted in tradition. Their contribution, performed by the men's Sunday school class known as the "Glad Hands," was made the night before, when they concocted their homemade barbeque and Brunswick stew. The stew was also steeped in white lightning handed out of the back of pickup trucks as the men labored throughout the night over wood fires and cast-iron pots. They stirred carefully at first and then carelessly as the night progressed. Their low laughter was sometimes punctuated with loud verses of "Work, for the Night Is Coming" or "The Old Rugged Cross," which got more rugged as the night wore on. As the flames died and the dawn rose, "Whisper a Prayer in the Morning" or "Rescue the Perishing" was about all they could muster.

The Presbyterians were, of course, predestined to have their church down the road, and sometimes their Scottish heritage prompted a little celebration of their own, concluding in the woods behind the church with a little barley or rye. Depending on what the occasion demanded, Pick could be either a Presbyterian or a Baptist. In either instance, all that preaching made him thirsty! Charles King also felt the call, and he and Pick soon bonded enough that Pick began to reveal to him his feelings for Mary.

And so began the polite and gentle courtship of a young girl on the verge of womanhood.

23.

The Rules!

THE RULES FOR THE COURTSHIP OF MARY KING WERE QUITE simple, though severe and strictly enforced. The enforcer was Grandma King, who hadn't trusted a man since Sherman invaded Atlanta. She guarded her granddaughter the same way she guarded the baking of her famous cornbread. She simply checked the temperature several times an hour.

Pick was already seriously overheated, but he wanted Mary and would do anything to attain her. He accepted the dreary fact that he would only be permitted to see her within the confines of her own home or at family outings such as church activities. He would not be allowed so much as a handshake unless Grandma was present, and he most certainly could not tell Mary of his interest. This might be allowed when she graduated from high school in a few months.

Suddenly his trips to Florida became more frequent and his stopovers in Americus much more pleasant. He had always enjoyed the charming little town and something exciting always seemed to be happening. He was there in

April of 1922 when Ty Cobb and the Detroit Tigers played an exhibition game. He had known Ty briefly from his Sears baseball days in Chicago, but Ty's surly temper and unsportsmanlike conduct made them a poor match.

Pick was also in town in May of 1923 when Charles Lindbergh bought his first plane from an Americus manufacturer, S & W Airplane Co. It was a World War I surplus "Jenny" and sold for $500. Lindbergh snapped it up and made his first solo flight at nearby Souther Field.

Baseball's shamed "Shoeless" Joe Jackson was coaching baseball in Americus at about the same time. He had been banned from the majors for life after suspicions about his part in the scandal throwing the 1919 World Series for the Chicago White Sox. Pick had no respect for Joe, but he loved baseball and was very happy to have a pickup game with him whenever he was in town.

But baseball was not the big thing on Pick's mind nowadays. June of 1929 had finally arrived, and Mary was about to graduate from high school. He watched her cross that stage in her long, flowing white gown, holding the red roses he had sent. He was so excited that he was sure his face was the same color as the flowers. Having remained in the shadows of her life all these months, he might finally be permitted to court her openly.

Alas, "the rules" changed only slightly after Mary's graduation. Pick progressed to conversations in the swing on the front porch, but still in full view of Grandma King, who scurried about like a mouse chasing cheese. There were occasional dinners with the family at the Americus Country Club and several fierce matches of tennis there under those same watchful eyes. Pick and Mary were both good athletes and enjoyed the friendly competition of those games. Mary was playful both on the court and in person. She simply delighted in her youth and life and was popular everywhere she went. She soon began to think, "All of these boys my age are so immature in comparison to Pick. I think I may be falling in love with him. I wonder what Daddy will say if I tell him. Maybe I should wait a while and let him first get used to the idea."

The summer hurtled forward in a blaze of sultry heat relieved by country rides in Pick's brand-new 1929 Packard Speedster 626 two-seater roadster. It was gorgeous and great for quick getaways. Low to the ground with running boards and an eight-cylinder engine, the two-door convertible had a rumble seat and radio. The best part of the package was that rumble seat. Too much cornbread and too many years on the front porch swing had caused Grandma King to swell to fairly magnificent proportions. It was a sight to behold as her short, fat legs collided with her bust and bottom and wound up halfway in the rumble seat and halfway over the spare tire on the back. It was all Pick could do to keep a straight face, but he sensed this was a critical moment. He asked himself, "Will she get in or stay out?" Fat overcame her protective fervor, causing her to roll off the back tire and onto the ground.

Seeing his chance, Pick grabbed Mary and they sped off, leaving Grandma King in a state of nervous collapse, shouting, "I do declare," and "I Never." That was Southern speak for "You sorry son of a bitch!"

The country air turned crisper as fall arrived and it was time for Mary to make some decisions. She wanted Pick, but her parents wanted her to go to college and insisted she embark on the two-year teacher's certificate program at Georgia Southwestern in Americus. Although that seemed a reasonable compromise, Pick gritted his teeth for another long wait. He figured, "If I have waited this long, I guess I can hold out for another two years. But maybe her folks will change their minds."

The wait was shorter than expected as the Great Depression came thundering in that October and dollars went rolling down the hill of depreciation. After a few months, it became apparent that this was going to be a long stretch of hardship and Mary's parents began to review her prospects for the future. She loved Pick and so did they, but he was not the solution they were seeking for her future security. He was too old for her and spent too much time on the road. She needed a young professional with an acceptable financial pedigree who would secure her place in Americus Society for a lifetime.

Not everyone had lost their money in the stock market crash, and there were several local candidates for Mary's hand. Her mother said, "You can take your choice of any of them except Pick," to which Mary replied, "But Mother, he is the only one I really want." No amount of tears on Mary's part would change her mother's mind, and since Mary was still under her parents' rule she had no choice. Her cries of "You can't do this to me!" went unheeded. She knew that an elopement was completely unacceptable and out of the question. Her mother was set on a big society wedding for her daughter, and the only thing lacking was a suitable groom.

Pick realized this was one time his prayers would not be answered, so he sped back to Atlanta alone in his little roadster. His heart was heavy as he vowed, "I will never fall in love again!"

24.

The Farmer's Daughter

PICK KEPT HIS WORD: HE NEVER LOVED ANOTHER WOMAN. BUT he continued to love Dorothy and Mary for the rest of his life. In the strange pivots upon which fate often turns, both women would reenter his life at a much later time and reprise their roles upon the center stage of his soul. In the meantime Faye had to be dealt with and the stage had to be really big because her role would be queen—or more likely, drama queen. No one would ever play it better or longer.

After Pick's defeat in Americus, he continued on the rollicking roller coaster that was his life. He still loved women, he still loved cars, and he managed to have lots of both. By 1937, with the Depression careening toward a close, Pick, never one to panic, had not only held on to his stock in Sears, Coca-Cola, and GM but continued to buy more shares. He was cash heavy at a time when other automobile dealers were going out of business, so he bought their entire inventories at rock-bottom prices.

Fall was always a good time for car sales in Georgia as farmers now had a little crop money and were able to trade in old products or buy new ones. Despite the still slow economy, the nation had not lost its love affair with wheels; in fact, throughout the Depression the automobile had remained the dominant industry in the United States.

In August of 1937, Pick arrived for a several-week stay in Tifton to help local car dealer Ben Brown with an auto-mobile auction scheduled for the end of tobacco season. Tifton, unlike Americus, was a small farm town known more for its peanuts, peas, and tobacco than for its culture. In lieu of a grand movie theater, it had only a small, dusty building that came to life to offer an occasional escape from the harsh reality of the Depression outside. Going to the movies remained the most widespread form of commercial entertainment during the 1930s. Most films of that era were set in upper-class surroundings and featured glamorous women in evening dress and men in tuxedos. Expensive cars and luxurious homes completed the scenes and allowed a glimpse into high society—far from the rural life of Tifton, Georgia. These unreal images, some of which also appeared in magazines, fed the imaginations of young girls like Faye.

Because rural families in the 1930s had very limited resources, farm girls never made it to the best-dressed list since their clothes were not store bought. On the contrary, their clothes were usually made from feed or white flour sacks sewn at home, then later mended and patched and "made do." The sacks were imprinted with the manu-facturer's label, some of which could not be washed out. Faye, whose underwear was made from white flour sacks, had two pairs of panties marked "My T Fine" in bold print and a homemade bra that boasted "Self- Rising."

As a marketing ploy, feed and flour manufacturers eventually began packaging their products in colorful prints of sturdy cotton fabric. The average dress required three such feed sacks, and farmer husbands were instructed to buy particular patterns in order to complete certain garments. Chicken feed had some of the prettiest patterns, but those were not the kind of feathers Faye wanted! Having been to the movies, she wanted ostrich feathers, minks, and high-heeled shoes. Instead, she was stuck with flour sacks, a single cloth coat, and hand-me-downs from her well-to-do relatives in town. In seventh grade, she owned only three dresses, which she rotated over the five weekdays. Meanwhile, the girls who lived in town wore clothes from Sears Roebuck. That was when Faye learned envy, a trait that was never to leave her. If envy were baggage, she guarded it as closely as her pocketbook.

Faye had just graduated from high school in the summer of 1937 and, as usual, was stuck on the farm picking vegetables, which was hard and hot work in the sizzling heat of a Southern summer. Vegetables had to be picked at their prime. The tomatoes, peas, string beans, butter beans, and bell peppers were ripening in the endless sunshine, so the picking usually started just after dawn. And then came the canning, pickling, and drying. The work was tedious to a teenage girl with dreams of fashion and fun.

Getting away from the farm was still constantly on Faye's mind. As she and her sisters hoed cotton, picked peas, and pulled corn from its stalks, the talk was always about movies, clothes, and what was going to happen when they got to Atlanta. Faye had never been anywhere outside of Tift County, but she knew she could get ready in a hurry when her chance came.

It came with a brand-new 1937 Lincoln Zephyr four-door sedan. The Zephyr was the first moderately priced Lincoln the company had built. It had just been introduced in an effort to keep the brand name alive during the Depression. Despite its cheaper price, it was still twice that of a regular Ford and already an unqualified success. It was about to get a really close look when it rolled into Tifton.

Pick had brought the car down from one of his dealerships in Atlanta to show at the auction being held by Brown Motors. Faye, meanwhile, had accompanied her father on one of his trips to town to see their cousin Ben Brown, who was offering an advance look at the cars coming up for auction. Ollie needed a new truck and was hoping to trade in his old, weary, and worn-out model. Faye was hoping to trade up too, only she wasn't talking about a car!

No sooner had they arrived at Brown Motors than Faye set eyes on the new Zephyr as it pulled into the lot. On her first look at that Zephyr, she thought her dreams had come true. The fact that it was driven by a good-looking, charming, and urbane man was just about more than she could stand. Her big blue eyes popped wide open and her long, red hair practically strangled her as she turned to get a closer look. This was the pivotal moment of her life to date, and she simply could not and would not resist. Begging her cousin for an introduction, she swung that hair and those hips in perfect rhythm, and soon that Zephyr was taking her out to dinner and down a road that she thought was clearly signposted "Atlanta."

Faye was so young and impressionable that her heart went pitty-pat at the mere sight of Pick and that car! She never had a chance, nor did he. His opening line just tore at her heart, hopes, and fantasies. She had no idea about a man on the prowl, because in her limited social life, they didn't exist. So when he said, "I asked your father if you two could join me for dinner, but he said, 'Just take *her* on because I need to hang around here a little while to talk to Ben,'" she grinned.

Then, with a smile, he asked, "Faye, would you like to join me for dinner? We can go anywhere you like—unless you don't want to be seen out with an old man like me. I'm sure your girlfriends will tease you about going to dinner with a man old enough to be your father."

Well, it didn't take Faye five seconds to make up her mind about that. "Yes, of course I would love to go to dinner with you!"

Secretly, she thought to herself: "My girlfriends will certainly talk about me, but only because they will be jealous. Golly, he is so handsome I think I will just die if I keep on feeling this way. I've heard of love at first sight, and I think I've fallen for him here right in front of this Lincoln Zephyr. He is as gorgeous as the car. I never expected to find love at a car palace, but then I'm not sure just where I *did* expect to find it." She knew immediately that this feeling was as real as her red hair.

In the meantime, Pick was having a bit of a panic. This beautiful, young, innocent girl had actually agreed to go out with him. She was quite a contrast to the sophisticated women he usually dated, which intrigued him. He couldn't help but wonder if this would be another easy conquest or a real battle. He decided to risk it and thought, "She will make quite a change. I have always liked younger women—What man doesn't?—but this one may be a bit *too* young. Let's start with dinner and see what happens. After all, I'm not going to be in town very long, and I don't want to shop around if I don't have to. I'm about the same age as her father, but if all else fails I can win him over with a few thumps of the Bible."

Faye had never been out to dinner before and suggested the Lankford Manor, which, in Faye's view, was Tifton's version of the Biltmore. Her dining out had been confined to church socials and family suppers punctuated with the constant chatter of cousins, aunts, and preachers. The highlight of those events was presentation of the famous Southern coconut cake—the ultimate dessert. Now she was being treated like *she* was dessert. She loved it, and she wanted more.

Pick and Faye were engrossed in learning about one another. He was fascinated by the innocence and simplicity of her life, and flattered that such a lovely young girl would be attracted to him. She was intrigued by his adventurous life, his sophistication, and his apparent interest in her. It was exciting to be out on a date with a real man, not a farm boy whose only vehicle was a pickup truck smelling of the fertilizer it hauled.

However, winning over her mother was going to be far less easy than winning over Hill Pickett.

25.

An Uphill Battle

CAROLINE MAE LOVE, A FIREBRAND WHO REGRETTED HER LIFE of drudgery on the farm, wanted better things for her girls. Born during the reign of Queen Victoria, she ruled her kingdom of five girls and four boys with the same stern hand that had governed the British Empire for more than sixty years. Mae had an opinion on everything, and if you didn't agree with her you were in for a long and determined siege. Her opinion of Hill Pickett was that he was a very nice man—polite, well mannered, soft-spoken, and intelligent— who was obviously successful business, but he was also obviously too old for Faye. He was thirty-seven, and Faye was only a few days past eighteen. Mae, who was suspicious when it came to men, often exclaimed, "I *know* what men want, and I have nine fine examples to prove it."

On the other hand, Faye's father, Ollie, who was just ten years older than Hill, found him compelling and was snared by Hill's ability to quote chapters of the Bible without pause. Religion in the Love household was not just for Sunday. It was lived every day and in every way possible. Ollie was highly regarded as a faith healer, and people came from all over the county for his laying on of hands. Amidst the dearth of medical care everywhere in the nation, ordinary folks grasped at whatever relief they could find for their various ailments. Ollie's own deep faith was apparent in the gentle manner in which he quietly listened, touched his hand to a forehead, or soothed away the tears of a teething baby. His calmness and reassurance were often all it took to calm a troubled spirit. He never turned anyone away and never made a charge for what he considered to be a gift from God.

Faye's third date with Hill was supposed to be a weekend sightseeing trip to Jacksonville in the company of another couple, friends of Hill's from Atlanta. But when Hill came calling for Faye in his new Lincoln Zephyr, Mae let out a loud screech that sounded like a fat pig trying to squeeze through a tight feeder. Her shouts of, "He may have a fast car, but *I do not* have a fast daughter!" went unheeded. For once Ollie overruled her. Having decided that a man as religious as Hill could certainly be trusted, he gave his permission for his daughter to go on the trip.

That Lincoln was barely out of Georgia when Faye felt the call of nature. So did Hill, but it was not his bladder that was calling him. Faye's curves had been fighting with the curve of the road for too many miles, and having her that close was intoxicating. He knew she was an innocent, and he steeled himself to withstand her obvious charms. However, one more sharp curve in the road, and she landed squarely and enticingly against him. She knew how to throw a curve! Whether by design or destiny, a motor court blossomed into view.

Tourist courts as they were called, were well-known to Faye. Her Aunt Lulu had owned one for years, and Faye often helped clean these units. Tourist courts were the forerunner to more modern motels, and Aunt Lulu's was extremely basic, with no extra frills. Tourist courts generally consisted of a small collection of individual wooden cabins set among pine trees and located along popular long-distance routes. The trunks of the pine trees were often painted white to make the site more visible from the road, as billboard advertising was yet to come. The tourist courts functioned like small private houses and offered an array of amenities such as heat in the winter, electric fans in the summer, private bathrooms, kitchens, linens, radios, and garages.

Hill arranged for Faye to use one of the cabins to powder her nose. Examining the various luxuries in the cabin, she stopped and turned on a big and exciting frill, the radio, something she did not have at home, where there was no electricity. The moment she turned the dial, she also turned Hill on. Faye was curious and interested in sex, but an inexperienced virgin. Though she had some idea of what it was about and, while living on the farm, had been exposed to the basic principles of sex, she had no firm idea of the actual mechanics of it. Mae was determined to keep it that way, and in accordance with the times there were no mother-daughter chats on the subject and absolutely no information about birth control.

It was a highly delicate subject, and at that time very few grown women even had knowledge of contraception. Mae was one of those women who had been reared to believe children were God's gift and there was nothing to do but accept each and every one of them as they came. Unwanted pregnancies were never a subject of discussion. It was absolutely unthinkable.

The birth control pill would not arrive until 1957, when the FDA approved it, but even then only for severe menstrual disorders. Shortly thereafter, an unusually large number of women were seeking medical care for severe menstrual dysfunction! In 1960, the pill gained approval for contraceptive use and was an instant hit. Finally, women had a choice regarding pregnancy.

However, the women in Faye's family did not have that choice or even basic sex education; it was all hush-hush. The boys in the family had strict instructions about preserving the purity of their sisters' minds, so when the rooster started chasing the hen the girls were ushered inside the house. The same was true with pigs. Only one male pig was allowed to breed; the others in the herd were castrated, This made them "feeder pigs" and also prevented them from growing large tusks for fighting. Their huge tusks could cause severe injury to farmers and inflict serious damage, such as udder wounds, to cows and other livestock. When a female pig, or sow, was led down to the barn to be bred, there was another round-up going on at the same time. Again the girls were sent to the house and forbidden to visit the barn.

Faye was about to have her own version of the barn dance. When she came out of the bathroom, she fiddled with the radio, trying to tune into a show she had heard about— *Amos 'n' Andy*. But Hill had the radio tuned to an entirely different station. When she turned from the radio, he wiggled his index finger and simply said, "Come here." She went confidently and quickly into the arms of the man she knew had the power to make all her dreams come true.

When it was all over, she didn't know whether she was supposed to be pleased or not, but he seemed to be. So she made what she thought were appropriate noises and settled in beside him. She was a bit alarmed about the blood on the sheets, but he assured her it was perfectly normal, and neither of them gave it a second thought. To Faye, sex would always be not about passion but about purpose. Her purpose now was to completely capture this man. And although inexperienced as a seductress, she was a quick learner. She practiced her new skills the same way she practiced the piano, loudly and vigorously!

As she lay in bed with this new wonder all about her, she couldn't help but think: "I wonder what's going on at the farm. Somebody has got to be doing my chores, and I can just imagine how mad my sisters are going to be. But that's all going to be behind me now. Here I am with the man of my dreams. I have been wrapped in his arms for two days with a Lincoln Zephyr parked outside that I am just sure is going to take me to Atlanta!" She decided that she must be in love.

Faye wasn't sure what to say about what had just happened so she waited for Hill to speak first. They were still wrapped tightly together when he mused: "Faye, I'm sure you have some questions about all this, but remember there is only *one* first time. My first time was a long while ago, but I still think about it sometimes. I want you to remember this as a very special thing. We've have just shared something wonderful that was a completely new experience for you. Is it something that you will want to tell your mother?" He fervently hoped not.

Faye was horrified at the thought and said, " I will never tell a single soul about this, especially not my mother. She would probably call me a strumpet, a whore, and throw me out of the house. Do you think I'm a strumpet?"

He laughed, then replied, "Well, I think you are just a sweet little girl who thinks she is in love.

Faye then asked the inevitable. "Do *you* love me?"

His response was measured, "Faye, when you get a little older you will understand more about what love really is. In the meantime, just enjoy what we have together at this moment."

She didn't quite understand just what he meant but, like Scarlett, decided to think about it the next day.

26.

The Daily Grind

THE LINCOLN ZEPHYR DID GO BACK TO ATLANTA, BUT NOT WITH Faye in it. For the farmers of Tift County, the tobacco sales and automobile auctions were over until next year. Pick had spent about two weeks in Tifton and was now headed back to his old life without giving much thought to Faye. He had not fallen in love, but she had—whether with a man or with a dream, it didn't matter. Of course, he told her he would be back, and of course she believed him. But her road to Atlanta had developed some serious potholes, and apparently there was nothing she could do about it. The man was not interested.

Life on the farm continued much as before. While the crops had been laid by, Mae was busy canning and putting up rations for the winter. First the vegetables had to be picked, cleaned, and sliced. Then the food, jams, and jellies were processed using sterilized glass jars with metal lids and a tight rubber-seal insert. Mae did not have a pressure cooker, so the filled jars were brought to a steaming boil in a huge pot on top of the wood-burning stove. In the summertime, this released a lot of heat into the kitchen, and Faye made sure she was out of the way of that work.

In fact, she tried to get out of the way of work as often as she possibly could. It seemed endless as kerosene lamps had to be cleaned of their soot, carpets taken outside and beaten with a broom to relieve them of their dust, fireplaces emptied of ashes, and windows washed of their constant collection of grime from more soot and ashes. Faye knew about Cinderella, and she was damn ready for that prince to stride in, but the magic wand seemed to be out for repairs. Now that she had graduated, she was held captive by domesticity and her time and activities were entirely dictated by Mae. For instance, it fell to her to make lunches for her siblings. She had to wrap their sandwiches in newspaper as waxed paper, used by the other kids, was deemed too expensive. She didn't like that it set them apart, along with so many other simple things they did.

Faye was not much of a candidate as a farmer's wife. She had never learned to sew because she took all the sewing projects from her home economics class to her own home for Mae to complete. She could cook, but hated it. And she wanted nothing to do with babies; there were too many of them around the house anyway, and she was always having to diaper or change one of them.

Mae did insist, however, that Faye make at least one apron. That was a necessity in any farm woman's wardrobe as it was multifunctional. For one thing, it was easy to wash; for another, it protected the dress underneath and was easier to wash—a good thing since Faye had so few garments; and for a third, it doubled as a potholder, a hanky for drying children's tears, and a secure basket for carrying eggs from the barn. Mae's apron was always busy: if not filled with freshly shelled peas, apples, or kindling wood for the stove, it was dusting the furniture in the event of unexpected company. There was no telephone in the house, so family and neighbors routinely arrived without advance notice.

Visitors to the farm, however, were rare. Neighbors were too busy with their own chores to waste daylight time chatting. There were, however, a number of traveling salesmen who frequented the small country roads selling a variety of goods, and Mae always made time for them. Starved for adult conversation, she listened attentively while they made their pitches. Faye would be looking over her mother's shoulder, always on the lookout for a prospect who knew the highway out of Tifton. Mae's favorite salesman was the Rolling Store, whose driver brought a large covered truck filled with candy, fabric, thread, needles, and other necessities. The best parts were the books that came with him. Mae loved to read and would spend all night devouring an encyclopedia by kerosene lamp. She read encyclopedias like novels, memorizing every word to pass on to her children in their lesson the next day. Faye liked to read, too, but was more interested in reading maps that showed the way to Atlanta. She didn't think Atlanta was on the list of rolling store destinations, and she wasn't about to consider any intermediate stops.

Sometimes as the dark crept close, Mae and Ollie would gather the children around them and sing, or play piano duets with them. Those evening activities were also conducted by kerosene lamp, or sometimes by candlelight since they were without electricity. In fact, in the 1930s, only about 15 percent of farms had electrical power. So the dark brought stillness as there were no noises from cars, refrigerators, radios, vacuum cleaners, or the shrill interruptions of telephones or TVs.

Early evenings were often quiet as well. Because people on the farm lived by the sun rather than the clock, and had to make the most of each daylight hour, they would spend early evenings on their front porch swings punctuated only by the noise of farm animals, the soft flutter of birds, and the creak of the swing or a rocking chair, the sighing of the wind, or chattering children. Chasing fireflies in the soft summer evenings was about as entertaining as it got, unless there was going to be a peanut-boiling or watermelon-cutting party. Faye didn't think of this as bliss, but rather as a prison wrapped in a velvet night. And she envisioned herself as being held captive by her parents, with no option but to do their bidding and abide by their rules. Her only hope was for a man to rescue her. The days of a liberated woman with limitless opportunities were far in the future and something she could not even imagine.

However, not everyone in Tift County was a farmer, and the townspeople all had electricity. In fact, Tift County was prime peanut country, and every family had its own favorite recipe for cooking them. Groups would gather in the late afternoons, with each household bringing a pot of its own, usually cast iron, setting up a wood fire, and getting down to business! There was an annual competition for the best peanuts. Peanuts were simple to cook in just water and salt over a hot boiling pot. But there were endless variations on the theme, depending on how much salt was added, what kind of wood was used, how many peanuts were cooked at once, and how long they were cooked.

Watermelon cutting was another summertime favorite. The same groups would converge on a single household with a load of their best watermelons just picked from their fields. The back porch or backyard would be filled with sawhorses and planks placed across the tops of them to make primitive tables for the watermelons, which would be carefully positioned—all in a row, like enormous green glistening marbles. Then, using a very long, sharp knife, someone would cut their centers, and the children would run in for the kill. There was nothing as good as a cool watermelon on a hot summer day and nothing as much fun for a child as having watermelon juice as thick as blood running down their face and arms.

Soft summer evenings were the peaceful reward after many hours of long and hard work in the fields. Families went to bed with the waning of the light as sun up would soon signal another day of hard labor.

The fatigue and peaceful silence that came with the dark would soon them off to an easy slumberland. One evening, however, that silence was punctuated by Mae's cries of alarm!

27.

A Ripened Georgia Peach

ALTHOUGH THERE WAS NEVER ANY MONEY, THERE WAS ALWAYS plenty to eat in Mae's kitchen—all homegrown and homemade—thanks to the huge supply of vegetables and meats Ollie provided for his large family. The only thing "store bought" was the ice the iceman delivered each week and installed in the upright wooden two-door chest with its insulated tin liner. This primitive refrigerator served to cool meats that had not been smoked or cured, along with a few other perishables.

Mae had a large walk-in pantry in the kitchen with shelves to the ceiling. Her homemade products were stacked in neat and beautiful rows all along the three sides of this fortress of food. The gleaming glass jars reflected the bright red tomatoes, the green beans, yellow corn, and plump peas that would feed and comfort them through the winter. This was her "office." It was also the place she went to when despair overcame her. On those occasions she would begin "cleaning out the pantry," which meant she had free license to throw anything she could grab at anybody who happened to walk by.

One evening, Ollie made the mistake of strolling by and was suddenly turned into a coloring book of vegetables. Green okra pods hung from his ears; tomatoes had put out the cigarette he always smoked; and there was corn so far up his nostrils he was about to suffocate.

Never one to panic, he simply looked at Mae and said, "Well, what is it this time? Are you expecting again?"

She replied, "No, but Faye is!" and let go with another jar of tomatoes. If Ollie had not caught her hand, she would have demolished an entire two-year supply of peaches as well, with a single blow. She was in a true Irish fury, and there was nothing he could do but let it burn itself out.

He finally persuaded her to come sit in her little rocking chair by the fire. Its warmth had a calming effect on her. Slowly the tears came and the anger left, only to be replaced by a very deep sadness. She had long had such high hopes for her beautiful daughter, and now all was lost.

Ollie let her cry it out and then gently asked, "Who is it?" to which she replied, "It is all your fault."

Now, Ollie didn't take too kindly to this as he was absolutely sure that Faye's pregnancy had nothing to do with him. But knowing that logic, anger, and women sometimes collided, and that he had endured enough collisions for the day, he simply waited for Mae to continue. Her next words truly surprised him. "They had three dates; he has been gone for three months; and now Faye is three months gone! If you hadn't let her go out with that man from Atlanta, this never would have happened!"

All he could say was, "Aw, shucks." Then he retreated to the small table where he kept pen and paper, and instructed Faye to write Hill Pickett a letter informing him of her condition. She had no idea how to contact him directly, so she wrote to him care of the car dealership in Atlanta that bore his name.

Hill, of course, was off on one of his many buying trips and did not get the letter immediately. But when he did, he was stunned with the news. Here he was, thirty-seven-years old, happy in his carefree life, and suddenly the door slammed with the same force as a Cadillac at full speed careening into a Tin Lizzie. His first thought was, "What in the hell am I going to do now? I do not want a wife, and I am certainly not prepared to be a father." Ollie, however, gave him no choice in the matter, and his life was irrevocably changed on December 14, 1937.

28.

The Bride Wore Black

FAYE BECAME MRS. HILL PICKETT IN AMERICUS, GEORGIA, in the presence of her eldest sister, Gwen. She wore a black dress that Gwen had lent her and a colorful hat from the same closet. Gwen had married two years earlier and was living in Americus. While Gwen's circumstances had improved since her earlier life on the farm, money was still tight and her own wardrobe was limited to the basics. She was an excellent seamstress and could have easily made Faye a wedding gown, but time was more important than attire. The scandal of a forced marriage was overwhelming and the fear of every living and breathing mother and daughter. Faye had crossed that terrible line of respectability, and her family knew that every single day up until the birth would be calculated and clucked about by every woman in the county. It was a solid pastime and better than Bingo!

Ollie and Mae did not attend their daughter's wedding. The shame of the pregnancy stuck to them and to Faye like the smell of a skunk on a hot summer night. Faye and Hill, standing before the justice of the peace, exchanged vows that were deeply rooted in the religion and tradition of the day but had no real meaning in their own minds and hearts. They were practically strangers. Hill barely remembered this young girl who was now his wife and the soon-to-be mother of his first child.

Faye, on the other hand, had her map out and was in the car as soon as the marriage certificate was signed. There was no reception, no dinner with friends and family, no round of parties, and certainly no announcements. This was to be kept as quiet as the dark secret that surrounded them. As for Faye, her thought was not "I'm going to be a mama!" but "I am finally on my way to Atlanta!" She clutched her hands in her lap to avoid clapping them with delight at the thought and admired the gold band now solidly on her finger. It was official: she was now a missus and about to be a resident of the New York of the South.

Her trousseau consisted of her three homemade dresses and her one pair of shoes. She had no frilly lingerie, or cedar hope chest filled with linens, china, and silver. The only hope she had was for a better life in the city of her dreams with a man she barely knew. The fact that he was old enough to be her father was actually quite comforting, and his soft voice spoke politely as they made their way northward.

While Faye felt comfort, Hill had a host of worries. In the swath of the Great Depression, Atlanta had gone bankrupt. Although the previous year Coca-Cola had come to the rescue by agreeing to back Atlanta's payroll, allowing city scrip to be honored at face value by banks, the tremendous financial tension would not be relieved until the outbreak of World War II, when the military and its associated manufacturing would rescue the city's finances.

Hill had these thoughts to contend with as well as his swift and unexpected marriage. He was more on edge than she as the miles carried them toward an unknown future. He remembered the headline in the *Atlanta Journal* about the Reverend Thad many years ago. It quoted him as saying, "Church spires go up to Heaven while People go down to Hell." For the first time in his life, Hill had been uneasy in a church and thought to himself, "I wonder if I am about to go down to hell." He would soon discover the answer.

29.
Faye's Movie

SO FAR, THE MOVIE WAS FOLLOWING THE SCRIPT THAT FAYE had imagined. She was in Atlanta at the fabulous Winecoff Hotel and on her honeymoon! The Winecoff was not only the premier hotel in Atlanta but one of the finest in the entire Southeast. Constructed in 1913 of brick and stone, it was fifteen stories tall and thought to be fireproof, so there were no sprinklers, alarms, or fire escapes. Tragically, the most terrible hotel fire in US history occurred there in 1946, killing 119 people.

For the moment, Faye was enthralled with everything about this hotel. There was electricity, indoor plumbing, and heat—all of which were unavailable on the farm. She watched breathlessly as beautifully gowned women came floating down a wide, central spiral staircase made of gorgeous hand-carved wood. There was also an elevator attended by a full-time operator in a smart-looking uniform. When she stepped inside, she wasn't quite sure what he was there for and mistook him for the usher at the movie theater. As she started looking for a place to sit down, the thing started moving, throwing her off balance and into the arms of the attendant. He took one look at the couple and asked Hill, "How old is your daughter, sir?" That question would be repeated many times in the future.

Faye had never seen anything like this before. In fact, living in a one-story frame house, she'd not even had much experience with stairs other than those leading up to the loft in the barn. The hens were prone to nest up there and lay their eggs in the warm hay, all the while depositing a lot of droppings on the steps. This caused considerable soiling of her one pair of shoes, and cleaning them up afterward was just one more daily chore she would be glad to kiss good-bye. This hotel palace was far from a chicken coop, and she finally quit expecting feathers to fly as she glided up in the magical elevator. She had made it! Her real-life movie had started, and she was the leading lady.

All this excitement had made Faye hungry, and eating for two made her ravenous. Hill couldn't take her down to the dining room because her homemade dress would be an embarrassment not only to her but to him. So he ordered room service, and that was when he cottoned on to the extreme naïveté of his beautiful and intelligent new wife.

When the waiter knocked at the door, Faye opened it and gasped. Before her stood a very large cart making a loud clattering noise and covered with a white cloth. Thinking it was going to be a magic show, she waited for the entertainment to begin. Suddenly she herself became the entertainment as she tried to cope with the assorted dishes and platters laid out before her. Not knowing what to attack first, she surveyed this bountiful bonanza and decided the most efficient method would be a frontal assault.

She grabbed what she thought was a biscuit and began piling on everything she could reach. The biscuit turned out to be a delicate vol-au-vent filled with crab and cream. Because its flaky pastry was not able to withstand the mountain of ham and chicken that Faye tried to force on it, the entire concoction collapsed in midair on the way to her mouth. She tried to catch it, but it wound up fluttering to rest on Hill's good suit. He covered his growing laughter by simply taking her hand and, like the child she was, drawing her gently to him, saying, "Faye, I think there may be some things I need to show you." With that, he sat her down and began to introduce her to the art of fine dining.

At home, her meals had been a clamoring frenzy of knives, spoons, and forks as the family took up position to grab the best piece of fried chicken or get to the pie before the last piece was captured by another hungry hand. It was hard work and you had to be fast! Hill led her gently and quietly through the meal, explaining the order of service with each course. Extremely embarrassed by her lack of sophistication, she kept reminding herself, "I am no longer on the farm. I am the star of this new movie. I am going to learn everything this man can teach me, and I will never be embarrassed in this way again."

30.

The Starlet

FAYE LOVED HER NEW LIFE STARRING HER FAVORITE SCREEN personality—herself. It was all so exciting, and happiness seemed to fill every corner of Peachtree Street. It was the Christmas season and the crowds and stores captivated her. She and Hill were still at the Winecoff because he needed time to figure out a few things. The biggest question on his mind was, "What in the hell am I going to tell Mother?" Laura was a preacher's widow who walked a path so straight and narrow that a snake couldn't crawl through it. He thought to himself, "Telling her is going to be just about as easy as hitching a ride on an ambulance headed for hell with a drunken driver trying to find the road to it."

He certainly couldn't take Faye home without some decent clothes. He knew nothing about attire for pregnant women, but he'd had a lot of experience with women's clothing. He called the manager of JP Allen, Muse's, and Regenstein's and had them send over an assortment of dresses in what he thought might be Faye's size. Those elegant shops featured models who presented the latest fashions to customers seated in plush lounge chairs sipping champagne. Having bought clothing for his various girl-friends at these high-end stores, Hill was a valued customer, and the store managers were happy to accommodate him.

Faye wasn't really showing much yet, so Hill quickly selected a suit and a day dress, unaware that they were to be her first store-bought garments ever. Once she was suitably attired, he took her to these stores to complete her wardrobe. As they were both seated and the models paraded by, Hill said decisively, "We will take that one, that one, and this one. She will also need undergarments, hats, gloves, and some shoes immediately." Faye was too overcome with all the gifts to protest that she would have liked to choose *some* things herself. As it turned out, until Faye learned how to dress in accordance with her new life, Hill would continue to select her clothing—which was fine because he had excellent taste and was teaching her the nuances of style.

Shoes were another matter since only she could decide which shoes fit her comfortably. Her old shoes were bulky oxfords that Ollie had chosen on his own and purchased from the general merchandise store in Tifton. He rarely took the children, or even Mae, into town to shop with him as he knew he would never be able to get them what they wanted, so he went on his own, guessed at sizes, and limited his selections to items he could afford. Now faced with a dazzling selection of shoes and unable to believe she was allowed to have several pair, Faye went into a frenzy of delight and confusion, leaving the shoe salon looking like a corn picker in high season had just been through it.

With the clothing situation resolved, nothing stood in the way of the inevitable. Laura had to be confronted.

31.
Mother-in-Law and Marriage

NEITHER LAURA NOR MARRIAGE WAS WHAT FAYE HAD expected. Her private script was developing some unpleasant subplots. The initial meeting with Laura was surprising because she was the type of woman Faye had already experienced. After all, her own mother had been deeply religious and raised all her children on the same strict principles that Laura had raised her brood. After the introductions and news of the pregnancy was broken, Laura's only comment to her son was, "I would have never expected this of you. I never! Why, I do declare!" (We all know the translation for that by now.)

Both Hill and Faye were gratified when the stern Laura simply embraced her and said, "We should try to be good friends because you will see a great deal more of me than Hillyer."

That warning bell went off with a clang, and sure enough, by the first of the year, Hill was gone again, scouting for and selling cars. Laura had suggested that Faye and Hill stay with her for the duration of the pregnancy as his travels would keep him out of town for extended periods. This suggestion delighted Hill and confused Faye. She knew nothing of city life, and had never driven a car or even ridden a streetcar. Worst of all, she didn't know a single person in Atlanta other than Laura.

Faye thought: "This is not what I had in mind. If I don't get away from this little old lady, I am going to go stark raving crazy. She is as bad as Mama and watches me like a hawk, afraid I am going to get into trouble. Well, come to think of it, damn it, I already *am* in trouble, and it is all her son's fault."

She said to her new husband, "I thought we would have our own place. I don't want to live with your mother. I feel like she will be calling me a sinner every time she looks at me."

However, Hill was adamant. "I have to make a living, and you will have to be looked after. You don't know about anything but the farm. I can't hang around to teach you all you need to know, but Mother can. I have to get back to work, and that means I have to travel," he said. He would not have the time or interest to babysit a sulking, swelling, eighteen-year-old redheaded and red-tempered girl.

He added, "You can either stay here in Atlanta with *my* mother or I can take you back to Tifton to *your* mother. Make up your mind." With that, he was out the door. The hormonal hellion he had married was not about to go back to that farm. It would become her mantra, and she reminded herself of it several times a day, even in her sleep. "No matter what, I am never going back to that farm, I am never going back to that farm," she chanted again and again. So she settled in for a long winter with Laura.

The house on Euclid Avenue in Little Five Points was a modest brick home that Hill had bought for his mother a number of years ago. He and his brothers also provided a housekeeper-cook named Essie Mae. She was an enormous, black, and friendly woman who came to work every day in her black rayon uniform with stiff white cuffs. An equally stiff and starched white pleated cap perched on her curly head of black hair and a frilly white apron completed the ensemble. Essie Mae became Faye's much-needed friend and confidant who helped her understand a great deal about her new world.

Essie Mae was patient as she answered endless questions about life in Atlanta and, for that matter, life in general. She quickly became a substitute mother figure prepared to tell the young girl the *real* facts about life in a big city. Faye would find that Atlanta maids were a rich source of information on who was who and who wasn't, what to do and what not to do. They also knew who was doing what.

Faye was well mannered, as Mae had insisted on that, but she was not accustomed to city ways. Essie Mae introduced her to proper etiquette in many aspects of life. She taught her how to use the telephone properly, how to serve at the table, what to wear where, what to cook for dinner parties, and how to set those tables. She also kept reminding her: "Now, Miss Faye, don't be goin' out in the street or uptown unless you got yo' stockings on. Nice ladies don't be showin' their bare legs. Now, you don't want to wear that dress what you done put on less you is goin' somewhere special. It bees too fancy for shopping and it sho won't do for church." Essie Mae felt really important telling Faye what to do, as if she finally had some influence in this household, and Faye was as eager to learn as Essie Mae was to teach.

While Faye busily absorbed all that Essie Mae could teach her, she kept remembering what life had been like at home. She also remembered some of the old familiar school traditions that had begun with an assembly of students in the auditorium, followed by a recitation of the Pledge of Allegiance to the Flag, the Lord's Prayer, the national anthem, and a final flourish with a resounding rendition of

"Dixie." Faye realized she was homesick and that she missed her school friends and the company of her many brothers and sisters. But she didn't miss the lack of electricity and plumbing. Actually, electricity did not come to rural communities until after World War II. In 1945, the rural electric cooperative known as the REA (Rural Electric Association) finally brought light—and with it, domestic freedom—to the farm.

Faye found the new freedoms in the city delightful, but she still had a lot to learn about modern conveniences. At her home, the toilet had been a small wooden structure way out in the backyard. Known as an outhouse or privy, it was located far enough away from the house so that the odors emanating from it would not infuse the household. The simple structure consisted of a wooden shack large enough to accommodate two to four people; erected over an open sewer, it had a plank nailed between the two back sides of the building with several round holes in it for comfort. Toilet paper consisted of the Sears Roebuck catalog. Relieving oneself on a cold, dark night took courage, and Faye had often prayed for constipation. It only took a quick recollection of this outhouse to replace her initial shame at being a "fallen" woman with a loud, "Yahoo, I can go to the bathroom any time I want to now." Indoor plumbing became more and more important to her as her developing pregnancy increased her trips to the new and wondrous facility known as a bathroom. Sometimes she went because she really *had* to and sometimes just to make sure the wondrous toilet was still working.

Of all the modern electrical conveniences in her new life, it was especially important that Faye learn about the stove because somebody had to cook on Essie Mae's day off. Accustomed only to a wood-burning stove, Faye had no clue what to do with this mechanical white monster any more than she knew what to do with the electric iron, another important device. Her previous ironing had been relegated to heating heavy irons on the wood-burning stove and then applying them to sturdy fabrics. She hated ironing and managed to burn enough clothes to be eventually relieved of that task. Now, however, she had acquired some fine dresses and wanted to take special care of these new symbols of her prosperity.

Clothes would become Faye's shield against any hurt, and she would learn to wear them like a warrior. She would flaunt them with the same pride that she flaunted her stunning beauty. Nothing again would ever be good enough for her; she wanted only the best, and even that could never be enough. She kept trying to wash the dirt of the farm off her soul with her growing collection of fashions. No one must ever know she had begun life as a simple farm girl wearing flour sacks for dresses!

Hill did his best to be a good husband, but his work kept him constantly on the move. Since there was little time for the newlyweds even to get to know each other, Faye's resentment began to flare like a volcano aching to erupt. It challenged his attempts to quell his mounting impatience for her to grow up. To make matters worse, each scene had to be played out in front of Laura.

Faye wanted to get away from her mother-in-law, but the Depression of the 1930s had brought housing construction to a halt. As a result, Atlanta had an acute shortage of homes and overcrowding was rampant. Eventually, Hill was able to find a large, contemporary home out in Stone Mountain that he and Faye could share with another couple, Nell and Arlie Hitt, old friends of Hill's, and their young son, Arlie Jr. It seemed an ideal arrangement, with two separate bedroom wings and a large common area for dining and entertaining. It, too, came with a cook and housekeeper, so Faye was again spared rigorous domestic activity. Soon after moving in, Faye recognized that she had learned a lot from Essie Mae and missed her, but was prepared to learn whatever Nell could teach her. However, Nell was not interested in the problems of a teenage bride and had no time for her. She and Arlie owned a furniture store and she was busy all day helping with their business.

Before long, Faye began to feel isolated. The Hitts, who were much closer in age to Hill, had known him for a number of years as they had played and partied all over Atlanta together. Hill had always been available as an "extra man" for dinner parties and card games. So while Nell tolerated Faye, she was a bit miffed that he was now out of circulation. Worse, Arlie Jr. who was only five years younger than Faye, and she would often be called on to supervise him when his parents were away at one of their many social events. Faye wanted to go along, too, but her pregnancy was not easy and she was uncomfortable a great deal of the time.

Every upper-class and most middle-class families in the South at that time employed a cook or housekeeper. They were almost always black, always underpaid, and their duties were strictly regulated. Segregation was at its peak and rigidly enforced. Blacks and whites were not allowed to sit at the same table, had to use a separate supply of plates and flatware that were kept in a different cabinet and also washed and dried separately. However, Faye was bored and lonely and wanted someone to listen to her tales of woe, so she spent time talking with Susie, the black cook, Susie was acutely aware of her "place" and careful not to cross any lines. Also, social interactions between the two were only allowed in the kitchen—because that was Susie's domain.

Finally free of her mother-in-law, Faye had become desperately lonely. And now that she had a long-term and very large stomachache, she couldn't seem to quite get the attention she felt she deserved. Soon she found that she got the most attention when she complained of an illness, real or imagined. And while her husband made an effort to be home for most weekends, that didn't really resolve Faye's loneliness because on the weekends he came home he just wanted to relax or play bridge with Nell and Arlie. They were formidable bridge players, and Hill loved any form of cards, so they played constantly. Faye didn't know how to play cards and was shocked at the thought. It was wicked! She vividly recalled a scene at her mother's when Faye's sister and brother-in-law were home for a visit. Mae caught them playing cards in the front bedroom and made then go spend the night in the barn.

Besides, the card playing at Stone Mountain sometimes involved alcohol. Now that Prohibition was over, liquor was easily and gratefully obtainable. Hill made good use of it on those occasions when Faye began to throw one of her tirades. He would send her to bed like the child she was and continue the card game enjoying his bourbon and branch, a Southern term for water. The drinking helped dull his disappointment with his new wife. And while he never got drunk, he would sometimes feel remorse. On those occasions, he would wake her from an angry sleep and preach a good sermon right there in the bed! At times it made him feel better, but it didn't do much to endear him to Faye.

Her response could sharpen a knife in midair. She didn't just bicker; she went in with that tongue like a meat cleaver on a mission to clobber an entire cow. That is when she really felt her power. She discovered that anger gave her energy, and she was just bristling with it!

Hill, by contrast, was always soft-spoken. Even when riled he never shouted, but Faye was pushing him to his limit. He decided his trips needed to be longer and further away. He needed lots of distance from her if he was going to survive this marriage.

Realizing that Faye was probably lonesome for her family, he brought her younger sister, Sara Mae, up from Tifton to be a companion during her final weeks of pregnancy. It didn't seem to make much difference as Faye stayed in her room most of the time, leaving Sara Mae to her own devices.

Relationship building was not something Faye or Hill was adept at. Faye wanted everyone's attention and felt entitled to it. When that didn't happen, she simply vacated the scene—or better yet, made a scene! Sara Mae didn't really notice it much because she was becoming excited by the same discoveries Faye had made a few months earlier. There was a refrigerator full of ice cream, a radio, electric lights that enabled Sara Mae to read day and night and—wonder of wonders—the telephone. The only real thought she gave to Faye was trying to figure out how her sister could complain so much while living in what she considered the lap of luxury with a maid to wait on her.

There could never be enough attention for Faye. Nevertheless, she was soon to get a considerable share of it as her delivery date approached.

32.

A New Star Is Born

HILL HAD JUST RETURNED FROM A BUYING TRIP ONE NIGHT
when Faye announced that she was in labor and thought
they should leave for the hospital. With great deliberation,
Hill made sure that her bag was properly packed, the house
secured, the cat chased out of the kitchen, and messages left
for Nell and Arlie. Since there was no phone at the farm,
there was no way to immediately contact the Love family to
let them know a grandbaby was on the way. He would send
a telegram later.

Crawford Long Hospital, in downtown Atlanta, was a
considerable distance from Stone Mountain, so Hill's plan
was to waste no time and yet focus on getting Faye there
safely. Sadly, he did not focus on the gas gauge until the car
had come to a complete and unexpected stop! Hill had run
out of gas. It was late at night; there were no streetlights; and
the traffic was scant.

After an agonizing wait, Hill finally managed to flag down
a small delivery van. The driver was on his way to deliver a
load of corn and beans to a downtown restaurant and agreed
to make a detour to the hospital. The tiny van could only

accommodate the driver and one other person in the front seat, so Faye was carefully secured up front while Hill hopped into the back. There was no overhead light, so Hill had no idea what was in the back of that van. He got his first clue when a long, moist tongue started licking his wrist. Hoping for the best but fearing the worst, he decided not to lick back. He had a fine example of unbridled passion already in the front seat and he couldn't handle another one. However, that tongue persisted and wouldn't be put off. Was it a dog? he wondered.

No, as he reached out, he felt a hairy hand run up his pants leg, and he nearly jumped through the roof. Desperate to get away, he started shouting and crawling down between the layers of corn stalks to find a hiding place. His cries could not be heard above the loud noise of the engine in the front, and it seemed they only further excited the hand that was pursuing him.

The van kept traveling steadily but at speed, and careened around corners like a go-cart on steroids. Faye was starting to wonder if she would deliver this child now or in the hereafter. The van finally came to a halt, and Hill began to back out, looking more like a corn casserole than an expectant father. As he slowly emerged, he spied the source of the passionate tongue as a smiling monkey gave him a last lingering kiss! Too grateful to complain to the driver, he hurried after his wife, leaving the monkey to linger in its unrequited love.

The attention that Faye so badly craved was now centered between her legs as she tried to disgorge the heavy burden that had lain in her womb for nine long months. Once in the hospital door, things moved so rapidly that Hill became a father at about the same time he finished picking the corn off his clothes. With Faye's final push and a last curse, Ronald Gibbs Pickett glided into the world on June 7, 1938, with a beautiful smile on his tiny red face and an obvious sense of relief at the release from his long captivity. He was perfectly formed with long limbs and a mountain of hair. Immediately Hill breathed a sigh of relief when he saw it was not red!

Faye, too tired from her struggle to have much energy for her new baby, said, "Well, I hope you are satisfied." Hill was elated and couldn't seem to get enough of his new son. He had not expected to feel this rush of love and responsibility for another human being. His heart was beating with the same rapid rhythm of a train clicking over its tracks. Having calmed down a bit following his harrowing ride to the hospital, he was now ready for action.

Always fastidious in his appearance, he was eager to get into clean clothes and begin the list of chores Faye had compiled for him to complete. But first, he had to retrieve the car. He took a taxi to the dealership and sent two of his drivers to fetch the car. Meanwhile, he cast an eye over the showroom, hoping to bring his wife and son home in the style she had come to expect.

A Super Eight Series Six four-passenger Packard—a cream-colored convertible coupe—had just come in and was shimmering on the showroom floor. Packard had remained the luxury car of the 1930s and the company prided itself on making vehicles that were highly refined, fitted with luxurious coachwork, and powered by proven engineering. As the world entered the Great Depression, Packard was one of the few luxury automobile companies that had managed to survive. In fact, it outsold all its competitors combined. Hill thought to himself, "That creamy color would be a beautiful backdrop for her red hair." He was once again besotted with his sexy young wife, even more now that she had given him a son. He was giddy!

So, on the day of discharge the happy little family wheeled back to Stone Mountain where Faye's sister Gwen greeted them. The two girls had always been close. They had no secrets, and Gwen was about to hear all of Faye's.

33.

Sob Sisters

THE FACT THAT FAYE HAD BEEN PREGNANT WHEN SHE married Hill was not a secret among the families on both sides. This shame was one she had learned to bear, but not one she needed or wanted to continue to share with the world. She wanted to belong to the "right crowd" in Atlanta, and a forced marriage was not going to be an asset. She sobbed out her sorrows to Gwen, who simply counseled that marriage and birth dates not be discussed in the same conversation or with the same people.

Despite the Great Depression, life in Atlanta in 1938 still took place on a generous scale, and Faye desperately wanted to be a part of its social scene. She had heard about the debutante parties where girls were presented to society by their parents and entertained lavishly at teas and receptions. There was always a gay round of parties for a bride elect, which included trousseau teas, luncheons, open houses, and buffet suppers. College students home for the holidays were entertained at open houses and invited to come by between 8:00 pm and 10:00 pm.

The party Faye found most disturbing, but also amusing, was the Washday Tea. Ladies entertained in their homes at a seated tea in the washday spirit, with checked tablecloths and black Mammy place cards as they were waited upon silently by their own black maids! Now, Faye certainly knew a lot about washing, but it never included place cards, so she decided she could skip those events entirely. But she didn't want to just read about parties; she wanted to attend them.

In the midst of lunch just weeks after returning from the hospital, she cried out to Gwen, "I want to go to parties and wear pretty dresses and dance to a *real* orchestra, but Hill is not interested. I think he is too old for me!" Faye had celebrated her nineteenth birthday four days before her son was born, having gone from being an ignorant farm girl to a wife and mother with no taste of the heady party days that other girls her age had enjoyed.

Hill, at thirty-eight, was having to make adjustments of his own. In addition to being old enough to be her father, he was now a husband and a real father trying to cope with these dual roles. He had always loved parties and dancing, but he had done enough of it and, very much a chauvinist, didn't see these as suitable activities for Faye. He could excuse himself, but not her: many Baptists of the time prohibited dancing as sinful since it might promote physical intimacy, although lots of folks got around that by describing a dance as a "foot function."

Whatever it was called, Faye wanted out of the house and onto the dance floor, but Hill was adamant. Faye believed she now had the upper hand as she had so recently produced a son. Thinking that would give her whatever she desired, she screamed, "I want out of this damn house. I am tired of being stuck at home with a baby and having you gone half the time. Let's have a party, or even better *go* to a party. You seemed to know how to do that *real* well before you married me."

It was true but Hill, never one to raise his voice, quite fairly rebuffed her with, "That was before I became a father and a husband. Those things are no longer important to me now. I have responsibilities, and so do you. You should be old enough to recognize that by now. Whether you realize it or not, motherhood means you mother your child; you do not gallivant all over town. You want to be out every night, and I want some peace and quiet—which I don't seem to be getting from you."

Ever the peacemaker, Gwen persuaded Hill to let them go out on "girl excursions" around the city, thinking that might relieve Faye's boredom. Since Faye didn't know how to drive a car, Hill's personal driver, Sam, was sent from the dealership, and the girls escorted in fine style to Atlanta's shopping and movie districts.

Faye began calling him Sam Spy and soon complained, "I never get to go anywhere by myself. That driver is always following me around. I want to learn how to drive." She nagged Hill constantly about teaching her, but he wouldn't budge. He observed, "Faye, even if you knew how to drive, you are hopeless at directions. Why, you can't even find your way to the bedroom anymore."

To his mind, something had to be done about that, and he wasn't going to draw her a map. If she was no longer interested, he still knew plenty of ladies who would be, and he began to look for his little black book. He had never been with a new mother before and didn't understand how her libido had been trounced by motherhood.

This was part of Faye's sob story as she and Gwen lunched together another day. Lunch was almost an afterthought because the primary purpose was to discuss Faye's problems—whatever they might be at any given time. She always had a wealth of woes, and Gwen was patient Faye made it clear that Hill was becoming a nuisance. She barely had enough energy to focus on Ronald, much less a fuddy-duddy old husband who was now too old to play, or so she thought.

Gwen counseled her to be patient as she would soon get over her post-pregnancy problems and Hill would eventually come around.

34.

A Rich History

B EFORE CONTINUING THEIR "GIRL EXCURSIONS" AROUND Atlanta, Faye and Gwen extensively researched places to go and things to do. Three of their top choices for future visits ended up being Rich's Department Store, the Lighting of the Great Tree, and the Frances Virginia Tea Room. Rich's Department Store, they discovered, had become synonymous with the South and almost as revered as that of General Robert E. Lee. Founded by a Jewish Hungarian immigrant, Morris Rich, from Cleveland, Ohio, the store had come to symbolize retail shopping at its finest. The establishment opened in 1867 as a dry goods store on Whitehall Street and was financed with a borrowed $500. It quickly became an institution known for its customer service and a strong interest in Atlanta and the broader community of Georgia itself.

Rich's was more than just a store. At its peak, the massive building included fifty-four escalators that ran 650 miles a day, covering territory between the various floors and its two buildings. More than 14,000 meals were served daily in its seventeen restaurants, cafeterias, and snack bars.

Rich's was deeply committed to Atlanta and could always be counted on for assistance. When Atlanta called, Rich's was there with a helping hand and checkbook. One excellent example would occur in 1914, when Georgia farmers were to suffer a dramatic drop in the price of cotton, creating a huge financial crisis for the farmers of Georgia. To ease the situation, Rich's, despite a large financial loss to itself, would accept bales of cotton in payment for merchandise.

A second example occurred during the Great Depression when the city of Atlanta was too broke to pay its teachers' salaries. Rich's agreed to cash the worthless checks of the teachers until the city government could reimburse the store. In years to come, Priscilla, the Pink Pig introduced in the toy department, would ride on a track near the ceiling to the giggling delight of hundreds of children and even some adults.

Department store dining during the 1930s had been a mecca of refinement, though, in the South, still racially segregated. The rooms were well appointed with prissy chairs, prissy ladies, and resplendent wallpaper echoing the glorious history of the region—including lots of flowery wallpaper with Tara strewn about in the scene and fat matrons in print dresses with hats, white gloves, and matching pumps. The devoted foodies feasted on daintily prepared menus that would soon send their girdles snapping. Some of the clerks in lingerie referred to their salon as the Meat Packing Department.

The Magnolia Room at the renowned Rich's was awash in style, food, and fashion. For decades, among the ladies who lunched, Rich's set the gold standard. A favorite menu included frozen fruit salad (a real delicacy for most because of refrigeration), a delicate chicken salad, feathery light triple coconut cake, and of course the Southern cocktail for all occasions—iced tea. Most of the women were known by name and were regulars on the constant circuit of shopping, polite dining, and refined gossip.

Gossip wasn't just a pastime; it was a religion all its own and included a choir and a preacher. The church was the tearoom, and the preacher was the one relating the sometimes sad, sometimes juicy story. The story included the preacher's opinions and sermonizing about the behavior in question. The chorus was the rapt audience murmuring soft sighs of "I do declare!" or "Bless her heart!" We all know about "I do declare," but "Bless her heart" is a treacherous trap. In Southern speak, it could mean, "I am so terribly sorry for what has happened," but more often meant, "Get over it. You got what you deserved, you silly cow." One had to pay close attention to capture the nuances of raised eyebrows and subtle smiles in order to make the correct translation.

Rich's was not just for gossip, however. The store had always been a trendsetter in the South. Its elevators glided up to gracious floors, while attended by smartly uniformed elevator operators sporting white gloves and singing a continuous litany of "First floor: Shoes, hats, and gloves. Second floor: Lingerie. Third floor: Evening wear and furs," and so on. Doors were instantly held open for elegantly attired women burdened by large shopping bags and hatboxes.

The flagship store in downtown Atlanta offered a pianist on the mezzanine floor. Also a local radio host, he gave popular performances to a regular audience. In this instance the store offered both a favorite entertainer and a venue for the after-lunch ladies. A different performance was of special interest on August 7, 1939, and not on the mezzanine! On that day, Rich's was absolutely mobbed with a fascinated public who came to see the first live demonstration of television in the Southeast.

Meanwhile, mass media was still a thing of the future and television would not come into its own until well after the war was over. Radio was still king and telephone service still poor. In fact, with the onset of World War II, expansion of telephone central offices stopped. Even after the war, it would take years and massive reconversion of equipment and manufacturing to bring this service to the general public. It would require cables, wires, and intricate equipment to be connected individually, without interrupting current service to the few households who were already "on the phone."

In rural areas such as Tifton, multiparty lines would become common. Each subscriber had a particular set of "rings" to alert them to their own phone calls. Of course, eavesdropping on the conversation of others was a popular, though discreet, game. However, the expense of private lines would remain out of reach for much of the public, and many years would pass before rural families could hear the ring of a telephone.

There would be lots of ringing in Atlanta on Thanksgiving Day, but of a different nature. The Lighting of the Great Tree at Thanksgiving became a festive tradition throughout the South, officially announcing the start of the holiday season. The tree was seventy feet tall and sat atop the five-story Crystal Bridge joining the two buildings, the main store and the home store. The tree had 2,500 twinkling lights and 200 five-inch gold ornaments. There were an additional 280 ornaments the size of basketballs containing sixty-watt bulbs. It took four miles of lights to circle the tree, and it was all topped with a seven-foot tall star!

The Lighting of the Great Tree was one of the biggest nights in Atlanta since there were no sprawling suburban malls in those days, so people poured into that exciting city from all over the South to do their Christmas shopping.

Choirs rehearsed year-round for the occasion, which would attract more than 150,000 people. An expectant hush quieted the crowds; babies intuitively stopped crying, while toddlers scrambled to the shoulders of their dads. Nearby streets were closed to traffic, and all lights for several blocks went dark. The magic moment started with an announcer, who read, "And it came to pass in those days . . ." As the Christmas story was read, the choirs would begin their response. The first voices to be heard would be from the children's choir on the lowest level of the bridge. Then more of the story would be read and the next choir would sing and so forth, until all the words and music had traveled up all five floors.

The Frances Virginia Tea Room was another legendary establishment. It had opened in 1927 and become Atlanta's best-loved spot for the ladies who lunched. "Tearoom" was a genteel Southern name for a restaurant. Women at that time were not allowed to own restaurants, though it was acceptable for a woman to own a tearoom. It was a safe place where men could be counted on to act like gentlemen and ladies could dine unescorted. The white-clothed tables were set with fine china and silver, and attended by polite waitresses in black and white uniforms. Waiters were also in black and white and always served guests with a polite smile and a folded napkin over their arm.

Southerners were as proud of their politeness as they were of their plantations and good manners were a requirement. "Polite society" was not just a well-worn phrase; it was a way of life in the South.

35.

The Ladies at Lunch

FAYE AND GWEN BOTH LOVED RICH'S DEPARTMENT STORE IN downtown Atlanta. Faye especially enjoyed the piano and headed for the mezzanine every time she could. She knew how to play because Mae was a piano teacher and had made her practice long and hard. To Mae's mind, Faye's crippled finger had been no excuse. You could do whatever you set your mind to, and, like it or not, Faye was going to play that piano. In truth, Faye was later grateful.

After a few trips to Rich's, Faye decided she had to have a piano of her own and began a long campaign that was never to bear fruit. Hill was more focused on providing food and shelter in those severely straitened times and told her the piano would have to wait—another grievance she would chalk up on her list.

Faye was among the throngs crowded around the television on that August day in 1939. She was surprised to see an upright wooden box that looked like a small china cabinet. Along with everyone else, she clapped with pleasure and excitement as not only sound but pictures began to float across the screen.

She, of course, wanted one but was still focused on getting that piano. She could always go out to the movies, but a piano was a performance piece she could use at home. Besides, not many people had one, a fact that would put her one up on the rankings list. Then, too, since Hill liked music maybe that would keep him home more often. She still didn't understand that travel was the basis of his business and something he could never give up for a musical interlude.

Faye was like a deprived child in a candy store. Everywhere she looked there was a new experience to savor, a new treat to buy, or some new luxury she wanted with all her heart. It was a case of too much, too late!

Gwen and Faye would meet at Rich's during the holiday season for a round of shopping and lunch. Gwen's two little girls, Jane and Judy, rode Priscilla until the pig nearly went off the rails with their laughter and delight. In the meantime, Faye and Gwen continued the dissection of Faye's problems. She was never happy, never joyful, and consistently poured out her heart to her sister. Whatever her situation was on any day, she would lean on Gwen for acceptance. And she always found solace in the unconditional love she received in return.

Gwen might not have agreed with Faye's choices and lifestyle, but she knew it was pointless to offer advice. All she could offer was love, something she did well not only with Faye but with everyone she encountered. Her sweet nature and even disposition served as calling cards that, combined with her ability to be at peace with life, enabled her to be generous of spirit—unlike her tempestuous sister, who never seemed to know a moment's peace or be able to spare a thought for anyone's troubles but her own.

Mothering came naturally to Gwen because she had had a lot of practice as the eldest of nine. In fact, she had been as much a mother to her brothers and sisters as Mae had been. It was a role she would never relinquish as she was greatly loved by them all.

A trip from Americus to Atlanta for Gwen and her family was a big event requiring an overnight stay and a lot of advance planning and budgeting. Because it was such a long and difficult trip, the destination might as well have been NewYork. And money was always tight, so the little girls had excitedly saved their allowances all year to help make this special "Priscilla" excursion.

The family preferred to stay at a small, inexpensive downtown hotel close to Rich's so they could make the most of their annual shopping adventure. There was always a game of hide and seek in the store to keep the girls from seeing the presents that were carefully selected to be tucked away for Christmas. Their daddy kept them busy while Gwen did the shopping. Rich's was the closest thing to Disney World that the South would see for a long time.

Gwen and her husband, Jim, also wanted to be close to downtown so the girls could see the Lighting of the Great Tree at Thanksgiving and not be trampled by the crowds. They couldn't come every year, but each time they did, it was a magical memory.

Gwen's daughters, Jane and Judy, were breathless with excitement waiting for the moment when the magic would begin. It was better than the picture show, better than Roy Rogers and Trigger, and almost as good as ice cream! They bounced from one foot to the other as they impatiently waited for the instant their daddy would hoist them high in the air to better view the spectacle. At the end of the event, Gwen, Jimmy, and their tired little girls would retire for a good night's sleep and, upon waking, leave this brilliant ballet of color and return to their quiet and happy lives. But not before Gwen had one last lunch with Faye! She wasn't looking forward to more of the same, but it was part of the ritual.

When Christmas arrived, Faye and Gwen were among the lucky folks to be in Atlanta. At least Faye thought so. But Gwen was just waiting to hear her sister's latest tale of woe before grabbing her pocketbook and rocketing out of there. She loved Faye, but just wasn't in the mood for her complaints that day.

As the sisters enjoyed their lunch another day at the Frances Virginia Tea Room, Faye thought how thrilled she was to be there and remembered everything Mae had taught her about how a lady should behave. Posture had to be perfect, legs crossed at the ankles, and one hand correctly positioned in the lap. This code was as strict as a girdle and enforced by a sea of Southern eyes. Their conversation was low, polite, and punctuated by a murmur of, "Yes, ma'am," from the waiter.

Faye took great pleasure in ordering aspic. These gelatins were only available at restaurants or in the kitchens of the rich who could afford refrigeration. Faye wanted to be seen ordering one as though it were an everyday occurrence. Dessert was also a special event as Southern ladies would not dare consume liquor in public. But Tipsy Trifle—pies with sherry, whipped cream, and fluffy wine sauces or rum creams—were always an acceptable and popular alternative. And after a couple of hours listening to Faye, Gwen had about decided she needed *all* of those tipsy desserts!

It was a busy lunch as the women attempted to eat and talk at the same time. Faye finally confessed, "I don't really know what to do, Sis. Hill wants to have 'relations' (polite Southern speak for sex), but I'm afraid of getting pregnant again. Although I love my little boy, I don't want another one. Babies are way too much work, and I don't want to end up with a houseful like Mama. I want to have some fun for a change."

There was not a whole lot of advice Gwen could give as she knew little more about birth control than Faye. Sex was definitely a taboo subject buried as tightly as Tutankhamun's mummy.

Gwen didn't really have an answer, but Hill did.

36.

The Southern Charmer

BY 1939, MOST CAR CONSUMERS WERE NOT FIRST-TIME BUYERS but rather replacement buyers. Hill had a long list of clients—commercial, municipal, and private—who depended on him to keep them supplied with reliable transportation. He traveled nationwide buying fleets of cars for police departments, taxicab companies, and as individual "prizes" for his luxury clients.

He loved the thrill of finding that special car, and the sport of buying it was as addictive as horse racing. Consumers were at a complete disadvantage because sticker prices did not reach the windshield until the mid 1950s. There was no Internet, *Auto Trader* Magazine, or other pricing tool available to the general public. Only the salesman and the manufacturer knew the actual cost of a car. It was Hill's job, therefore, to inspire confidence and trust in a prospective buyer. He certainly knew how to do that, and he was still particularly successful with the ladies.

Hill had done his best to remain faithful to the fiery Faye, but her increasing demands and rising suspicions were making life more and more difficult. Faye was born with a

keen and intelligent mind. She was also born with a highly
suspicious nature and should have been a detective. She was
constantly on high alert for anything she felt might affect the
movie that was always playing in her head.

She was suspicious that Hill was seeing other women on
his travels as he resumed his extended buying trips to
Chicago, New York, Miami, and Detroit. She had certainly
lost her zeal for sex once she discovered it could also be
complemented with babies! She didn't want any more of
those, so she had a "headache" that no amount of aspirin
could cure. Hill was beginning to wonder if she had a brain
tumor and sent her to his friend, Dr. Fred Turner, who
pronounced her "as fit as a fiddle." While that might be true,
it didn't have much effect on Hill's ability to fiddle with Faye.
So he thought, "If this is how it's going to be, I will just play
another fiddle," and pulled out his little black book again. His
Southern charm and good looks still worked, even at thirty-
nine.

Faye got lonely during his frequent absences and often
begged him to take her with him. About as far as she got was
back to Tifton. He would often drop her and the baby off at
Gwen's in Americus or at Ollie and Mae's farm in Tifton. She
thought going back to the farm was just his way of punishing
her. She complained constantly to Mae and Gwen about the
lack of running water, radio, electricity, telephone, bathroom, and on and on. She also complained about Hill with
every breath, saying, "I know he is cheating on me. Why,
how could he do this to me—and on top of getting me
pregnant? It's all his fault. He took advantage of me!"

While Gwen was always sympathetic and consoling, Mae
had more starch in her apron and told Faye, in no uncertain
terms, "You've got no one but yourself to blame. The only
thing he took advantage of was your raging desire to get
off this farm! That's all you have ever talked about. Why,
when I was carrying raisin pies down to the cotton fields

for the workers, I could hear you and Gwen going on about getting to Atlanta. Well, you got what you wanted, and you better get on back up there and take care of it or start toting in some wood for this stove. I've still got a bunch of young'uns of my own to tend to, so you go feed the chickens yourself. While you are it, milk the cow so your son will have some milk to drink when he gets hungry. You don't seem too inclined to breast- feed. Afraid it will spoil your figure?"

That little speech was all it took for Faye to realize just how close she was to coming back to what she had only recently escaped. Her bags were already packed, and when Hill rolled up the next day she threw herself into the car without a single good-bye. Her mind was now set on getting a house of their own in Atlanta. Though she got along with Nell and Arlie well enough, she was tired of sharing a house with them and wanted more independence and privacy.

37.

Take It on Faith

FINDING A HOUSE THAT WOULD PLEASE FAYE WAS JUST ABOUT impossible. In the first place, there was nothing available to buy. No one was building new houses, and there were very few rental properties for single families. The nation's first public housing project, Techwood, had opened in Atlanta only a few years earlier. Dedicated by FDR in 1935, it was for whites only and was near the campus of Georgia Tech. That was not the kind of home Faye wanted.

Shared housing was a common practice during the Depression because of costs, but crowding was rampant. Thousands had flocked to Atlanta hoping to find work. Many lived in shanties without heat or plumbing in such places as Buttermilk Bottom. The city's populations had risen dramatically to almost 300,000, and about a third of the residents were black, many fresh from the farm.

Hill finally found a small, detached rental house in Northeast Atlanta on Sutherland Terrace. Faye loved it because the streetcar line ran right by the corner. She could now get to the movies by herself and continue to escape to her dream of a glamorous world somewhere out there. The only entertainment at home was the radio, and she always had it on because she loved listening to all types of music.

Many Appalachians had come to Atlanta to work in the cotton mills during the 1920s and 1930s, bringing their music with them. As a result, Atlanta was now an important center for country music recording and recruiting talent. Faye fantasized about auditioning for one of the programs, but her only musical talent was the piano. And while she played beautifully, her voice was not trained. Hill might have disagreed. He thought it was superbly trained to nag and could produce an entire symphony of sounds when she got riled!

Things were a little better once they had a house of their own. Faye had learned her way around Atlanta by streetcar and was now able to join friends for lunch at one of her beloved tearooms. These restaurants were filled not with little old ladies but with dynamic, independent women, bachelors, businessmen, and occasionally entire families. Faye meticulously took note of who was there, what they wore, and who said what. She wanted to learn all the nuances of fine society.

She read the society page of the newspaper each day and noted with great and growing envy the announcements for debutante balls, tea dances, and weekly orchestra dinners held at glamorous locations like the Georgian Terrace Hotel or the Atlanta Biltmore. WSB, broadcast from studios on the top floor of the Biltmore, signed off at 1:00 each morning with the orchestra of Bob Crosby.

Faye dreamed of being a part of these glittering social occasions and practiced and preened every time she saw a mirror. She knew she was beautiful. Others agreed and constantly told her so.

Hill was not interested in society. He was a businessman now and that consumed all his energy and thought. He wanted his wife at home, not gallivanting all over town. He never raised his voice or a hand to her, but he also never changed his mind once it was made up. His personality could not allow otherwise. He was an expert negotiator in business, but he didn't negotiate with Faye at all. He simply told her, "There are two ways of doing things—my way and the wrong way, so we will do things my way." He was an autocrat, and there was no changing him at that stage of his life. He became stern and critical as she became resentful and angry. The differences in their ages, personalities, and life experiences were growing so great it seemed the two might never bridge.

He continued his travels, and she continued to be suspicious. Meanwhile, he began to have some doubts of his own. Just what did she do while he was gone? While Faye was completely faithful to him, he didn't believe that any more than she believed he was faithful to her. They would fight, then she would leave in tears and seek solace with Gwen for a few days; soon she would return, and they would make up. The cycle just kept repeating.

Faye was itching to go to the fabled movie *Gone with the Wind*, which was scheduled to open at the Georgian Terrace Ballroom in Atlanta on December 15, 1939. Tickets to the movie alone were ten dollars—forty times the regular price! The town talked of nothing else. The governor had declared it a state holiday, and a million visitors came for the three-day celebration.

Because Hill was out of town, Faye had begged a ride with a neighbor to this sparkling event. And she was among the eighteen thousand fans outside the theater when Clark Gable and Vivien Leigh made their grand entrance. At barely five feet, she was too tiny to see over the huge throng, so she did what she always did when she wanted attention and was having a hard time getting it: she collapsed on the ground in tears and pretended to be sick. Well, nobody wanted to have her throw up on their finery, so they took her inside the theater and sat her down with the ladies room attendant. Faye figured that sooner or later Vivien would have to make an appearance there, and sure enough, the actress glittered into Faye's sight. It was more than Faye could deal with, and this time she *did* faint and fall to the floor.

Once revived, she talked of nothing else for days but never admitted that she had fainted on the spot in front of Scarlett O'Hara herself. This glorious image of glamour would remain with her forever. She did wonder, however, why she had fainted. She was not the sickly type, but she had been feeling a little off lately.

A doctor's visit soon revealed why—she was pregnant again, dammit! The last thing on earth she wanted was another child, and when she delivered a healthy girl on May 26, 1940, Hill made a startling comment, saying, "I know Ronnie is my son, but I will just have to take it on faith that she is my daughter." So, in a fit of fury, Faye named her infant Faith.

Hill, of course, regretted the comment, but he had occasionally thought, "Well, if she slept with me out of wedlock, maybe she will do it again with somebody else. I know she is ambitious. I'm always looking for a better deal on a car, but she is just always looking for a better deal on life. She is never satisfied."

With that, he pulled out of the driveway and was soon on the road again. Faye continued to be remote and resentful, always on the lookout for any evidence of Hill's infidelity. When he returned from a trip, she grilled him like a pork chop, probing to find out what, if anything, he might have been up to. He was hardly in the door before she called out, "Well, who did you sleep with this time?" or "Why are you so late coming home? Have you been giving another one of your famous driving lessons? Why don't you teach me to drive?" All he could think of was, "She already knows how to drive me crazy. I'm damned if I do and damned if I don't, so I may as well 'do.'"

Hill, forever caught between his life and his religion, was never able to resolve the tug-of-war. Faye grew to realize that when he began one of his bedtime sermons, the likelihood was he had been up to something she wasn't going to like. One day she walked in on a scene that confirmed her worst fears. She had just come home from the movies, and after looking in the door it seemed she was still in the theater.

Her daughter was now two months old and could be left in the care of the college girl, Lois, who had been hired to help with the children. Faye could diaper, but Pampers were unknown, so it was a smelly job washing all those soiled cloth diapers and constantly emptying and cleaning the nasty diaper pail. That job was done by Lois—who now had her arms wrapped tightly about Hill's neck! Faye let rip with a stream of words that made a worse racket than a woodpecker on a pine tree. Among them were "You little tramp, how dare you?" She favored Hill with, "You sorry son of a bitch, get out of my house and take your little slut with you." To her surprise, he did.

38.

Intermission

HILL MADE NO ATTEMPT TO PERSUADE FAYE HE HAD BEEN AN innocent victim in the situation with Lois. He adored the two children he had sired, but the very *last* thing he wanted or needed was another teenager to raise. He had already been through that with Faye, and he wasn't going to repeat it with Lois, who had been looking for a father figure ever since her father died when she was ten years old. "I am not a candidate," he told her and sent her home.

Faye turned twenty-one a week after her daughter was born, though she was still as self-absorbed as ever and behaved like a teenager. Motherhood had not imbued her with a grain of serenity or sensibility. Her first response to the crisis with Lois was, of course, to flee to Gwen in Americus.

This time she arrived not by car but on the Greyhound bus, with two crying children in tow. She had written Gwen, telling her long-suffering sister to expect her, but gave no details. Since World War II, mail remained the most reliable form of communication; in fact, even in 1945 fewer than half of US households had telephones.

However, Gwen was not quite as comforting as on past occasions. She said, "Faye, you must think about these children. They need a home, and right now you don't have one. You're making a terrible decision. What are you going to do? How will you take care of them?" Faye had no idea what she was going to do, but she knew one thing for sure: she was never going back to that damn farm—never, never, never!

When Faye had ordered Hill out of *her* house, she had overlooked the fact that it didn't actually belong to her. It was a rental property for which Hill held the lease. However, she had made up her mind: she was not going back to him. She would never forgive him and didn't even want to try.

Gwen attempted to persuade her to give this some careful thought, but Faye replied, "I don't know if I ever really loved him or not, but I do know he didn't love *me* when he married me." She had failed to consider the fact that they had only seen each other three times before the wedding, making it highly doubtful that either of them had loved the other.

The only thought she had now was to get back at her husband. Lighting up the first cigarette of her life, she felt victorious and defiant. She said decisively, "I am finally an independent woman. Even if he gets down on his knees and begs me, I will never give him another chance to hurt me." Hill was not one to beg, and Faye not one to forgive, so they faced an insurmountable impasse.

Gwen was aghast, but knew her sister well enough to make no further attempts at reason. She herself felt that reconciliation was an obvious answer to this difficult situation. After all, he did take care of her, provide for and love the children, and was not a brute in any sense of the word. Gwen asked, "Couldn't you try to forgive him for the sake of the children?" But Faye was impetuous and, when facing a crossroads, inclined to take the most dangerous and difficult path. She would never understand that she carried others with her on this journey and that her children's lives could be damaged by her own selfish choices.

Whereas logic would have told Faye that it was still very much a man's world, she was ruled by her emotions. In fact, she was about as logical as a lizard on a lazy Susan—she could never quite figure how to jump off. In those days, women were at the financial mercy of their menfolk. A cheating husband was not considered a good enough reason to throw away hearth, home, and financial security. The wife was supposed to look the other way and go on with her life.

Even after reviewing her limited options, Faye would not back down. She had to deal with the fact that she had only a high school education, no training or business skills, and couldn't even type as the typewriter keys were too stiff for her damaged digit.

At this thought, Gwen began to get a little frantic herself. After all, she was married and had a home and husband of her own to look after, so Faye could not remain hidden away there forever. In desperation, Gwen went to the local college from which she had graduated only three years before. As it turned out, the school had a training course for beauticians, and Faye's tuition would be paid by the state of Georgia because of her crippled finger. Without consulting her, Gwen signed Faye up for the course and went home to break the news.

Faye was not pleased. She didn't know what she was going to do, but it certainly shouldn't have to involve putting her hands on someone's dirty head. Once she got the dirt of the farm off her shoes, she had become obsessively fastidious about cleanliness and neatness. She would never again tolerate so much as a spot of dirt on her dress, hat, shoes, table, or person. Nor would she allow so much as a matchbox to be out of place. It drove everybody around her crazy, but she simply smiled and said, "I will not have anything around me that reminds me of life on that damn farm, and dirt is the biggest reminder of all."

Gwen didn't give her any choice about the training program. She told her: "I will look after the children until you finish the course. Then you will have to get a job somewhere else and try to support yourself. I cannot jeopardize my marriage just because you have jeopardized your own. If you will not go back to Hill, then you will have to suffer the consequences, and it will not be easy." Faye would hear these words for the rest of her life, but, to her mind, none of the precipitating problems were her fault.

Faye couldn't wait for the course to be finished, and as soon as it was she made a trip back to her mother's. Mae agreed with Gwen that Faye had made a foolish decision, but she saw her daughter was determined. In the end, she took the little grandchildren to live with them at the farm for a while. She still had children of her own at home and two more would hardly be noticed.

Faye was finally free to go back to Atlanta. She promised to visit as often as possible and come for the children when she finally got settled. Her movie was not turning out the way she had planned, but since there were always new movies coming out, she figured she could star in another one.

In fact, her movie came perilously close to an unhappy ending almost as soon as she left her children and Tifton behind. The children were adored by everyone in the Love household, especially Sara Mae, or Mae Mae, who became particularly attached to Faith during a crisis in the baby's health. One winter afternoon when she was about six months old, little Faith came down with pneumonia. Penicillin, discovered during the war, had saved the lives of thousands of GIs but was not yet available to the general public; for them, antibiotics were a thing of the future, and prayer the most prevalent medicine of the time. The doctor visited Faith, only to say that she was gravely ill and should not be moved to the hospital as nothing could be done for her there. Faye was not contacted since it was determined that a letter would not reach her in Atlanta for quite some time, that even if she knew about her daughter's illness it would be difficult for her to make the trip, and that she might very well lose her job if she left abruptly, especially for an extended period of time.

That evening Mae Mae, frightened about Faith's condition and aware that the heat from the fireplace was not sufficient to warm the room, gathered her up and took her to her own bed, where she comforted and cradled her throughout the long night. The baby finally slept, but not Mae Mae. Because rubber pants used to cover diapers were no longer available now that rubber had been diverted to the war effort, Mae Mae ended up wet from head to toe. When the light of dawn finally enabled Mae Mae to clean up both the baby and herself, she said aloud, "I am glad I was here to help, but why am I always doing Faye's job. She got away with everything when she lived at home, and, by golly, she is *still* getting away with everything."

But that was about to change, and the events that would befall Faye and her little family no one could have predicted.

39.

Now Playing

FAYE'S CURRENT ROLE CAST HER AS A YOUNG, SINGLE MOTHER torn between her children and the single, free life in Atlanta. She didn't need acting lessons to make it plain how much she hated the man she thought had ruined her life—that came naturally. Hill would forever be cast as the villain, and she the innocent victim. The older she got and the more unhappy she became, the more she blamed him for everything wrong in her life. Her hatred flowed like Niagara Falls—fast and furious, spectacular and constant. It became her life's blood.

If she was in the mood, Faye could sometimes still be witty, but she was rarely in the mood. She could also converse on a variety of subjects if she was interested enough to learn the facts. Like her mother, she could spend hours with a good book. She had a phenomenal memory and was very good at math, so her bills were always in order. She had no problem counting money! Her home was always well kept and exceptionally tidy—in fact, too tidy for most.

Also, fashion came easily to her because she had a great eye for color and style, and could always put an outfit together with just a few garments. She had learned how to recycle and restyle, and many girls sought her out for fashion advice. This would come in handy as she packed her bags and left married life. Her greatest attribute—or perhaps her greatest flaw—was her determination. It was as fierce as her temper and never left her, no matter how hard things became. She used it to untie the knot of a broken marriage and then again to knit together a new life in Atlanta.

However, single mother was not a role for which she had any taste. The part she really wanted was more along the lines of a beautiful and carefree upper-class lady. She saw herself as a sort of Lana Turner and yearned to emulate the seductiveness of that silky siren with silver-blonde hair. In years to come, she would, indeed, color her hair blonde and wear it in the fashion of the famed film star. In the meantime, she still had a lot to learn about hair and a particularly harsh lesson was on the way.

After finishing beauty school, she got a job as a hairdresser in the Peachtree Arcade. The 1917-style building was in an area known as the Great White Way, famous for its illuminated streets and sidewalks, which had been designed to make the area attractive to evening customers. The arcade stretched an entire city block between Peachtree and Broad Streets and was the city's first enclosed shopping and entertainment mall.

While the 1940s were a time of great glamour, it was a difficult appearance to achieve; it was also very high maintenance. Hair dyeing was done with a paste made of ammonia and mixed with peroxide and soap flakes. The pageboy style, emulated by ordinary women, had been popularized by actresses such as Ginger Rogers, Rita Hayworth, and Veronica Lake, known for their seductive waterfalls of hair. Faye styled her own long hair in the same fashion as theirs.

Hair salons of that era were known as beauty parlors, and hairdressers were referred to as beauty operators. That was probably because they were often required to implement a particularly odd method of beauty aid in the form of a permanent wave machine. Women with straight hair longed for curls, and some went so far as to use false hairpieces to achieve the desired effect. Others braved the permanent wave machine!

When Faye went to work at the Peachtree Arcade, she encountered this particularly loathsome contraption that offered long-lasting curls through a combination of chemicals and heat. This permanent wave gadget looked like a milking machine infested with a nest of long-legged spiders hanging from a round cage and about to descend on an unsuspecting victim. They were actually rods containing a heated circuit with clamps on the ends. The idea was to apply a chemical treatment to the hair and then attach the hair to the heat machine with the use of the clamps. There was a setting on the machine to differentiate between spiral and other kinds of curls. The heat settings had to be carefully regulated.

A day at the beauty shop was literally an entire day spent in one process or another. Permanent waves were especially time-consuming and expensive. The cost of each rod or "curl" was one dollar. The hair had to be washed, curling rods put in with rubber pads, then spacers and finally chemicals added. At last, the client was hooked up to the permanent wave machine.

The beauty school had only one of these machines for the entire class, so Faye hadn't had a lot of practice. Faye's first thought was, "It looks like some mad scientist has gotten loose and wants to torment women. Why doesn't he attack balding men instead? They could do with some curly hair!" She had no need for a permanent wave herself as her own locks were perfectly and naturally curled by Mother Nature.

Her first customer was a well-known Atlanta matron, Mrs. Thompson, who was also known to be very difficult to please. Faye had heard about her and dreaded the appointment. As the woman descended upon the beauty shop, she announced that she had a very important dinner engagement and a new hairstyle was just what she needed.

Mrs. Thompson was not just difficult to please, she was next to impossible to satisfy. She referred to Faye as "girl" and was constantly ordering her about. "Girl, get me some coffee!" or "Girl, hand me my purse," or "Girl, go to the café and get me a sandwich." Faye hated being ordered about and especially hated the term "girl." She later swore that her dislike had absolutely nothing to do with the outcome of the attempted beautification of Mrs. Thompson. She even managed to say it with a straight face.

When Faye finally got her hooked up to the machine, Mrs. Thompson looked like a gigantic chandelier. Tired from the long day of both standing on her feet and dealing with her demanding client, Faye then sat down to take a break and smoke one of her frequent cigarettes, an activity that had become more an addiction than a statement of the "new woman" she felt she had become. While lost in the smoke of her cigarette, Faye began to smell a different kind of smoke. Looking up from her movie magazine, she saw that Mrs. Thompson appeared to be in considerable distress. The spiral rods were wound so tight on her head it looked as though she would never blink again. There was steam coming out of the machine from all directions and tears rolling down Mrs. Thompson's face. The chandelier was on fire!

Faye took a long, slow, deliberate stroll over to the chair and began to review the situation. She couldn't throw water on an electrical fire, and it would take too long to undo all those rods that bound Mrs. Thompson to the dreadful machine. Her only option was to grab the scissors and cut her client loose! Once that was accomplished, everyone but Mrs. Thompson began to laugh. Her hair looked like a haystack in a high wind, and her fury was like a hurricane! She grabbed Faye by the hair and was about to create a new style for her when the manager intervened. Obviously, Faye would have to go, and go she did—right up the street to another misadventure.

40.

The Newsreel

AFTER THE DISASTROUS AFFAIR WITH MRS. THOMPSON, FAYE decided she was not cut out to be a hairdresser. It was hard work and definitely not glamorous, so she found a new job that allowed her to work downtown and remain a part of that busy and bustling business scene.

By the time the United States entered World War II on December 8, 1941, Faye was at work at her new job as a switchboard operator at the Hotel Atlantan. A switchboard was a telecommunication system used to connect phone calls between subscribers. It consisted of a large panel with rows of keys, lamps, and cords. One key was a Talk key and another a Ring key with lamps that lit up to signal that a call was incoming. After connecting the parties, the operator would close the Talk key and go on to the next caller.

This position at the hotel was strictly reserved for women and one that Faye felt capable of handling. Sometimes things there were so dull that the operators would chat among themselves. The favorite topics, of course, were men and fashion. Faye could now participate in conversations about men as her divorce from Hill had, at last, become final.

Dissolving the marriage had not been easy or quick. The Great Depression of the 1920s and 1930s had forced many couples to stay together out of economic necessity. However, during WWII divorce rates began to spike because, as some historians have suggested, many families were strained under the burden of living with war-injured men. So while there had been an increase in marriage during the war, there had been an increase in divorce, too. Between 1939 and 1941, the divorce rate increased by 3 percent, though it was still highly frowned upon and divorced women, in particular, were seen as social pariahs.

At the time, there was no such thing as no-fault divorce. The injured party had to prove the defendant had committed a crime or was guilty of sin, such as abuse, adultery, or abandonment. Faye went for adultery. Judges and attorneys were driven by social mores and tended to drag things out as long as possible. They felt morally compromised if they had done otherwise. Their advice was always to attempt reconciliation. Gwen had not been able to make this happen, and Faye sure as hell wasn't going to let a judge persuade her! Her response to the judge's admonition was, "Well, you go live with him because I'm not."

After a year of waiting, the judge finally agreed to dissolution of the marriage. As was the custom of the time, Faye was awarded custody of her children with extensive visiting rights for Hill. However, he would have to visit them in Tifton, where Ronnie and Faith remained tucked away in the care of their maternal grandparents, because Faye was living in a boardinghouse in Atlanta where children were not allowed, even if they had been wanted.

The nation was now fully engaged in a world war and, despite the divorce, General Faye continued her ongoing battle with Hill. She was constantly on the attack, unrelenting and unforgiving. An entire regiment could not have persuaded her that she'd had any responsibility in the situation. She had decided it was all Hill's fault and always would be.

To succeed in her campaign, there were many things about her time with Hill that she would have to forget. At the top of the list was the inescapable fact that she was now branded as a two-time loser. She had been a "fallen" woman and was now a divorcee, all of which happened within the space of three years. In addition, although she had attained her dream of a new life in Atlanta, her dream had not included two children and a cheating husband. And while she had never been terribly interested in sex and denying the bedroom to Hill had been a relief to her, she had not quite made the connection with the impact this would have on her marriage. Nor did she realize just how much effect her temper and demands would have on an experienced older man who had known a lot of women and was well aware of what to expect from most of them. Volatile tempers and tantrums were not the norm—most especially down south! But then, he was not experienced with teenagers. Faye was a fiery young furnace, and he kept trying to turn down the heat until he'd finally grown weary of the effort. Further, she hadn't realized that if the kids weren't crying she was, and consequently Hill, unable to find any peace at home, was frankly glad to be back on the road.

Faye was born in 1919, just a year before women got the vote and began their long battle for independence and equality—a journey that would speed up dramatically during World War II but was off to a slow start for Faye. As for being a two-time loser, Faye convinced herself that she'd been in the trenches of a society stuck in the mire of stiff morality and Southern refinement. "Nice" girls and "ladies" did not have the soubriquets attached to them that she had since earned. Regarding the other issues she yearned to forget, she found it easy to cover her tracks. Her children were safely out of sight, so she could make up any stories she chose about her earlier self. She stole bits and pieces from other women's lives until she finally had a suitable pedigree.

One thing she never revealed was that she had grown up on a farm. When asked why she was working as a switchboard operator, she would reply, airily, "I got bored at home, and this seemed like it would be fun. I meet all kinds of nice people here. And besides, I want to do my bit for the war effort. You know how critical communications are right now."

It wasn't long before they got more critical than she had counted on. Switchboards could get really busy at peak times of the day, and operators had a hard time keeping the keys, lines, and cords going to all the right places. Faye did pretty well with that; her failing was leaving the key open, which allowed the customer's conversation to be heard from both sides. She had mistakenly left a key open while taking a quick cigarette break. When she returned, there were six pairs of eyes staring at her with hostility.

It was not uncommon for switchboard operators to become well acquainted with the male hotel guests. It was easy to develop such a friendship, as the operators were constantly answering and placing phone calls for the guests. However, this kind of friendship was severely frowned upon by management, and the operators made every effort to keep any liaisons private. Little did Faye know that her cigarette break would cost her another job.

The open key was to a room occupied by a high-ranking military officer who, at that moment, was encouraging a switchboard operator named Gladys to make personal calls from his hotel suite. Luck would have it that the hotel manager walked by at the same time and overheard the officer's remarks. Instead of firing Faye, he fired Gladys, who left in a storm of denials and tears. Faye decided she might as well leave too because all those eyes were descending on her like a coop full of hostile hens!

So Faye had to find a new job—a mission she figured would not be too hard. Jobs that had previously been held by men were now vacant as the GIs, those enlisted in the army, rushed off to war. Thousands of them came through Atlanta from all over the Southeast for training at Fort McPherson. Atlanta was awash in uniforms. There was also a large army base at nearby Camp Gordon, just outside Atlanta. Additional installations included supply depots and military airfields as well as an increasing number of military suppliers and manufacturers of war materials.

Trucks, rail lines, and buses were in great demand for moving the military and its supplies, and soldiers were always given priority. Civilians got a ride on anything they could whenever they could. Greyhound buses had the cheapest fares but also took the longest time. To save rubber on tires for the war effort, a 35 mph speed limit had been imposed. In addition, seats were hard to get, as Greyhound had become the major carrier of troops heading to the East and West Coasts while also transporting personnel to work in the shipyards and munitions factories.

Bus companies were barely able to handle the demands made by the military, much less transport all the civilians who wanted to travel. Ad campaigns discouraged ordinary citizens from travel, with slogans such as "Serve America Now, So You Can See America Later" and, more specifically, "Don't Travel unless Your Trip Is Essential." As the war progressed, 40 percent of bus drivers were called up, and consequently women began to be trained as drivers.

Driving a bus was more than holding a steering wheel. It involved handling heavy bags and sometimes settling disputes between riders. In addition, it required some navigational skills. Faye couldn't drive a car, much less propel a 45,000-pound bus down a busy highway. Nor would her petite frame allow her to handle her own bags, let alone anyone else's. In fact, she always made sure there was at least one strong guy hanging around to take care of whatever luggage or box she was taxed with. On top of that, she had absolutely no sense of direction. Bus driving was out.

She also wasn't cut out to be Rosie the Riveter. That popular World War II icon was too forceful a figure to fit in with Faye's self-image. She wanted to appear fragile, delicate, and perfectly ladylike. That tallied with her fantasies of glamour, and she also hoped it made her more appealing to men. Besides, Rosie would have to get dirty, and Faye wasn't about to do anything that might soil her hands.

So she stuck with receptionist and telephone operator positions. As soon as she heard of a better paying option, off she went down the street to a new office. She was open to dating the few men she might meet at work, but, for the most part, these turned out to be over- the-hill characters who were too old for the war. She'd already had one older man and was not interested in another.

There was no shortage of men, and she didn't have to look long or far. In addition, Atlanta already had a large number of single women who'd come from all over the South. Faye loved being among those courageous young men and equally hopeful young women. It opened up an entirely new social life that she really enjoyed. Getting a date was easier than getting a doughnut; men were plentiful but sugar was not!

Dates were most often evening trips to the movies. It was convenient, inexpensive, and gave the couple much to discuss. The movies were not only for entertainment but provided a venue for the public to review the newsreels about the war and learn about war bond drives.

The talk of war and its dreadful toll did not become a reality to Faye until Ollie Jr. rushed to join the army air corps and flew off into the clouds of combat. She adored Ollie and felt closer to him than any of her other siblings except Gwen. When Ollie left for flight training. He told his parents, "Watch out for Faye. She can't seem to stay out of trouble." He was absolutely right.

While other women were feeling victorious for political reasons, Faye still felt liberated and victorious every time she lit up a Lucky Strike, the American Tobacco Company's top-selling cigarette. The brand had recently been repackaged from its former green and gold color scheme because the war effort needed the titanium contained in Lucky's green ink and the copper contained in the gold; the cigarettes were now dressed in an all-white background with a red bull's-eye. This delighted the female smokers who had hated the earlier packaging since it clashed with their dresses.

As the war pushed on, President Roosevelt made tobacco a protected crop, and cigarettes were included in GIs C rations. Immediately tobacco companies began sending millions of free cigarettes to the soldiers, mostly the popular brands. Consequently the home front had to make do with off-brands like Rameses or Pacayunes. Tobacco consumption became so widespread that a shortage developed, and by the end of the war, cigarette sales were at an all-time high.

Nevertheless, in 1940 a woman smoking was thoroughly frowned upon, a reality that didn't faze Faye a bit. She loved smoking and especially enjoyed the airy gestures of lighting up and then waving the cigarette around in her hand as she talked. Yet, while tobacco was still regarded as something ladies did not do, ladies did do the USO.

41.
Movie Madness

THE UNITED SERVICE ORGANIZATION (USO) WAS FOUNDED in February of 1941 by several volunteer organizations: the YMCA, the National Catholic Community, the Salvation Army, and the National Traveler's Aid Association. FDR had asked for recreational services that would boost morale to be provided to servicemen and women; nationwide, a giant effort was made. Subsequently USOs were held in churches, barns, museums, log cabins, and anywhere else space could be found. Their purpose was to provide a "home away from home" for millions of GIs. Recreation included dances and movies as well as free coffee and doughnuts; USOs also provided a haven for quiet moments to write home. The USO later partnered with the Department of Defense and began its long tradition of putting on celebrity shows for troops overseas. As a result, Bob Hope became as much a symbol of the war as Hitler himself.

USOs were in every small town, including Tifton, where Faye's sister Sara Mae was a hostess. She was eighteen and a beautiful dark redhead who had just been crowned Tobacco Queen of Tift County. It was summertime, and in the fall she would be heading for Drake University. To make college money, Sara had a part-time job as an usher at the local theater, which was just across the street from Tifton's USO club.

Sara was a real showstopper. Her bright smile, stunning figure, beautiful face, and mountains of long hair were just too much for one of the theater patrons, whose name was Mal. Mal was in uniform and about to be shipped off to a northern base to begin his military training. Originally from Virginia, he epitomized the true Southern gentleman. He watched Sara lead him to his seat and instantly and totally lost his heart. Mal couldn't wait for the movie to end because he wanted to see that little bundle of beauty. So as soon as "The End" popped up on the screen, he was on his feet and out the door, hoping for a date. But she was on duty at the USO, so he had to share her with dozens of other soldiers. The girls were not supposed to go out with GIs they met while on duty, so Mal stayed until they locked the doors! He was not going to let this girl get away from him. He hadn't counted on the fact she would be leaving for college the next morning.

Undaunted, he was at that train station bright and early to see her off, and they both pledged to write. The letters began to fly, and it was obvious they were falling deeply in love. Her letters were about college, and his were about the war, but they still managed to create an unshakable bond through the magic of the written word.

They next saw each other a year later. She came to visit him at his parents' home in Virginia, where he had prepared a quick campaign that resulted in complete victory. They were married a month later! Their movie, a true wartime romance, was to last through seven decades and several wars—including the one between Hill and Faye, which only seemed to get worse as the years went by with no truce in sight.

42.

Supporting Cast

FAYE FINALLY LANDED A JOB IN THE MOVIE BUSINESS! THE
Paramount Theater was downtown on Peachtree
Street in the same block as the Loew's Grand. Movie
theaters of the period were grand affairs, and the
Paramount was a glittering example. Its lobby was a two-
and-a-half-story vaulted room with a grand marble
staircase leading to the promenade and balcony. Its decor
resembled that of an ornate seventeenth-century Italian
palace. A huge antique bronze and crystal chandelier
hung from the ceiling of the balcony, casting a soft light
over the entire theater.

Many of the movie theaters built in the 1920s and
1930s were so grand that people referred to them as
movie palaces. Inside the palaces, smartly uniformed
ushers escorted ticket holders through grand hallways,
plush carpeting, and extravagant decor. The ushers not
only escorted viewers to their seats but also handled large
crowds. The Paramount, Loew's Grand, and the famed
fabulous Fox Theatre were all enormous. The Fox had
4,678 seats and filled them regularly.

Theater patrons were treated to pre-movie entertainment such as a ballet, orchestral music, or a performance on one of the Mighty Wurlitzer organs. The organ at the Fox rose to the stage from a hydraulic lift and opened the evening's entertainment with a startling bellow that could be felt all the way to the top balcony.

Ladies' lounges in these theaters were equally luxurious and attended by a uniformed black maid. Her only purpose was to hand the patron a clean towel for hand drying. A small tip was expected.

Although Atlanta was receiving hundreds of new black soldiers and war workers on a daily basis, segregation was still rigidly practiced. Theaters had a separate entrance and separate ticket window for blacks, and seating was strictly enforced. Blacks were relegated to balconies and not allowed to drink from the same water fountains as whites, nor use the same restrooms. Some theaters simply chose not to have facilities for blacks at all.

Even in the 1940s, Depression-era sales tactics were used to lure people to the movies. These included ladies' night with lower rates for women, free dishes, and raffles for appliances and automobiles. A night out at the movies could be very profitable. And all of this activity required a large staff of secretaries, musicians, ushers, ticket salespeople, and ticket takers. Some theaters even employed a nurse and a fireman. Faye's job: a receptionist in the business office.

As wartime attendance rose to astronomical numbers, it paid Paramount Pictures to own an extensive chain of over two hundred movie houses across the nation. Their studios produced sixty to seventy movies a year featuring their huge stable of stars. Those same movie stars were often booked through Atlanta on either war-bond drives or simply to promote their current film. Faye was elated—she could see all the movies she wanted for free and her job in the office gave her access to stars such as Marlene Dietrich, Bob

Hope, Bing Crosby, Lauren Bacall, Veronica Lake, and her favorite redhead, Rita Hayworth.

But Faye had a knack for ruining her own good luck, and she soon did it in her usual style.

Faye often acted impulsively, with no thought to consequences. As a result, her decisions were rarely good ones. In fact, what began as an ordinary day in her new dream job at Paramount Pictures soon spun into a considerable crisis as her first star sighting was almost a disaster. From the moment Rita walked through the door, Faye was speechless. The star was clad in jewels and fur, platform high-heels, and real silk stockings with seams down the back. Her makeup was flawless, as was her creamy skin. She had penciled eyebrows, a patriotic bright red lipstick, and fabulous false eyelashes. Her hair was in an elegant updo and topped off with a saucy hat. She was every inch *the star.*

What caused Faye to act impulsively this time were the stockings, which made her angry. Silk was scarcer than sugar. At least you had a ration book for sugar, but silk was out of the question as it was needed for parachutes, making silk stockings an extremely prized possession. As for stockings themselves, Faye didn't mind not having any since she hated the uncomfortable girdles and garter belts that held them up; panty hose were way off in the future. In the absence of stockings, Faye, like most other women, used a piece of black charcoal to draw a line from behind the knee down the length of the leg to simulate a seamed stocking. It was a messy business that had to be repeated several times a day—depending on how many times a woman crossed her legs. Fortunately, Faye had finally learned to keep her own legs crossed!

But as she took a look at her black-spattered legs, she let out a screech of jealous outrage that could be heard all the way down to the Fox. Instead of a polite, "How do you do," her greeting was a snarling, "Where in the hell did you get those stockings?"

Rita wasn't used to anything but adoration, and Faye seemed to have insinuated that she was unpatriotic. Hence, Rita gave Faye a quick and unexpected slap across the cheek accompanied by a snarl of her own. She roared, "None of your business, you bitch!" Red hair and red tempers were flying like nervous saucers under tittering teacups. In the midst of returning the serve, Faye's hand was grabbed by the manager before she could even the score.

She was immediately sent home to cool off and also think of some appropriate way to save her latest job. She was pleasantly surprised when, the next day, her boss told her she was not going to be fired and she was directed to simply find some way to obtain a pair of silk stockings and send them to Miss Hayworth with a polite apology.

As usual, she took her problem to Gwen. By return post, a letter and two pairs of silk stockings came up from Americus. The stockings were beautiful and had been given to Gwen just before the war as a birthday present. She had been saving them for a special occasion, and there was no time like the present emergency!

Faye was reluctant to send them on to Rita as all nine girls she shared the boardinghouse with had seen the package and was hoping to have a chance to wear them. The girls shared a lot of their clothing, but Faye was not about to give up those stockings. She would send Rita one pair and keep the second one for herself. The other girls would simply have to wait till the war was over—whenever that might be.

Meantime, her continuing war with Hill was about to ignite into an explosion with huge casualties.

43.

A Double Feature

FAYE ONLY SAW HER TWO YOUNG CHILDREN ON THE RARE occasions when she was able to visit them in Tifton. Even if she had owned a car, she wouldn't have known how to drive it there. In Atlanta, she rode the electric streetcar to and from work or play. Her visits to the farm, however, had to be by bus or train, making each journey long and expensive.

The boardinghouse she lived in was a well kept but crowded six-bedroom house near Piedmont Park. It was owned by a recently widowed woman whom the girls called Mom Dunbar. She was very protective of them and vitally interested in their lives. "Mom's" house was always noisy, filled with the chatter or tearful wails of an assortment of women, which made it more like a college dormitory than a boardinghouse. Everyone knew everything that was going on in everyone's lives. There were no secrets, except the ones Faye tried to hide.

Clothes, hats, and shoes were draped over curtain rods, doorknobs, or dresser drawers. Items were constantly traded so that the girls could expand their own limited wardrobes.

But Faye, while happy to give fashion advice, refused to share clothes, or even so much as a hairpin. Obsessively neat and clean, she ensured that her things were carefully hung up or folded away, and no one dared touch anything with her label on it. All her life she had been forced to share her belongings with her sisters, and by God she was not going to share with this new bunch!

Boardinghouses were generally old homes whose owners had fallen on hard times and so rented out rooms in order to keep a roof over their own heads. In the Deep South, they were always segregated racially and sometimes by gender as well. Usually, single rooms were rented out and paid for by the week, but often guests doubled up or slept three to a room.

Some boardinghouses offered meals and some just kitchen privileges. There was rarely more than one bathroom in the entire house, but there was always a radio and sometimes a piano. A boardinghouse was not just a place for occupants to share space, it was also a community—and Mom Dunbar ran a very tightly knit community of young working women. She made sure they got a good breakfast before dashing out the door to what she thought must be exciting jobs. Food rationing was in high gear, and many items were just impossible to get, especially meat. Vegetables, on the other hand, were fairly plentiful as most people had planted victory gardens in place of lawns.

Faye always enjoyed the pretty white rabbits scampering through Mom Dunbar's back lawn, which she was sure were kept as pets—that is, until she bit into what appeared to be chicken one night at dinner. She thought it tasted a bit odd and asked Mom if it was spoiled. Mom replied, "I always spoil those little things a bit before I cook 'em." It suddenly dawned on Faye that she had just taken a bite out of Bugs Bunny! Her eyes grew as wide as her mouth, and she let out a haunted cry. "Eeeeeh! What's up, Doc?" was about to switch to "What's *coming* up?" With that, she left the table and didn't eat another piece of fowl for the remainder of the war.

Faye had become a fan of Bugs Bunny immediately upon seeing him in several two-minute US war bond commercials called "Any Bonds Today?" He first appeared, however, in *Porky's Hare Hunt*, a Walt Disney cartoon produced in 1938, with an accent crafted to be a blend of pronunciations heard between Brooklyn and the Bronx. By 1941, he would become a mainstream cultural icon, and he would later achieve fame as the most popular character of the entire Looney Tunes cast, eventually having his own star on the Hollywood Walk of Fame.

Mom Dunbar always served a simple meal promptly at 6:00 pm. Afterward, the girls could either listen to Faye play the piano or indulge in the theatrics of radio. Their favorite characters were Amos and Andy, Jack Benny, and ventriloquist Edgar Bergen and his wooden pal, Charlie McCarthy.

In the summertime, the radio was taken out to the porch, where it was cooler. Air conditioning consisted of high ceilings and lots of hand-held paper fans flying back and forth across perspiring faces. The sounds of children playing and laughing on the porch often reminded Faye that she had two children of her own. One afternoon while trying to distract herself from motherhood, she mused, "I wonder where my new boyfriend, Bob, is going to take me tonight. This is payday, and I think I need to get that blue dress I just saw at Rich's. Maybe he will take me to out to dinner and then to that new movie playing at the Fox. I sure want to eat somewhere besides this damn boardinghouse."

Mom Dunbar was particularly interested in Faye's job at the Paramount. She had a daughter in show business who later became the "legs" for a cigarette company called Pall Mall. The ad campaign targeted women and featured a Pall

Mall cigarette package placed on top of a set of gorgeous dancing legs. That was Dixie Dunbar.

Faye and her two roommates, Sara and Pauline, were living in Dixie's old bedroom. Dixie had favored lots of ruffles, and her curtains and bedspread were covered in pink—Faye's favorite color. There was a small makeup table similarly dressed, with a large mirror hanging over it that the girls used as a bulletin board for notes and messages. A pink ruffled shade on the lamp completed the decor.

Faye loved this room. Her room at the farm, which she had shared with all her sisters, had two simple frame beds dressed in one of Mae's many homemade quilts. They would now be considered beautiful works of art, but Faye never could see beyond the "homemade" label and hated them all. She knew she could not live there again, even for her infant daughter and son.

When thinking of herself as an occasional mother and a full-time city girl, she preferred the latter. It was a less demanding role. However, a great demand was about to be made upon her, and it would shatter her very soul.

44.

The Child Stars

FAYE FINALLY HAD A CHANCE TO VISIT HER CHILDREN FOR THE weekend. When she got off the bus in Tifton, she was met by Ollie Jr., who was home on a short leave. Ollie and Faye spent a few hours together at the farm before he was off again to the skies and to the war.

She was glad to see her children, who were now barely two and four; but they hardly seemed to know who she was. Her occasional visits didn't allow their little memory banks to grasp that she was their mother. Ronnie remembered her vaguely, but Faith just smiled as she received a pat on the head from the strange, glamorous lady.

Faye was not one to cuddle a child, or anyone else for that matter. She only wanted to *be* cuddled, but she could not reach out to another. Her maternal instincts were buried beneath her mattress just as deeply as the ledger she kept about what Hill owed her. The alimony and child support she was awarded by the court could not begin to keep her in the lifestyle to which she aspired and felt she deserved.

Her first and last thought each day was, "He ruined my life and he should pay for it." The more she thought about it, the more she thought he had ruined her life and the more she thought he should pay. By this time, there wasn't enough money in Fort Knox to handle the bill, but she would not and could not let her hatred go. She constantly bounced it around like a basketball player shooting for victory.

By happenstance, Hill had also arrived in Tifton that weekend to visit their children. He had been on his way to Florida and taken a detour for a few days. He had not heard from Faye in some time and, unsure if she was still living at the boardinghouse, had stopped calling her. However, since they were both in Tifton at the same time, he decided to ask her to dinner to discuss the children. She refused, saying, "You are interfering with my visit to the children. You are down here all the time and can see them whenever that fancy car of yours gets pointed toward Tifton. I have to ride the damn bus; it takes a day to get here and a day to get back, so I don't have much time with them. Leave them alone, and leave me alone. I don't care if I ever see you again, you son of a bitch! Just send me my check every month, and don't be late."

Faith and Ronnie knew their father because he had made it a point to stop in Tifton whenever his business took him anywhere near the farm. That particular weekend, he had been asked to preach at the little country Baptist church in Brookfield. The congregation had come to know him as Faye's husband and continued to welcome him to their church as a powerful preacher.

He knew that Mae and Ollie, who never missed a Sunday, would bring Faye and the two children to the service. Note sure what the topic of his sermon would be, he was still wrestling with it as he approached the pulpit. But then he looked out into the audience and saw Faye sitting primly in her usual pew with one of *his* children on either side and he knew an apocalypse was about to come. Aware that the sight of those two small children whose lives had been so tragically changed was almost more than he could bear, he launched into a lengthy discussion of the Book of Revelation. It had been one of Thad's favorite scriptures, and remained popular among many fundamentalist preachers, as it predicted the Second Coming and an apocalyptic end— perfect drama for the scene about to unfold. Despite his soft-spoken nature, his voice began to soar with a terrible pain, and he was unable to continue. Tears streamed down his face as he finally stepped down and said to the congregation, "Please pray for my family." With that, he left the church and left Tifton.

But he did not leave the battlefield. Needing a little time to complete his plan and implement his strategy, he went back to Atlanta with nothing else on his mind.

45.

The Director

HILL WAS EXTREMELY EFFICIENT AND COULD GET THINGS DONE in a hurry, but he wanted to think his plan through very carefully because there was no room for error. Accustomed to being in charge, he had become an autocrat. He didn't ask for permission; he simply gave directions, which were usually obeyed without question. Now he directed his attorney to draw up new custody papers and said he would get them signed at a later date.

He had always been very respectful of Ollie and Mae and appreciated their taking responsibility for the children. Yet, seeing the little ones that last weekend made him desperately want to raise them himself even though he knew it would be a wrench for the little ones to be separated from the only real home they had known. Mae and Ollie had been wonderful and loving grandparents, and the children were obviously happy with them. But Hill loved his children and now wanted them with him.

Atlanta was growing daily, but still small enough that he would occasionally spot Faye around town. Like everyone else, he was also aware of the huge numbers of military personnel moving in and out of the city. He knew it was only a matter of time before Faye would find another man to take care of her. That was fine with him, but he did not want another man raising his children, especially not a soldier. They had already lost one father to divorce, and Hill refused to let them risk losing a second one to war. Such a loss was entirely possible if Faye were to marry a GI, but at forty-two he himself was now too old to be drafted.

Military mobilization created great changes for the entire nation. As men were called up to serve their country, others had to be found to replace workers in shipyards, metalworking industries, and other initiatives needed to support the war effort. America was on the move, and Hill was very much afraid Faye would be moved along with it. In particular, he had no doubt that a uniform would soon catch her eye. One of her brothers later commented, "Faye never could resist a uniform. It didn't matter if it was on a bus driver, taxi driver, delivery driver, or train conductor, she just loved a man in a uniform. Why, I remember that when she came down from Atlanta she always had a date on the way back up with whatever uniform had been driving."

Hill would subsequently use this information to justify the terrible action he was about to take.

46.

Flirty Faye

IT WAS TRUE THAT FAYE HAD MANY MEN TO CHOOSE FROM. THE United States had almost 16 million men in uniform, and all those from the Southeast came through Atlanta. She and her roommates were regular volunteers at their local USO club, where Faye loved hostessing. There she had lots of competition since girls from all over Atlanta were quickly discovering the delight of giving delight to the GIs who flocked to those doors. Southern girls were well-known for their poise and beauty, and the occasional Yankee who landed there was overwhelmed by their obvious femininity. The Southern girls considered Yankees special prizes since they seemed much more sophisticated than their own Southern boys, usually fresh off the farm.

Faye could bat her eyelashes with the best of them and do the boogie-woogie at the same time while easily pivoting from one partner to the next. The only time she sat a dance out was to smoke a cigarette, all the while blowing smoke rings while tossing her curls at some enamored GI. She especially enjoyed practicing her skills on the innocent farm boys. Knowing all too well what their previous life had been like, she pretended to be a gracious society girl doing her "bit" for the war.

The men she most wanted to practice on were the few who came from old-monied families, a lifestyle she would have liked to fit into. She planned her strategy like a general. Able to spot money at a hundred paces, she moved like a first lieutenant in the heat of battle. After considerable observation, her roommate, Patricia, cautioned her, saying, "Faye, you need to slow down some—you're like a dog trying to tree a possum," to which Faye replied, "I only need to tree one, and he needs to be fat."

She thought her chance had finally come when she met Bob Webster. He was an army colonel with a West Point background and a large family fortune earned in the Chicago stockyards. Bob thought Faye was charming and certainly among the most feminine women he had ever met. He was smitten and took her to all the best places, including the Wisteria Garden Night Club in the heart of Atlanta. There they danced the night away to a popular orchestra while dining on lobster and steak. Faye had never been much of a drinker, and Bob, who enjoyed only the finest wines and was amused at her lack of knowledge on the subject, undertook her education bottle by bottle. Their last bottle of wine had to be consumed quickly because he had just received orders that his unit was being shipped out the next day. He couldn't tell her where, of course; but they both knew his military background would send him into the heart of the fighting.

He wrote often for a while, and then his letters became less and less frequent. Finally they stopped altogether. Faye never knew if he was lost in battle or victorious in the arms of another woman. Yet she continued to wage a war on two fronts—one with Hill and the other to find another rich man.

47.

The Director's Cut

HILL WAS VERY METHODICAL IN HIS PLANNING AND OVER-looked no detail. It was 1942, and the war was quickly drawing to a close, but Hill's war with Faye was escalating. From Hill's point of view, Faye was not particularly inclined to raise the children but didn't want him to have them either. So the war was going in her favor because she had full custody even though Ronnie and Faith were housed with her parents. She also had the final say on all matters involving the children.

It infuriated Hill that she seemed to be more interested in having a good time than in looking after the children. Hill was not accustomed to being sidelined, especially when it came to having control over his children's lives—something he would not tolerate. More than that, it irritated him that Faye appeared to delight in the drama and her ability to flaunt the situation, enjoying his discomfort while she had him on the run.

Hill knew it was hard for her to make the long trip to Tifton because of the transportation issues surrounding the war, though to his mind she did not seem to be putting forth much effort on that front anyway. He did offer her a ride down from Atlanta one weekend, however, and they spent it discussing the children.

It was more like a firefight than a discussion. Hill tried to be calm, polite, and keep his voice low, but Faye was armed for battle.

He asked, "Would you like to try to work this out? What can we do to make it easier for the children? Do you think we should try again?" Privately he thought to himself: "My children need to be with me *and* their mother. Why can't she see that? Has she just completely lost interest in them? I wish I knew what to say that would bring her to her senses. But she seems determined to think only of my past mistakes and nothing about the future of these kids. Maybe she is finally having the good time she missed when she was growing up on the farm. If that's the case, then there is absolutely nothing I can do. I can't compete with what she never had."

She was adamant and said: "I am through with you. The only thing you can do is leave me alone. You wouldn't quit traveling; and when you were home you never wanted to do anything I wanted to do. While you were gone, I was stuck in the house with a bunch of smelly diapers and nothing else to do. I was too young to be stuck with an old man like you unless you were are willing to make serious changes, and you weren't."

He replied, "Faye, do you understand that I have to travel to make a living? That's how I bought you all those pretty dresses and hats you carried on about all the time. With the war on, cars are even harder to get now, so I have had to keep looking for them."

She said, quick as a flash, "Well, you could sell some shoes or suits! You sure are a hell of a salesman because you sold me a load of goods and it wasn't a suit. Now, go sell somebody else!

Hearing that, Hill just about choked but managed to reply, "Yes, I could sell suits, but the only ones being sold now are uniforms and the government has the concession."

Under his breath he muttered, "Just how in the world does she think I could sell enough suits to buy all the things she demands. I would be better off selling ice cream in hell."

It was a long, unpleasant conversation that left them both angry and went nowhere. He did not offer to drive her back up to Atlanta on Sunday.

He realized there was going to be no compromise and he would have to take other steps. The first step would be financial. US automobile production had completely ceased in February of 1942 as those manufacturers were now turning out tanks, jeeps, and airplanes. By the end of that year, used car prices had become so high that the government had to impose price controls. Hill promptly sold his entire inventory and left the automobile business for good. He also intended to leave Atlanta, but there were a few other things he needed to do first.

One of them was to visit his mother. Laura had never disapproved of Faye and had treated her in a kindly fashion, but she did disapprove of divorce. When Hill broke the news that he was giving up and leaving Atlanta for good, she said, "You were called to be a preacher, not a husband, and I see you have failed at both. You will never be happy unless you answer God's call." With that, she placed her Bible in his hands and left the room without a backward glance.

In her heart of hearts, Laura realized that Hill was only one among millions of people who were relocating. Twenty percent of the entire population had already left their homes to follow well-paid jobs created by the war. Perhaps it was best that he start his life over again in new territory. She, of course, had no idea what his real plan entailed. Even if she had, she wouldn't have been able to stop him since once Hill decided on a course of action he never changed his mind.

He knew what he was going to do and had worked it out carefully. It was the old bait and switch. He made a date to take Faye out driving. She had always loved the thrill of fast cars, and he had the last 1942 Packard off the assembly line. They drove around town for hours, then he said, "The children need to have a home of their own and a secure future. You will not be able to provide that in your current state of employment, nor with your lack of higher education and your limited job skills."

Hill hadn't been a salesman and a preacher for nothing. He knew when to close the deal and when to ask for prayers. He concluded his pitch with what he knew she would find irresistible. "I am going to buy a farm for myself and the children from Dr. Turner in Conyers, and you can see them anytime you want. Although I have given up traveling, I will have a maid there to help look after them when I am not at home. In addition, I will give you some money to get you started off right." He didn't need snake oil when he could use money.

Maybe it was just one of his tricks, but to Faye the offer of money seemed like the perfect solution. Conyers was really just a rural suburb of Atlanta, and getting there would be much easier than the long, hot bus rides to Tifton that she so dreaded. She also began to think about how she could use that extra money.

Finally a deal was struck. He would have the children nine months out of the year and she could have them in the summer vacation months when they were out of school. It seemed that the war between them might actually be coming to an end.

Hill's parting comment was, "As soon as the papers are signed, I will come to Tifton, get the children, and bring them to my farm."

A month later, the documents were in his hands. He called Faye at her boardinghouse and said, "You better start spending that money because that's all you are getting out of this deal. I've got the kids and you will be lucky to ever see them again. I've got a farm, but it isn't in Conyers."

It turned out that Hill had instead purchased an eighteen-hundred-acre timber plantation and cattle ranch in Northwest Florida, three hundred miles from Atlanta! Although Hill had indeed secured custody for nine months of the year, the children would be farther away than ever, leaving no way for Faye to visit them.

48.

The Final Curtain

HELL HATH NO FURY LIKE FAYE TRICKED! HERE SHE WAS having a perfectly good time in the middle of the war and he had to go and pull a dirty trick like that.

She declared, "I *will* find him, and this time he will really pay!" Yet she also knew she'd have to think about what she'd done. After all, she had taken his money.

The first thing she did with it was quit her job and go to Des Moines to stay with her glamorous brother Ollie, who was stationed there and training to fly the P47 Thunderbolt, a massive weapon of the sky. At age twenty-three, he was slightly older than most cadets.

The average age for US pilots in World War II was twenty to twenty-one. It was considerably younger for England's RAF pilots. By the time the United States had entered the war, England's skilled pilots had been decimated by constant dogfights with the Germans. New pilots were being trained daily and often had as few as two to three hours of instruction. Some of these brave boys were not even old enough to have a driver's license. They rode their bicycles to the airfields and flew off into the skies of war knowing their chance of being killed was seventy-one percent.

Ollie was well aware that he would soon be sent overseas to fulfill thirty combat missions. He was also well aware that he might not return. All the air jockeys, as they were sometimes called, knew there was no such thing as an average pilot. You were either an ace or a target. He kept these harsh realities from Faye and his girlfriend, Marie.

He also withheld information about Faye's other brothers, who were also in the service—Larry in the navy, Bunny in the army, and Wallace in the merchant marines. All the Love men were serving their country, worrying constantly about one another, and trying to keep it from their mother. Mae and Ollie now had four sons at war and a life consumed by worry. Letters from the boys were infrequent, and, when they did come, gave very little comforting news.

Faye didn't have to worry about the father of her children being killed in action. He was thirty-nine, far too old to be called up. "I wish he would just drop dead," she often said. But the truth was that as much as she hated Hill she needed him around to provide for the children.

Ollie's girlfriend Marie had her own apartment and offered to house Faye for a while, unaware of what she was getting into. The three soon became regulars at the nightspots around Des Moines, where Faye appeared to have nothing to do but have a good time or complain that she wasn't. Marie was very much in love with Ollie, and if being with him meant putting up with his tempestuous sister, then so be it. But Ollie adored Faye and pampered her constantly, and soon Marie was starting to feel a bit excluded.

After the loss of her children, Faye seemed unable to either gain perspective or move toward forgiveness. Any hope of softness or tenderness was lost. She remained stuck in her childish and foolish fantasies of a glamorous life and distracted herself with clothes and parties. Her attitude became so bitter that not even Ollie could penetrate it. In truth, not wanting to relinquish the scenario, she had continued to replay those emotions again and again.

Marie had watched this drama until she was ready to declare a war of her own. By then, she and Ollie had married, and Faye had become so desperate for attention that her needs interfered with everything in the household. Marie wanted time with her husband, but Ollie was way too involved in trying to soothe his sister.

They almost came to blows one night over the meal Marie had so carefully prepared for Ollie, who was about to leave on a training mission of indeterminable duration. Marie had used every coupon in her ration book and asked Faye for some of hers to buy a few extras for the celebration. Faye, who guarded her coupons like she guarded her heart, wouldn't part with a single thing once it came into her possession, not even for Ollie.

Marie had been pleasant and forgiving ever since Faye arrived but now was in the mood for murder. She launched into a tirade: "You selfish, little haughty bitch! You walk around like you are some sort of movie star. You can't get enough attention to satisfy yourself for five minutes. Why, you even wiggle that fanny of yours at the garbage collector. Personally, I think that is just where you need to be because that line you keep feeding every guy you meet is nothing *but* garbage!" With that, she left the kitchen and also left a week's worth of meat ration on the stove. The meat was about as well done as Marie and promptly caught fire, no doubt from the smoke coming out of her ear.

This chaotic scene was nothing new to Ollie. He was more than familiar with the heat Faye managed to generate everywhere she went. He was practiced at calming his sister and soon managed to negotiate a peace settlement between the two. It took his entire week's pay, but he offered a night on the town, anywhere they wanted to go. Naturally, Faye wanted an expensive night out, and Marie just wanted a night out with Ollie, wherever that might be arranged. They went to the Officer's Club.

Ollie was almost as gorgeous as Faye, and the two of them made a sparkling addition to the Officer's Club that night. Ollie was full of charm, and his dark hair and soulful eyes were the stuff of movie stars. He also had a natural voice that beautifully complemented Faye's piano skills. They were a great team, and he and Faye soon became favorites among the GIs and flyboys hanging around the O'Club that night. They would perform at the drop of a hat. She had never had so much fun and attention, and she didn't want the evening to end.

It did come to an end as soon as Ollie got his orders. He was being sent to an air base in England where he would join other bright and beautiful young men in the continuing onslaught of aerial combat. Marie was inconsolable and finally asked Faye to leave so she could at least have these last few days alone with her love.

Faye didn't want to leave, but had no choice. Her parents, having made the long journey up from Tifton to see their son off to war, told her, "Get your things together, get in the car, and get some sense while you're at it. They need some time alone, and so do you. You need to think about what you are doing. You are a mother, and you need to see about those children instead of running around with a bunch of soldiers."

Faye had occasionally thought about her children and told Gwen years later,

"I always felt like I sold my children," to which Gwen deftly replied, "Sure looks that way doesn't it?"

49.

The Last Curtain Call

FINDING HILL WAS NOT GOING TO BE AS EASY AS FAYE HAD thought. There were no amber alert systems, email blasts, Facebook, Twitter, or cellphone alerts. Communication was still by mail and slower than usual since the war had generated huge amounts of correspondence for the domestic market, straining the postal service to the hilt.

When she got back from Des Moines, she found a new boardinghouse and a new job. The glamour of the military had begun to fade, and she was faced with the fact that her children were really and truly gone. For one thing, children were not allowed in boardinghouses. For another, the girls at the new boardinghouse—all involved in their own jobs, lives, boyfriends, and the war effort, and without children of their own—were unable to comfort her. Although many were recent transplants from farms themselves, enjoying the excitement of city life, Faye maintained silence about her own roots.

In addition, the landlady, Mrs. Peet, was not nearly as understanding as Mom Dunbar had been. Worn down from years of listening to sob stories from her boarders, now she just tuned them out. "Give me your money, not your problems" was her motto. Faye, having no shoulder to cry on, began to think she wasn't going to get the sympathy she depended on. It was no fun playing victim to a disinterested audience.

While Faye was beginning to feel a bit frantic at the thought of possibly never seeing her children again, she was relieved not to be burdened with the responsibilities of motherhood. That would have interfered with the parade of soldiers that marched through her life, as well as Gus, her latest catch.

Gus was a much older and widowed Jewish man with a fourteen-year-old daughter. He needed a mother for this girl, and Faye wanted a father for herself—someone to take care of her and provide all the lovely things she knew she deserved. Gus seemed to fit the bill in every way. Besides, he had two things Faye loved most: an expensive car and a women's clothing store! As far as she was concerned, it was another dream come true.

However, to her dismay, this dream was to be interrupted by some snoring. Gus soon got bored with Faye's constant chatter about clothes, cars, and movies! Faye was lively, beautiful, and fun—as long she was the center of attention. But what Gus wanted was another wife, not another child to raise. This relationship was obviously not going to work, he told himself.

Faye, still trying to figure how to find her children, was discovering at the same time that men did not want another man's children. In the remarriage game, she concluded, she had two major strikes against her—divorce and children—both of which she had to keep secret if she wanted to find a man.

Determined to find her children, Faye eventually took the bus to Americus, hoping Gwen could wave her usual magic wand and make things fall into place. All Gwen could think of to do, however, was drive Faye to Tifton to talk to Ollie and Mae. The distance was only fifty miles, but it covered a lifetime.

Hill and Ollie had always respected each other and got along well. But Ollie had not heard from him and had no idea where he was. He and Mae had both assumed that Hill had taken the children to Atlanta. They were not worried about the safety of Ronnie and Faith because they knew Hill would protect them with his life. However, they were distressed and concerned about what kind of home he would provide. After all, he was a single man. They decided that all they could do was talk to the sheriff of Tift County to see if he could find them some clues.

After several months of anxious waiting, Hill and the children were finally located through a friend of his who had sold him some property in Florida. But Hill refused to return the children.

Ollie and Mae decided to drive Faye down to Florida and work out a compromise between them. They traveled the two hundred miles over rough roads on worn-out tires in an old truck, with the three of them crowded into the small cab in front that would have been tight for two. Ollie, having used the last of his gas ration coupons, hoped they could get there and back on whatever gas they had in the tank. He also had to drive all night since there was no money to pay for a room at a tourist court. Worse, Faye was trying his usual quiet patience with her smoking, crying, and constant complaining, so he was eager to arrive at their destination. Deep inside, Ollie wished he knew more about the place they were headed because he was hoping to leave Faye there to free themselves of her theatrics on the way back.

However, it became apparent upon their arrival that there was to be no peace. Hill was adamant: "I want my children, I have them, and I am keeping them. *Period.* I now have legal custody nine months of the year. You get them in the summer only. But they will have to stay in Tifton with Ollie and Mae until such time as you are willing and able to provide a proper home for them."

Faye secretly didn't mind that part too much as she had little inclination to be a full-time mother. But she was furious about being tricked, enraged that his plan had been so skillfully executed that she had never suspected a thing. What was even more maddening was that despite her naturally suspicious nature he had beaten her at her own game and that no amount of spite, tears, tantrums, or enticements were going to make a bit of difference.

While this scene was unfolding outside on the lawn, the two young children were watching from the window. They had no idea what was happening or who the redheaded lady was supposed to be. She seemed awfully mad, and they wondered if it was their fault because she kept screaming their names over and over again. Soon they began to cry and wished it would just stop and that lady would go away. They wanted their daddy. He always made everything safe, and they didn't feel safe now.

Mae and Ollie, also bystanders in this drama, felt too helpless to intercede between the two equally determined opponents. Frankly, they thought Hill was probably right. Even if Faye had custody of her children, she would not be able to support them and fulfill their needs. In addition, she was too young and immature to fully understand just what parenting was about. Her temperament was certainly not inclined toward nurturing children. And then there was the fact that she wanted her life in Atlanta and would never be prepared to sacrifice it. People were very focused on practical matters after the war, and issues surrounding a mother's rights or a father's deceit meant less than what was plain for all to see—Hill had the means and the will to raise the children and Faye did not.

Realizing that Faye would go on forever Hill ended the confrontation, saying, "That's enough now. You need to leave. You can see them in the summer. I will take care of them and guard them daily. My life is now devoted to them for as long as I live. They will have the best of care."

Faye, knowing she was beaten, let loose with every adverse adjective she could give tongue to. It was a long and embarrassing list. Still her rage continued to boil over, and there was no stopping it. So huge was Faye's rage that it could have blown Stone Mountain off its foundation. Finally, she screamed, "You son of a bitch. You have ruined my life. Everything that has ever happened to me was all your fault!"

He replied, "Yes, it was. I married you when I should have left you on that farm you were so eager to get away from. Had I not done that, you could have stayed in Tifton and married some local farmer and spent the rest of your life shelling peas and picking vegetables in the hot sun. But that was not your plan. You wanted off that farm, and did what you thought was necessary to get away. As I recall, you even enjoyed it. I was not in that bed by myself. In fact, it was not exactly cold under that hood either. Your engine was racing like a new V8 just off the line and roaring to get some mileage. You got what you wanted all right, and now you're expecting me to pay the price for it."

He continued with what he hoped were his last words. "Faye, I have preached a lot of sermons in my life, and I will take the next one from Psalm 52, verse 2: 'Thy tongue deviseth mischief like a sharp razor, working deceitfully.'" With that, he stepped inside the house, took the children from the window, and ushered them into their new life.

Faye had never been able to confront reality, and in this last scene she acted out her usual part of victim, only this time she truly was a victim. Without another look at Hill or her children, she squeezed herself back into the little truck, swung her massive mane of hair forward, and lit up another cigarette.

She was still muttering like a demon when Ollie started the engine. Mae was trying to calm her but was helplessly wedged between an exhausted husband and a fire-breathing daughter who had smoke coming out of both ears as well as her mouth! Ollie had also lit up a cigarette, and Mae thought she was going to suffocate. She didn't know if it was from the tobacco or from the fumes of Faye's rage.

As smoke billowed out of the tiny cab, Faye's final words hung in its hazy cloud. She screamed over the noise of the engine, "I'll never forgive you! Never! Never isn't long enough!"

50.

A New Beginning

HILL, ALWAYS FOCUSED, NOW TURNED TO THE TASK OF RAISING his children. His life had been like a series of postcards with an ever-changing signature as he moved his bright and colorful stamp from place to place. He began life as Hillyer, became known as Pick, got stuck with Hill, and finally became Mr. Pickett to the citizens of the new town in which he had elected to raise his children. As for himself, his calling card simply read: H. Pickett.

Mr. Pickett had created quite a stir when he first entered the lobby of the Florida Hotel in late 1942, prepared to start a new life. It was evident that he did not fit the bill of a traveling salesman and, despite the open stares of staff and guests, was not at all intimidated by their obvious curiosity. He had driven up in a luxurious late-model car, which was cause for amazement in itself. The war was still on, and no new cars had been manufactured for several months. How and where did he get that? Most interesting of all, he had two small children in tow. The little girl looked to be about a two and a half, and the little boy nearly four and a half.

Despite their small size, the tykes were simply holding each other's hand and politely waiting while the tall man made his inquiries. They seemed as at ease as he and were obviously accustomed to being obedient. He eventually seated them in the dining room, ordered their meals, and assisted the youngest one as she ate her food. They displayed no crying, screaming, tantrums, or other noisy behaviors usually exhibited by young children. They behaved like tiny adults, which in some respects, they were. Their father believed in the adage "Children should be seen and not heard," and his children would be perfect examples. He knew they would remain the subject of endless gossip, but no one would be able to utter a single unkind word about their behavior.

He had trained them to obey his total will with a single raised eyebrow or an elegantly pointed index finger. Either motion would immediately bring silence or interrupt whatever behavior was occurring. There was only one rule to follow: "Do exactly as I tell you and when I tell you. Don't ask me a second time about anything and we will get along just fine."

With no woman to countermand his instructions, his rule was powerful and absolute. The children quickly learned not to challenge him and simply accepted whatever decision he made. Having no one to run interference for them except one another strengthened their bond. He was not a pushover, and they knew not to push back. Their only occasional success was when they joined together in a mutual plea for permission, which further strengthened their bond. Careful not to openly celebrate these small successes, they privately hugged each other in shared delight.

The area where Pick had chosen to live was called Open Pond. There he had bought a spacious white home set far back off the road with a circular drive. It had lots of outdoor living space with two screened porches as well as adjoining, brick-floored open verandas. There was a large screened back porch adjoining the kitchen, which was unusual for the designs of that time. It also had brick floors and a large built-in barbeque pit and oven that could hold an entire pig.

The home had been built by a wealthy retiree from South Florida who had brought his outdoor Miami lifestyle with him. As soon as Hill bought the place, he had all the rooms and windows measured and drew a rough floor plan of the house. He then took the plans and measurements to the interior design department of Rich's in Atlanta. There they made a selection of beautiful fabrics, furniture, lamps, carpets, china, pictures, and everything else needed to completely outfit Hill's new home. He couldn't help but worry, "I wonder how all this stuff is going to look when it gets here. I know a lot about cars, but I don't know a damn thing about carpets and chairs." However, when the furnishings arrived by truck they were such a perfect fit that he thought it all looked like a magazine layout. Not a thing had to be changed.

Open Pond itself was originally settled by Scots, and their influence was still obvious in the clannishness that was so strong you could almost smell it as you entered the town. The village itself was reminiscent of an outdated world, one that was rapidly drawing to a postwar close. The "Golden Age of America" was on the horizon, and Mr. Pickett wanted the town to be a part of that modern gold rush which would bring innovation, enormous creativity, and power to a great and proud nation.

However, local residents were painfully slow to accept not only outsiders but anything outside their own realm of personal experience. Resistance to change is endemic to the world at large, but in this instance it bordered on blind prejudice. After all, Open Pond was a very small, close-knit town where everybody knew everybody and most were related by blood. With centuries of clannish behavior behind them, the locals were programmed to resist any idea not generated by one of their own. It was the armor that protected them and kept their individual interests at the forefront. Some clans were farmers, some were shopkeepers, some bankers, and of course, some just plain loafers. None, however, had the slightest interest in cooperating with the others for fear it might dilute their own strength.

This behavior also had a fierce social component that was played out daily by the local women who behaved like either wounded soldiers or victorious generals as they went into combat over teas, suppers, bridal showers, or church socials, and scored victories as masters of social climbing.

The Scots were also loathe to part with their money and would squeeze a penny until Lincoln's head snapped off the copper coin. World War II remained the major focus of life in 1942, but the Scots had a suspicion of "outsiders" that was just as intense and far more personal than their antipathy for the Hun.

Mr. Pickett was not interested in the turf wars of the local residents. He was focused on his own plan to keep his children safe and secure. He never wavered from that goal, even if it meant he was sometimes a little overbearing. He would do anything necessary to protect them and would happily sacrifice his life to their care. If it became necessary to give up a personal life, he was prepared for that as well. But, truth to tell, he didn't see much chance of a personal life anyhow in a small town buried deep in the dense thickets of Northwest Florida's virgin pine forests. He set about raising his children with a single-mindedness that impressed those around him. While the local men discounted his presence, the women were enthralled by the very thought of an eligible male. After all, it was wartime and the only men left at home were the blind, disabled, and/or dishonored. He was a delicious and new curiosity to be gossiped about and dissected bit by bit. He might be an outsider, but he was tall, good-looking, smart, well dressed, and obviously well-to-do. Best of all, there was no sign of a woman in his household apart from the cook and a maid. "A cook and a maid, too, imagine that," the women whispered.

It only took a few days for every spinster and widow in town to begin to outline their own plan of seduction. Mr. Pickett had never been immune to women, but he had been a soldier in these fierce campaigns before and knew all the signs of combat. The ladies began slowly with a pat on the head for the children, a soft "tut-tut" for their lack of a mother, and then progressed to invitations to church socials, picnics for the poor little kids, and on down the lust ... uh, that is list.

Mr. Pickett was polite and charming but aloof. He kept to himself and made absolutely certain there could never be a word of scandal or gossip about his activities. There were, however, occasional trips to Atlanta on "business." That bustling city and other large towns were where he conducted his limited social life, certain to be far from local prying eyes and busy, curious, sharp tongues.

What maddened the locals most was the fact that Mr. Pickett really didn't care what they thought of him or said about him. Immune to their opinions, he was his own man and did not need their approval. It was neither sought nor required. But he did care what they thought and said about his children. He did not want them to be the subject of anything but good behavior.

He and his children occupied a very circumspect and quiet environment in a small town where people were obsessed with their neighbors' families and their faults. That was the town's favorite sport, and it was very competitive, indeed! No wonder the Romans built Hadrian's Wall to keep the Scots out of England! They were, after all, fierce and victorious warriors. When they locked their castle gates, no outsider would ever scale them. That was certainly true in Open Pond.

Ronnie and Faith lived a rather solitary life on the vast acreage they came to call home. They were best friends as they seldom had playmates come to call. In fact, because there was no mother in the home, other parents were reluctant to allow their own children to visit. Their activities were therefore confined to running through acres of land filled with brooks, small caves, and endless pines. They quickly learned to avoid the areas where rattlesnakes lived and to pick blackberries while standing on the fence, out of striking distance of those vipers. They could also easily climb a tree as well as any lumberjack.

In addition, sending them to school and making sure they did chores at home, Mr. Pickett made sure they were kept busy and out of trouble. Occasionally, he would play cards with them and even taught them the "art of the deal" for getting a better hand. He also taught them board games like checkers and dominoes. He was not much of a reader and lacked the soft touch, so the children read bedtime stories to each other.

As for Mr. Pickett himself, he hadn't forgotten how to play poker and, more often than not, dealt the winning hand at secret poker games played in the alley behind the drugstore downtown. The police chief was a regular and often allowed to win just to keep the game under cover. He wasn't much of a card player, but he was warmly welcomed! Those card games were about the naughtiest things going on in the alley. Yet there was plenty of activity going on in the building behind the fairgrounds. That space was usually reserved for the show animals during the annual county fair, but on many Saturday nights the squeals and grunts spiraling through the air were not from prize pigs but from certain ladies giving out some show prizes themselves!

51.

Dancin' Dorothy Again

LIFE IN OPEN POND WAS MUCH QUIETER THAN HILL HAD BEEN accustomed to in Atlanta.

It was an adjustment for him, but he wanted the safe environment it provided for his children. Here they were free to run over the open fields, and he was free of the burden of Faye, whom he rarely thought of anymore. And since the children didn't know her very well, he wasn't subjected to endless questions about why she wasn't in their lives. She was a thing of the past, and he wanted to keep it that way.

The first two summers were pretty easy as far as his custodial arrangement with Faye was concerned. The war was in full swing, and gas, tires, and transportation were growing tighter each day. So Hill knew that no one was likely to come get the children, and he wasn't about to take them to Atlanta himself.

As for Faye, she was deeply buried in her busy life in Atlanta, working and playing, so the time passed in a hurry. Suddenly realizing her children were now almost four and six, she asked herself, "I wonder what they look like now. Has Faith started to look at all like me or does she still favor her daddy? I wonder if Ronnie is still as sweet as he was the last time I saw him, almost two years ago. My goodness, it has been almost two years now hasn't it? I don't want any of my boyfriends to know about my children, so I can't ask them to take me to Florida to get them, even if they could get the necessary gas ration coupons. I guess I will just have to see what *my* daddy can do about all this."

In the end, Ollie did come to the rescue. He had begged his friends for gas ration coupons and traded a truckload of corn for an old set of used tires that he thought might make the trip from Tifton to Florida.

When he and Mae pulled into the driveway of the house at Open Pond, the children were elated! They remembered their grandparents with great love and were delighted to see them again. Faith squealed, "Grandmother, are you going to teach me to make chocolate pie when we get to your house? It is my *very* favorite." Ronnie was quick to ask, "Papa, I remember you have a pond. Can we go fishing in it?"

So, off they went to a new summer filled with the happy noises of the Love household. Mae and Ollie still had several children at home and they all welcomed the smaller ones whom they loved and treated just as they would another brother or sister. Faye would occasionally ride the bus down from Atlanta, but those trips were few and far between.

Hill, lost without his children, went about the long summer days missing their laughter and constant company. He ate at the Florida Hotel more often instead of having the cook prepare a meal just for him. He needed the companionship of others although he continued to resist the efforts of most women—that is, until the summer of 1946, when he had a telephone conversation with his old friend Mary MacKinnon, now known as Maye T. MacKinnon. "The reason everybody calls me Maye T," she told him, laughing, "is because I am from Tennessee. There were so many Marys and Maes at my house that I was tagged with something a little different. I got to where I liked it, so I never changed it."

Hill and Mae T. had remained friends over the years. She had known of his marriage, his children, and his divorce from Faye. They stayed in touch by telephone as Hill was never one for letter writing. One summer afternoon, Maye T. had called to tell Hill that her daughter, the beautiful dancing Dorothy, had returned from New York and was now living with her in Jacksonville, following her own failed marriage. Immediately Hill began to think about risking his heart again. He could not believe that Dorothy might actually reenter his life after all these years. He thought, "I remember the last time I saw her. She was up on that stage in New York looking like just what she was—one of the most beautiful women I have ever seen. I wonder what she looks like now?" So off he went to Jacksonville.

By the time he got there, his heart was beating as fast as a Cadillac in overdrive. He raced up to the front door and was amazed to see it opened by a woman who was still one of the most beautiful he had ever seen. As far as Hill was concerned, Dorothy, at age thirty-six, had retained her perfect looks. It was hard for him to sit still. All he could think about was, "I am not going to let this woman get away. I think I will take her back with me right now."

However, common sense prevailed and he spent most of that summer in Jacksonville courting the woman he could not and would not resist this time. He let his business affairs slide and gave up any pretense of work. He was on a mission to capture the heart of this beauty. He wanted a quick courtship and was ready for a quick marriage. It seemed that Dorothy was of the same mind. She had regretted their parting and had often thought of him over the years. He still held the same magic for her, and when he asked, "Please don't make me wait—marry me," her immediate response was, "Yes, of course, but I have to meet your children first.

They may not want me for a mother, and they may be jealous and think I have taken you away from them. After all, it has only been the three of you all these years now. We need to give them a chance to get to know me."

Hill thought that was just fine if it didn't take too long. He said, "My children are really a delight and won't need much time. They can figure out real quick if they want you or not."

Of course he planned to premedicate them with a little bit of instruction along the lines of, "Just look what I have brought home for you—something you have always wanted—a mother, and a beautiful one at that!" As far as he as concerned, there was going to be no choice in the matter. Finally, at the age of forty-seven, he was falling in love and wanting to settle down.

He hadn't been in the car business for nothing. He *knew* how to sell, and it was soon a done deal. He brought Dorothy to Open Pond and proudly showed her his home, which she loved immediately. Coming from New York, she was especially drawn to the patios and barbeque area, architectural features that would not become common until well after the war when there would be an unprecedented demand for housing and a generation of returning warriors who would benefit from the GI Bill's home loan guarantee program. From 1944 to 1952, the Veteran's Administration backed nearly 2.4 million homes for World War II vets, which allowed couples to afford independent housing rather live with their parents or rent small apartments. After being stationed in Europe, American GIs had seen enough of old architecture and wanted something new and modern. They also wanted privacy and so moved from the front porch swing to back porches and backyard barbeque pits.

Between 1950 and 1960, twenty million people would be drawn to mass housing developments on the outskirts of American cities. In terms of sheer numbers, the move to the suburbs outstripped the fabled westward migration of the

1800s. The individual credited for the development of suburbia was William J. Levitt, who built entire communities and became famous for his development in Levittown, Pennsylvania. By 1950, *Time* Magazine estimated, Levitt had built one out of eight houses in America. Called the "Henry Ford of Housing," he was heard to comment, "Any fool can build homes. What counts is how many you can build for how little." Suburban sprawl was thus born.

Delighted to be hundreds of miles away from the escalating acreage of suburban sprawl, Dorothy was enchanted by Hill's new home. She also adored the children and couldn't help but smile at their innocence.

Because they were living in a small rural community, some of her pronunciations were new to them. When she asked, "Please pass the toemawtoes," Ronnie and Faith had trouble understanding. As the maid continued to serve the meal, they mimicked, "May we please have some toemawtoes, too?" and began to giggle. Hill immediately sent them from the table, where they continued their giggles between themselves.

Together they discussed the prospect of having a mother at last, and thought Dorothy was just "peachy." Faith said, "I bet she knows how to give hugs real good, too, 'cause I've seen her give them to Daddy, and he gives 'em right back."

When the visit ended, Dorothy went back to Jacksonville to discuss plans with Maye T. for her upcoming marriage. Her main concern was her seven-year-old daughter, Lyssa, who would have a big adjustment to make. Lyssa had spent her early years in New York City, so living in a rural environment with a new father, brother, and sister would be a big change.

However, a bigger one was unfolding. Dorothy had suffered from rheumatic fever as a child, and unbeknownst to her, it had left her with a weakened heart. Since cardiac care in 1946 was still a new science, little was known about the long-term effects of the disease, and as she had had no further problems everyone assumed she was cured. After joining her mother in Jacksonville at the age of thirty-six, she opened her own dance studio and was enjoying this new form of success. Then while visiting Open Pond she was prepared to give up the studio and make a life with Hill. However, almost immediately upon her return to Jacksonville, she began working with her students and suddenly felt faint during one of her ballet routines. Before anyone could catch her, she slipped to the floor, unconscious—never to revive.

Hill was absolutely heartbroken. He cried, "How could this have happened? I finally got her back and now she is gone again, only this time forever. How will I explain to the children that once again they have lost a mother?"

He hardly had time to absorb this massive blow when another and then another struck. His only sister, Lenora, died of cancer two months later, followed at Thanksgiving by his mother, Laura. He had lost all of the women in his life within the space of six months.

It was unbearably hard to go on, but he had Faith and Ronnie to think of, and they kept him from suffocating in grief. He tried to comfort them with the hope that someday they might get another lady in their life. They did, but not quite in the way he imagined.

52.

The Frail Friend

ONCE AGAIN, WITH NO FEMALE GENERAL OF HIS OWN TO run the gauntlet, Mr. Pickett kept both himself and his children aloof. He never entertained or accepted the invitations of others. He absolutely would not have his children subjected to a bidding war and would not permit them to become pawns of any aspiring woman.

The one exception was Alma, a hemiplegic who had been crippled by polio in childhood and left with useless legs. She was like Speedy Gonzales on her crutches. She rarely used a wheelchair as she did not want to be pitied, and instead used every ounce of her strength to stand upright and walk as well as she could, her back straight as a rod. A large purple birthmark covering her entire left eye and cheek further afflicted her. Refusing to be defeated by her illness, she lived alone at the Florida Hotel, which was actually a local boardinghouse.

With her deformities, she was as much the town topic as Mr. Pickett's children. It was natural they should gravitate toward each other. And indeed, Alma adored Faith and Ronnie from the first moment she saw them in the hotel lobby. They were quiet little things who looked at her in some amazement as well. She was a very small woman, so when she bent over to say hello to them they could almost touch her nose. That was a thrill, because their father was so tall that when *he* bent over, they could barely see his face. They were also interested in her crutches, and she was amused by their careful examination of them.

She was a gentle person, as was obvious in her every gesture. For these little tots, she simply smiled and opened her crutches wide. They, in turn, wrapped themselves around her like an apron. The children had never seen crutches before, and their innocent curiosity made her smile. She would always smile when she saw them, and they were happy to be so welcomed by her. In fact, She was one of the very few to whom the children were entrusted and the only human on the planet who was occasionally permitted to advise their devoted father. Little by little, Alma was able to intercede on things as small as permission to attend the county fair.

Alma was, like every woman, a little in love with Mr. Pickett, but had the sense to know it would be unrequited. More than anything else, she considered herself a much-needed friend and maternal figure to the children. Fully dedicated to the Ronnie and Faith, she eagerly welcomed them to her small bedroom at the Florida Hotel.

Here, in her tiny abode, she gave them hugs and fed them special candies while reading them bedtime stories. They never tired of that and often asked, "May we please hear about Ferdinand the Bull again?" Alma sometimes said, "Would you like to read it to me instead?" Then she would very carefully help them learn the words and letters on each page. They sometimes drifted off to sleep in her bed, awaiting their father's return from one of his many business deals or occasional card games in the lobby.

Boardinghouses were often referred to hotels to move them a step up for some of the other residents. Alma had been living in her tiny abode for ten years before meeting the children. An independent and modern woman, she had a full-time job as a clerk at the Department of Agriculture, the one federal office in town, at a time when it was uncommon for a person so disabled to be working at all.

At work and at home, Alma was surrounded by people who could reach up to get things off shelves, turn lights on and off, drive cars, stand alone at a sink to wash their hands, and cook for themselves. Living long before the Americans with Disabilities Act was even on the horizon, she had quickly learned not to expect much help. Indeed, little was given. There were no motorized wheelchairs, grabbars, elevated toilet seats, lowered sinks or drinking fountains, walk-in showers, or bathtubs. Automated push-button doors were unknown, and certainly no buses or vans were equipped with hydraulic lifts. The disabled had to fend for themselves.

Without parents to lean on or children of her own or even nurses' aides to help her, Alma had maintained a solitary but useful life conducted largely from a tiny one-bedroom haven in a commercial boardinghouse inhabited by traveling salesmen. She made her little nest warm, comfortable, and inviting. And her little body only left the hotel for work, a special mission, or an outing to church or a friend's home.

Every day after breakfast, Alma, on her crutches, walked the slow tortuous journey to her office in an old log cabin in the center of town. She took a longer walk each Sunday after church, often accompanied by Mr. Pickett's children. Her mission on Sunday was to take magazines to the inmates of the city jail. The jailhouse was slap dab in the middle of town, though only four blocks from the boardinghouse. The occupants of this small, smelly, one-story building were more likely to be the town drunks than the town criminals. Open Pond was not a place where crime was rampant, probably because it was so small that if you were about to break the law someone would see you and tell your mother—resulting in a fate worse than any sentence to be handed down by a judge!

Alma was an avid reader with a wide knowledge and special interest in politics. She loved to poke fun at the local elections and was often heard to say, "I don't know why all this money is being spent on campaigns when we already know it's Joe's turn this year. His family has already decided on that to save the rest of us the trouble of having to go to the polls."

Her favorite, and only, perfume was Evening in Paris, introduced to her as a Christmas gift by Mr. Pickett. It did, indeed, conjure up thoughts of faraway places that she would only ever reach in her mind. Faith loved the perfume. Just opening it presented one of the few occasions she had to brush up against something feminine. After all, her household was comprised entirely of men, none of whom wore perfume. She loved not only the scent but the elegant blue bottle it came in. She also loved the allure of the name and, like Alma, imagined foreign excitement.

Evening in Paris debuted as Soir de Paris in France in 1929 and was an instant hit. The name alone evoked the gaiety, flapper fashion, and romance of the French capital. It was considered very sophisticated and, because of the war, difficult to obtain. Entranced by both the scent and the presentation, Faith would repeatedly asked Alma, "Please let me see Paris." The fragrance was presented in a cobalt blue hemispherical Art Deco flacon with a silver cap and attractively packaged in gift boxes, some in the shape of stars, sailor's hats, or a crescent moon. During the 1940s, there was special packaging bearing the statement: "This is a temporary victory package. The contents are unchanged." After the war, it would be touted as "the fragrance more women wear than any other in the world."

Alma was the only full-time resident of the hotel and took all her meals there at a large corner booth, where there was always room for the Picketts. Her eyes would always light up at the sight of them. She and the children shared the same pain of being "different" as she was a physical cripple and they were considered social cripples because they had no mother. All of them were constantly referred to as "poor little thing."

Boardinghouses in small towns such as Open Pond were somewhat different from the sort of boardinghouse that Faye had lived in while in Atlanta. Places like the Florida Hotel were hives of activity and boasted a social center all their own. They put on big spreads for the after-church crowd on Sundays and timed the fried chicken to keep the Baptists, Presbyterians, and Methodists from going to war if one of their preachers ran late. There was a delicate balance if a new minister came to town and the cook hadn't figured out just how long his audience could last. Many a penitent changed churches in favor of warm corn bread and hot fried chicken.

The lobby of Alma's boardinghouse resembled a poorly lit movie set. It was directly across from the dining room and contained a seldom-used piano, linoleum floors, stiffly uncomfortable chairs, and a card table that was busier than a cat running from a vacuum cleaner. There was a quiet corner for conversation and a tabletop radio where guests and locals gathered to hear the latest horrors or successes of the war. Aside from a few board games, like checkers and dominoes, there was not much else. Or course, there was no television, and entertainment was primarily confined to the latest news and gossip. The latest news was always the latest gossip!

The chairs in the lobby were carefully placed near the large windows to give a perfect view of any unsuspecting stranger that might appear on the horizon. When one was sighted, dining room patrons quickly positioned themselves to view this new intruder. Having refined the practice of looking down their noses at strangers, they maintained a long but instant checklist for evaluation. If strangers appeared to be traveling salesmen, they were quickly discounted as having very little real gossip value and being no fun to shun. They all knew what those salesmen were like anyway, and unless one of the friskier residents like Mary Helen or Bobby Sue got tangled up with them very little new could be said about them.

Lobby guests would peer over their bridge cards and out from under their weekly newspaper to inspect each new prospect. If it was daytime, bridge was being played, but if it was long after dark then the card game underwent an unspoken, quiet transition from bridge to canasta to poker. And it wasn't just the police chief who enjoyed that game!

53.

Reprise of the Starring Role

FAYE'S ROLE AS THE INJURED PARTY HAD BEEN CONFIRMED BY the loss of her children, but what she mostly felt was self-pity. Critical, selfish, and self-absorbed, she was masterful at inflating ordinary situations into full-blown dramas. Worse, the phrase "thank you" never entered into her vocabulary. In short, Faye had become more bitter and vindictive, never missing an opportunity to bemoan her fate to anyone who would listen.

Soon, she did the only thing she could think of and went back to Atlanta to continue her quest to become a rich man's wife. She reasoned that if she had more money, maybe she could get her children back and live the life of her dreams. And, of course, there would be the satisfaction of showing Hill what she was made of!

Because of her beauty, she was popular, but her bitterness and anger made her an empty prospect for a proposal. Even so, a proposal eventually did come, and she remarried in 1950 at the age thirty-one. By that time, it was an act of survival; she was tired of working and wanted someone to support her.

She thought she had finally found a suitable prospect in Al. Even though he had come from a similar farm background similar to hers, he was making his way up the ladder in law enforcement. He had started off as a policeman, but when Faye met him he was a mid-level bureaucrat at the Department of Public Safety where she worked as a receptionist.

Al, a childless widower, was a few years older than Faye and seemed to have a good future with the Department of Public Safety. He was attracted to Faye because of her looks and age. She seemed bright and eager to please him. She was still young enough to bear children and he wanted some, even though he was approaching forty. He also thought Faye might add a bit of the polish he needed. He had never quite shaken off the dirt from the farm, but Faye had, and he was sure she would take care of that problem!

She was ready and determined to marry someone in the right social class. She preferred a rich man, but at the time they all seemed to have been taken by much younger women. Besides, in this immediate postwar era, eligible men were beginning to be in very short supply; the war had taken its toll on an entire generation. Additionally, she was finding it difficult to find someone who wasn't scared off by the fact that she was a divorcee with two young children. So she had settled for what she thought would be a secure future with someone on his way up.

By now, Al was in touch with state government officials and was often asked to meet with the governor so his department could arrange transportation for official functions. That simply meant Al would be in charge of the security detail and would drive the governor to and from airports, meetings, and conventions.

Faye was thrilled. At last thinking she was going to get in the big game, she saw herself being wined and dined at the Governor's Mansion. However, she had misinterpreted Al's role; he was, in reality, a bureaucratic chauffeur for politicians. Occasionally, she and Al would be invited to some minor function, but that was more because Al had become a drinking buddy of the governor's than an embodiment of his own modest position.

All too soon, the marriage posed a price Faye had not counted on: she had become pregnant. As with her other pregnancies, she was short-tempered and uncomfortable for the entire nine months. Very unhappy about being pregnant again, she told Gwen: "I am thirty-two years old now, and this baby is going to absolutely ruin my figure forever. A woman my age shouldn't be going through this. Besides, I don't want to end up looking like Mama. Al will just have to be satisfied with one because I am never ever going to do this again. I just bet I will never be able to get into all my pretty clothes again. Al will just have to buy me some new ones—but that won't change the fact that I will have lost my figure! He better not even think about getting me in that bedroom again. I am giving him a child, and that ought to be enough!"

Her second son, named Al Jr., became the center of his father's life. And after giving birth Faye immediately began to fade in importance, reverting once again to cook and house cleaner.

To a man in midlife who had never been a father, this child was the pinnacle of his achievement. The fact that it was a boy boosted his pride to ridiculous heights. Nothing was too good for his son, and nothing would ever be withheld from him, except discipline.

Faye didn't have much experience as a mother, but she knew that every child needed guidance and she tried to train the boy. However, Big Al wouldn't hear of anyone saying "no" to his son about anything at all. The boy could do and say anything he wanted and his father just laughed and bragged about how bright he was. To Al, his son was precious; to everyone else, he was a pain in the ass. As time passed, his behavior worsened and he became increasingly unpopular.

Faye was not happy to be stuck at home looking after a spoiled brat. Worse, she had no idea how to handle his horrid behavior, which just increased her isolation as she still couldn't drive. Her only outlet was her neighborhood of stay-at-home mothers, and few of those ladies wanted to bond with a woman who couldn't, or wouldn't, control her own child.

To make matters worse, Faye soon experienced tensions in her marriage as she and Al had begun fighting over their son. At one point, Al Jr. wanted to take dancing lessons, and his mother thought he should since he was not interested in sports and might be talented in dance. But his father thought it would be too "sissy." Al, with his background in law enforcement, greatly admired displays of power and machismo. So he explained, "I don't want my friends to make fun of me or my son."

He and Faye went round and round over that issue. Then, after several fights and several drinks, Faye won.

Before long, Faye and Al were arguing as soon as Al walked in the door each evening. Without even saying hello one evening, Faye yelled, "That son of yours bit another child today," to which Al replied, "What was the other kid doing?" Faye said, "He was playing with one of Al's toys." Her husband retorted, "That kid should leave the toys alone. I bought them for Al to play with, not the neighborhood."

Al's brutish nature combined with Faye's fiery temper did not prove to be a recipe for a peaceful marriage. Day by day, Faye's dreams of life at the Governor's Mansion were soon fading and her anger rising. She had expected more than this from her second marriage—including having her own way and being admired and petted—but her hoped-for fairy tale was turning into a nightmare.

Also, Ronnie and Faith had hoped that Faye's remarriage might provide an opportunity to spend more time with her and get the maternal love they had always craved. Having spent all their previous summers with Mae and Ollie, they were now looking forward to having a mother, at least part of the time. During their first summer in Atlanta with her, Big Al became jealous of them and did not want them in his house. As his drinking progressed, they didn't want to be there either and began to dread those visits. They were afraid—and with good reason. The police were called on more than one occasion. The first time Hill heard about this, he drove all night from Florida to Atlanta and was on the doorstep at sunrise the next morning to get the children.

During subsequent summertime visits with their mother, Ron and Faith, who had been bought up quietly, found Al Jr. to be a strain on their nerves. When they were left to babysit him, he threw tantrums and sulked for hours. Ron, now a teenager, had no patience with that behavior, nor did Faith. But of course they were not allowed to punish him for his misbehavior.

Ron said to his sister, "Al's the worst kid I ever saw, even if he's my half brother. He needs to spend about a week with Hill Pickett. It wouldn't take Daddy but a few minutes to straighten him out, and pretty soon he would be a different kid."

Faith agreed, "Never again would he say, 'I won't, I won't. You can't make me!' About all he would be able to get out of his mouth would be, 'Yes, sir,' and 'Just how high would that jump need to be?' and 'Do you want me to start now?'"

Faye was impressed by how exceptionally well behaved her two older children were. She was not surprised as Hill had always been a stickler for good manners and discipline. He had even tried to discipline *her* when they were married!

As time passed, there was still much discord between Faye and Big Al. A recurring theme was Faye's discontent with her wardrobe. Since she was no longer working, she had no money of her own and was fully dependent on her husband. This situation caused endless disagreements because she had never learned to ask, as a good 1940s wife should; instead, she demanded. She'd say, "I have got to have a new dress. Myrtle next door got one that I thought would look real pretty on me, and I want twenty-five dollars to buy it. I will need a hat to go with it, so that will be extra." Faye didn't sweet talk or negotiate; she simply sailed into battle. Her voice had long ago lost its pleasant tone and now her words were uttered with a hard and bitter edge.

Her greatest combat campaign concerned an automobile. She wanted one, and by God she was going to have one. She began with, "I am sick and tired of being trapped in this house. Go find me a car, and I mean *now!*" She even reminded Al that when she was with Hill she'd always had access to cars, often the best.

Al didn't want her to have a car and had refused to teach her how to drive. He didn't want to spend the money; but more importantly he did want her to be able to come and go freely. He liked the idea of a wife at home and dependent on him, so he kept resisting. Besides, she was beautiful, and who knew what trouble she'd get into if she had more freedom.

With her usual determination, Faye wouldn't take no for an answer. She finally called an old friend at the Department of Public Safety and asked for his help. Later that day when Al returned home, he was stunned to find a car backing out of the driveway—with Faye behind the steering wheel! She had borrowed a car and was busy practicing.

After a furious battle that night, Al finally gave in and bought Faye a car. It was old and beat up, but she figured she would deal with that later.

The vicious battles between husband and wife escalated into violent quarrels precipitated by her anger and then triggering his drinking. She never seemed to make the connection. She had her own tympani of slamming kitchen cabinet doors and banging pots and pans with a ferocity not even Tchaikovsky could have conjured up. Her baton was a large kitchen spoon that beat in time with the other kitchen instruments. The music began slowly, with a single pot banging on the stove; then a door slammed, another pot rattled, another door slammed, and soon the full kitchen orchestra was in discordant play. Slam, bang, slam, bang, bang, bang, slam.

While that overture was heating up, Faye invariably began spewing hateful and vicious words about how she was not getting what she deserved. One of her regular complaints was, "I don't know what you do with all that money of yours, because you certainly don't spend it on me. But every time Al wants something, you can't get it quick enough! What about me? I want things, too."

54.

Mary, Marry Me

H E WAS SEVENTY-FOUR YEARS OLD WHEN MARY REENTERED his life, and Faye, of all people, was responsible! In small towns like Americus, everybody knew everybody else *real* well and liked them in spite of it. Faye's sister, Gwen, still lived in Americus and had known Mary all her life. She, along with many others, had often heard the story of the torch Mary still carried for an old love. Mary had accepted her parents' choice of a husband and had married a wealthy banker, Robert Simpson. They had an agreeable and long life together, and it was considered a successful marriage. Robert's death was widely reported and merited an item in the *Atlanta Journal*. When Faye happened to see it, she immediately sent it to Faith with a sarcastic note, stating: "Well, looks like one of your daddy's old girlfriends is having some trouble. Gwen told me her husband didn't have a nickel when he died. Said he had spent it all chasing women and whiskey all over the state. Serves her right! She was always so snooty to me when I would see her in Americus."

Of course, Mary had known of Faye and Hill's marriage and divorce and had kept up with them all through the years with polite questions to Gwen along the lines of "How is your family? I saw your sister Faye in church with you recently. How is she?"

Faith was now a grown woman. Once she got that obituary, she sent it to her father. She had heard about Mary all her life and was excited to think Hill might actually be able to see her again. He was excited, too.

He waited a decent interval before calling, and after a suitable period he once again began his visits and courtship of the still lovely Mary. Age hadn't dimmed her beauty. She remained remarkably unwrinkled at sixty-six and as regal in her bearing as ever. She was always immaculately groomed and looked every inch the grand lady. She was what Faye had, unsuccessfully, strived to be all her life: the personification of elegance and refinement—something Faye still misinterpreted as "snooty."

Hill took his time with this renewed romance. Americus and Open Pond were about 200 miles apart, but he still loved the open road and was once again a frequent visitor to Americus. The Windsor Hotel, still an elegant landmark, is where he stayed on his many trips to visit Mary. He would usually drive up for two or three days, and they soon developed a routine between visits as well: he would call her every Sunday, and she would write to him every Wednesday. Neither of them ever missed.

Mary rarely came to visit him. It was not that she was afraid of the drive, but because Southern society and its rules still governed her life she simply thought it improper for her to visit a single man in his home. She made her rare visits only when Faith came home for the weekend. Faith remarked many years later: "That was one of the sweetest images I ever had of my father. He was so tender with Mary and so very solicitous. I remember being there one weekend when she was visiting, watching him open the door of that Mercedes and carefully getting her settled. He then hopped in right beside her and directed me to 'get this thing in gear.' I had never seen him in the backseat of *anyone's* car, much less his own. I will always remember driving them down to the beach for a sunset supper and thinking to myself, 'This is so right, even if they are in the sunset of their own lives.' I was very careful to play chauffeur, but it was tempting to sneak a peek in the rearview mirror and watch them hold hands. He was nothing but smiles, and it touched my heart in ways that make me cry today when I think of it. At last, he had his love at his side."

Even at his advanced age, Hill was still determined to marry this woman. To celebrate his eightieth birthday in 1980, Faith planned a trip to Bermuda for her and her father. Naturally, Hill wanted Mary to go along, but she declined, saying: "I would love to go, but I have to think about what they would say in Americus. It just isn't right for me to go off out of the country with a man. Why I have eleven first cousins in Americus, and none of them will ever believe we are being chaperoned. Now, I still have my reputation and my family to think about."

By this time, Hill had once again proposed. Mary, reluctantly but gently, turned him down. She sweetly said: "Why, Pick, the first time you asked me everybody said I was too young, and now they will just say I'm too old. I *know* they are right this time. Goodness' sakes, I could never leave Americus—all my cousins, my children and grandchildren, and my friends. Besides, you could never leave all your property down there in Florida. Why, it has been your life's work. I have always loved you and will love you till the day I die, even if *I can't* marry you."

Hill was wounded, but he knew deep inside that she was right. It was too late for marriage, but not too late for love. At least they had that, and each would have to be content that life had brought them together again. Even if it was in their waning years, their romance would live on, and she would continue to be at his side and in his heart.

55.

The Unthinkable

THE COMING YEARS WOULD BRING MANY CHANGES. AMONG them, great tragedies as well as grand successes. The prep school chosen for Ron was Georgia Military Academy, located in the foothills of the Blue Ridge Mountains. His military training soon led him into the army for a two-year stint prior to enrolling at Florida State University (FSU), where Faith was already hard at work on her own education.

Faith loved college and the life at FSU. She also fell in love and was married at an early age. But that didn't stop her ambitions to have a career of her own, and she was soon running a large medical organization with a good-size staff as well as good-size headaches.

In the meantime, Ron, following his father's first love, had become involved in the automobile business in Atlanta and was loving it. That's where he met his wife-to-be, Susan. In time, the happy couple had a boy, Hillyer Jr., and a girl, Tammy. Faye was never thrilled with any of the women he dated, and his wife would be no exception. Faye was, of course, extremely jealous of the attention this new woman was getting from her son and thus did everything she could to make her life as miserable as possible. She constantly berated Ron for having chosen such a woman and said she was just not "classy" enough for him. That theme certainly sounded familiar, and Ron and finally had enough. Taking his wife, daughter, and young son, he returned to Open Pond. At least it was quiet there.

He led a comfortable life in the town he had grown up in and had many friends still living there. Among them was Bobby Thompson, a Florida State University alumnus who loved football as much as Ron did, and they often went to the games together. FSU had a particularly good football team in 1978. The now legendary coach, Bobby Bowden, had arrived two years earlier and, after a losing season in 1976, had turned the FSU football team into a winner.

Ron was a diehard FSU fan and didn't miss an opportunity to see a game, whether on television or at the stadium in Tallahassee. FSU's football schedule that year called for the team to play an in-state rival, the University of Miami, at the Orange Bowl in Miami. Ron had been taking flying lessons at the little airport in Open Pond and had just earned his private pilot's license. Very proud of his accomplishment, he thought a flight down to Miami to see the game would be a great way to "spread his wings." So he and Bobby rented a four-seat Piper Cherokee 180 Arrow, snared a couple of football tickets, and were off. As they passed over Open Pond, they turned the plane southeast on a course toward Miami, about six hundred miles overland. Given the fuel limitations of the Cherokee, they had to refuel in Ocala, about midway. They rented a car at the airport in Miami and made it over to the Orange Bowl in time for the early afternoon kickoff. It was an exciting game, and FSU won 31–21.

By the time the game was over, it was getting late, so Ron quickly filed a VFR flight plan and they roared off back to the north. Flying time was about five hours—not including a fuel stop. Ron calculated that altering their flight plan for the final leg would save at least thirty or forty minutes if they flew directly over the Gulf of Mexico, a course that seemed to be low risk as the weather report was favorable.

It was already dark when they made their refueling stop. All was well as they took off and crossed over the coastline. Ron had turned on the plane's basic autopilot to help him compensate for the absence of a natural horizon as he was keenly aware that he was not instrument qualified and he didn't want to incur additional risk over eighty or so miles of open water.

It is not clear what transpired next, but the accident reports concluded that Ron and Bobby encountered an isolated severe thunderstorm that was neither forecast nor visible from the cockpit. The storm may have caused the plane to stall then spin headlong into the roiling waters, killing the young men on impact.

The grief and shock for both families was palpable. Here were two thirty-eight-year-olds, both husbands and fathers, instantly taken away in the prime of their lives. For once, Faye's drama and agony were real. Her grief tore her apart, and for weeks she barely left the house.

Hill remained in control and stoically began to pick up the pieces of life again. His son's death had rocked him with an intensity of grief he had never known. He had no one to share this burden with except his daughter Faith and, of course, Mary.

At the funeral, the encounter between Hill and Faye was muted. Faye wanted to find some way to blame Hill for her son's death but could find no grounds for it. For once her drama was real and her grief piercing. She also wanted to apologize to the son she had given away as a little boy, but he was now gone forever. It was too late; he had been given to God. There was no longer a chance for her to ever say, "I'm sorry. I wish I had done things differently." It was over, and she was in shock. Moreover, she was shocked to see Mary there on the arm of her ex-husband.

Faye's second husband, Al, was now dead, and she clung to the arm of her remaining son, Al Jr., as he eased her into the car for the long and sorrowful trip back to the city, unaware that he would remain her strongest ally for the rest of their lives. Hill didn't want to see it. He had lost his only son and didn't need to be reminded that Faye still had another one.

At least she had *someone*. Hill knew that he had someone, too—his daughter, Faith. She was as grief stricken as he was, and the tragedy had drawn them closer. There was a tenderness about Hill that had been absent before. He was able to show Faith his emotions, and she was likewise able to share hers with him. Having inherited her father's iron will, determination, and capability, she managed to carry both of them through this extraordinarily difficult time.

Following Ron's death, Hill also needed Mary at his side. Even the funeral was made bearable through her help and enduring love.

Life has a way of repeating itself, and Hill, now seventy-eight, once again provided a home for a newly orphaned child. This time it was sixteen-year-old Hillyer Jr., his grandson and namesake. He tried to instill his own work ethic and sense of pride and fair play into the grieving boy; certainly, he gave him structure and stability and a strong work ethic. Ron's daughter, Tammy, had just started her first year of college and therefore was no longer at home. Their mother, Susan, had died of cancer the previous year, and so the little family had already known its share of heartache.

Hill knew what it was like to raise a child alone, with no feminine influence to help temper life's troubles. There was no mother to give a desperately needed hug when life got rough. Worst of all, there was no one to simply whisper "I love you" in the softness of the night. To his regret, Hill knew he lacked a gentle touch as his life had not been supported by a feminine companion to show him the ways of love.

He knew, however, that as good a father as he was he had not been able to replace a mother's love. He had suffered through this realization with his own children and was sorry that the pattern would be repeated for his grandson. He had learned to live alone and had accepted the fact that his colorful life was probably not meant for sharing, but he sometimes wondered what impact that reality had had on his children, especially as he watched young Hillyer grieve for his parents.

No one had thought Faye would take the boy. It was simply assumed that the responsibility for raising him would fall to his grandfather and not his grandmother. When it came to pass, Hill was relieved as he dearly loved the child.

All the while, even at the height of his grief he was not bitter toward Faye. He never expressed anger toward her, nor did ever rail against her; he simply never discussed her. The only comment he had ever made was, "I thought she was just a nice little country girl who would never give me any trouble. I was wrong."

After the funeral, Faye and Hill had said awkward good-byes, each lost in their own grief, and never saw each other again. Yet Faye had kept the anger alive. Her favorite form of entertainment remained the scene where she repeatedly replayed what a monster he was. She had wanted her children to hate him as much as she did, and even following Ron's death she could not let go and heal the rifts.

56.
Grandpa Hill

HILL STRUGGLED ON, WILLING HIMSELF TO STAY ALIVE. HE had enormous determination and that, along with Mary, kept him going. He tried to work through his grief in order to settle into life with his grandson at his side. There would be no self-pity. Having always been task oriented, he set about building himself a new home—a project he hoped would keep him occupied and help ease his heart. It had worked in the past, and he knew of no other way to get through this terrible pain.

The new house, like his current one, would be ahead of its time. His plan was to create a maintenance-free structure built of steel girders enclosed by metal siding. And indeed, by the time it was finished it was the talk of the town. From the outside, it looked like a barn, which was fine for him as it would discourage unwanted visits from travelers along the now busy highway five hundred feet from his front door.

When everybody thought the house was done, Hill didn't. He still had grief to work out, so he decided to add an additional kitchen on the back that was five hundred square feet and contained three wood-burning stoves. It also had a grill that could cook sixty hamburgers at one time. Hill had never before thought small! The remainder of the house included four large bedrooms, an office, a second kitchen, and a big living room. It also had several wood-burning fireplaces.

Hill had always loved fireplaces. They reminded him of his childhood. One chilly evening, he would confide to Faith, "You know, a fire is a lot of company. You have to constantly tend it, stoke it, add wood to it, and then watch it burn itself out. Sort of human-like, isn't it? Seems to me a fire is about the same as the cycle of life."

His own cycle of life was coming to a close, and as he aged, his body began to decline. He developed diabetes and coronary heart disease, but that didn't stop him. Not for a single moment. Hill Picket would work right up until his very last breath.

One of his final projects had been the restoration of an old building he owned downtown and wanted to convert into a restaurant. He had been working on it for several months when one morning he arose at his usual 5:00 and got his crew started by 6:00 am. He then went home to shave and shower. When he had not returned by 9:00 am, his foreman went out to the house to check on him and found him sprawled across his bed, razor in hand. He had evidently suffered a heart attack while shaving, and the pain had driven him to his bed, where he collapsed and died.

The three women he had left in life would meet again at his funeral. Faith stood between Mary, the woman he loved until his last breath, and Faye, the woman who would hate him until *her* last breath. Faye was not sorry to see him go and, turning to Faith, said, "Well, that old son of a bitch lived a lot longer than he should have. He may be your daddy, but he was a terrible husband, and I will never be able to forgive him for what he did to me." With that, she turned in the other direction and told her son, "Take me out of this damn place and back to Atlanta. I hope never to come back here again." As usual, he obeyed her orders.

Epilogue
Never Ending

AFTER HILL'S DEATH, FAYE DIDN'T CHANGE ONE IOTA. SHE continued to behave as if he were alive, cornering anyone who would listen to her tale of woe. Since she ended up outliving him by thirty years, she forced a lot of folks to be patient listeners!

After his death, she did, however, shift her fire and ire immediately to her daughter, Faith. Maybe it was because Faith reminded her of Hill. She had his can-do attitude, his business aptitude, and his generous spirit. She resembled her daddy physically, too.

Faith had inherited money from Hill and used it to build up the real estate business he had founded. To Faye's mind, however, this was *her* money, and she made sure everyone knew it. Rather than argue, Faith simply paid up and supported her. No way did she want to become bitter and twisted like her mother; in fact, she was proud to finally able to keep Faye in the style to which she had always wanted to be accustomed, though Faith got little thanks for it! She had Hill's optimism, energy, and strength, but she also had her mother's strong will—a combination that enabled her to succeed in business and in life. In addition, she inherited her father's spirit of adventure and his gift of gab, contributing to a wellspring of unusual creativity.

Faye was utterly determined to squeeze every last nickel out of Hill Pickett's legacy to his daughter. This was money she thought should have been hers, though she could never explain why. All the while, she steadfastly refused to touch a single dime of her own money. Her friends and family thought that was very mysterious, but Faith knew she was saving it all for Al Jr. She chose to overlook it and continued to pay for her Mother's care.

Faith said, "Mama, I'm not going to abandon you. You need to relax and just enjoy life a little." The irony was lost on Faye.

Faith came to realize that there was no changing her mother at this late stage. Her life had been defined by her relationship with Hill Pickett, and she would never let it go. Faith felt some pity because she knew that her mother had been a product of her times. In an age when men were supposed to provide for women and women were supposed to put up and shut up, Faye had been unable to play that game. If she'd been a gentler, more loving character and more forgiving, maybe their marriage would have worked; likewise, if Hill had been less autocratic and more faithful it also might have worked. Instead, Faye was left perpetually stuck in 1942, and in Faith's eyes she now cut a pathetic figure—bitter, vindictive, and faintly ridiculous. People pitied her not for what had happened to her but for her inability to see beyond it.

In many respects, Hill had been as much a victim of the times and social mores as her mother. If he had been allowed to marry Mary all those years ago, this whole story might have been different.

Faith knew she couldn't change any of it. She was just sorry that her mother never let go, never moved on, and never enjoyed her children and grandchildren.

Faye hurled her final insult when she willed everything to Al Jr.—not only all her money but her diamonds and her four mink coats as well. As Al was still unmarried and sixty-two years old, this was almost comical, had it not been so pathetic! Yet Faith felt the sting as though her mother had risen up out of that casket and slapped her! She didn't need or want her mother's money, but she had always needed and wanted her love.

Not only did Faye leave nothing to her daughter but she also left nothing to her grandchildren or great-grandchildren. In omitting Hillyer Jr. and Tammy as beneficiaries, it was as if she'd also written her firstborn, Ron, out of her life. That, more than anything else that occurred, made Faith feel sad and angry.

Yet Faith was not really surprised by any of it. Her mother's temperament had never changed. Neither generosity, thoughtfulness, nor love had been a part of her disposition. She had never known their meaning, but Faith knew it all too well. She stood by her mother until the very end, ensuring that Faye would glide out on nothing short of a gondola of comfort and caring. Faye had always had a terrible fear of going to a nursing home, but Faith saw to it that her mother was cared for in her own home and able to draw her last breath in her own bed.

Faye died at the age of ninety-four. She had clung on and hung on, desperate to live for her precious Al Jr. She fought death as hard as she had fought life. Perhaps because she had spent almost a century on the stage of malice, her last curtain call came with no rewrite in the final scene. Hate had always been her hallmark, and she wore it like a sunbonnet guarding her soured soul. If there was any rowing to be done toward forgiveness, it would have to come from the other team, and there didn't seem to be anybody in that boat. Hill Pickett was long gone.

However, Faith had kept the faith and remained loyal to her mother until that final chapter was written. Faye had lived a difficult and angry life, and Faith was determined that her own would have fulfillment and meaning, not only to herself but to others as well. Having chosen a path of service, she set forth to change the lives of many people as well as the future of an entire town.

As for Faye, even in death her anger had not dissipated; it remained written in her wrinkled but still lovely face. She had her make-up on, and her hair was perfectly coiffed. The red had faded to gray, but those angry eyes were finally dimmed and her voice silenced.

She had always said, "Never isn't long enough for me to forgive." She was now finding out just how long never could be.

About the Author

F. DIANE PICKETT WAS BORN IN ATLANTA, GEORGIA, INTO A family with over three hundred years of Southern heritage in its genes. Like one of the main characters in this book, her grandfather was a well-known Southern Baptist preacher who fought in the Civil War; the other characters are largely fictional. This is her first book.

Diane grew up in Northwest Florida and attended Florida State University, after which she enjoyed a successful career as a medical executive. She has owned several small businesses focusing on everything from personnel to retail. She also has a strong background in event planning. Her vision and leadership inspired the revival of the historic Florida Chautauqua Assembly (www.FloridaChautauquaAssembly. org) in DeFuniak Springs, Florida, which is widely acclaimed as one of the premier cultural and educational events in the region. All proceeds from the sale of this book go to that nonprofit organization.

To contact the author directly, please visit
www.uphillpub.com or write to diane@uphillpub.com.